HOW IT HAUNTS US

DANIELLE RENINO

Copyright © 2024 by Danielle Renino

All rights reserved.

Cover design by ebook launch.com

No part of this book may be reproduced in any form or by any electronic or mechanical means, including information storage and retrieval systems, without written permission from the author, except for the use of brief quotations in a book review.

ISBN: 979-8-9865241-7-7 (paperback); 979-8-9865241-6-0 (ebook)

1

RAE

Today's the day I finally get rid of Mother. She's been dead for almost a year but continues to breathe down my neck, telling me in a low, clipped voice to stop slouching, fix my hair, and make a good impression.

I do the opposite to spite her. We never did get along.

"Remember to call me if you need anything." Eliza, my half sister, tries to place a hand on my shoulder, but I shrink away.

She frowns, the light in her eyes dimming slightly. Most of the time her expression is open and inviting. She looks more like me when she frowns. Closed off, cold. It's almost enough to remind me that we really are related, and she isn't just some random stranger tasked with monitoring me.

We stand a few feet down the service road from where the other two members of the documentary team wait at the foot of Seaside State Hospital for the Insane. There's a bite of salt in the air and the coastline peeks out from between the trees, the slivers of glittering blue making my pulse race. Equal parts excitement and nerves brought on by the ocean, the brine, the promise of the building beyond the trees.

The documentary team hasn't spotted us yet, but heat still creeps to my cheeks.

"I can walk the rest of the way myself, you know," I mutter. "They'll think I'm some kind of freak if you drop me off like this is a playdate or something. I'm not a little kid."

Eliza sighs. "I know you're not, Rae. I just wanted to make sure—"

"I know what you wanted to make sure of, and I'm *fine*."

"If you say so... Just take it easy, okay? And promise you'll call me if things get weird. I'll pick you up early if you need me to."

"Yeah, sure." I don't bother to mention that things are *supposed* to get weird—that's the whole point of a paranormal documentary.

Eliza makes her way back to the gated entrance where she parked her Volkswagen bug, and to her credit, only casts one final, anxious look over her shoulder before driving off.

I inch the rest of the way down the service road, stepping up next to the others.

They nod in greeting, and I crane my neck to get a better look at the anathema in front of us.

Anathema. I learned the word a week before Mother died. She had written it on a sticky note over and over again and stuck it to the kitchen counter, her long, thin handwriting threatening to tear the paper in two.

"What do you think this word means?" she'd asked.

Anathema.

I told her that I didn't know what it meant, but it looked damaging.

It seems to fit Seaside State.

Two patient wards sprawl out from the central building. The female ward branches to the right, lovely in the way that broken things are beautiful. What used to be the male ward sits to the left, burnt beyond recognition.

The grounds stretch back hundreds of acres, dotted with smaller brick buildings and decaying homes with white-washed siding where the staff and groundskeepers once lived. Tall maples and oaks muffle the bustle of the busy street at the edge of the property.

I always thought that once a place is abandoned, it dies. But standing on the concrete service road in front of this mess of brick and broken windows, I know that's not the case. Vines strangle the windowpanes, and wind whistles through the cracks in the glass. The building breathes. It's organic. Alive.

My long, dark hair forms a curtain between me and the girl to my right, a living perfume ad with wide eyes and a perfect button nose. She smells of vanilla and lavender, the scent blooming around her like a mushroom cloud.

"Your nose is bleeding," she says, running perfectly mani-cured fingers through her strawberry blonde hair. "In case you couldn't tell."

Fluid trickles from my left nostril and three ruby-colored drops splatter onto my Doc Martens. Thank goodness Eliza already left. She'd lose it if she knew how much this has been happening lately. Between the nosebleeds and my increasingly frequent stomachaches, it's getting harder to deny that some-thing might be wrong with me... again. I dismiss the thought before it takes root. I'm fine now. I'm better.

"Sorry, it happens when I'm nervous," I mumble, blotting at the careful trail of red with the sleeve of my hoodie. It's two sizes too big and makes me sweat despite the crispness in the air, the hints of summer draining into fall.

"Nothing to be nervous about," Mason, the guy who invited us—no, practically begged us to come here—chimes in. I recognize him from his Instagram profile picture, though he looks a lot younger in person. He's crouched to my left fiddling with his camera lens. It's a standard DSLR, the kind that shoots video along with still frames—not exactly the type of equipment I'd expect for a serious documentary. Everything about his appearance, from his ripped jeans and flannel shirt to his hoop nose ring, screams art major wannabe.

"Unless you're afraid of ghosts," he adds with a smirk.

The three of us—strangers before today—stand in a tight semicircle at the foot of a massive brick building, the administrative center of the asylum.

"I love ghosts," the blonde chirps, and it strikes me that Mason hasn't bothered to introduce us. I bite my lip. How can I ask for her name now? We've been standing out here for too long; she'll think I'm socially inept for not asking sooner.

"I used to trespass here all the time my freshman year of high school," she continues with a half smile. "It's beyond cool to actually be *allowed* here."

The sugary tone of her voice is enough to make me hate her. I know plenty of girls like her, the kind who are pretty and know it—who think it gives them the right to do whatever they want. The kind that coat themselves in polish and gloss, pretty perfumes and softness to distract from what rots beneath the varnish.

Still, I promised Eliza that I would try to make friends. I owe it to her. She defends me whenever her father complains about my moods, my short answers, my unwillingness to sit down and eat a nice dinner with them. As if "nice" and "dinner" were two words I'd ever pair together.

"I've only seen this place in pictures," I offer. "My mother was obsessed with the tragedy of '65. She used to pin photos and articles up all over the house." My stomach clenches when I realize I failed to ask the blonde for her name again.

She's not asking for your name either, I remind myself, but it does little to help my twisting gut.

"I'm the same way, actually." She grins, revealing a row of perfectly straight, shockingly white teeth. "Whenever I think of this place, I get butterflies in my stomach. Like I'm thinking about someone I love."

My brow furrows. Why the hell is someone like her here?

I was chosen for the documentary because of a rain of stones that fell on my house a few years back. Mason found an article online detailing the aftermath. The damage. All the shattered glass and battered siding that peeled like half-healed scabs from the flesh of my home.

The stones weren't the first instance of unexplained phenomena, just the most widely documented.

If someone were to follow the rabbit hole of articles back far enough, as Mason did, they'd find enough to make their blood run cold. Small things at first. Hairline fractures in the front windows that appeared out of nowhere. Mother's flower beds uprooted seemingly without cause, again and again. A slow boil of destruction. Until the stones.

Until the kids at school blamed *me* for every bad thing that happened to our house.

The thought that I would be connected to that much damage is laughable at best and horrific at worst, but Mason was insistent. In his eyes, I'm some kind of supernatural tuning fork, and I cause paranormal activity to spike in my presence.

I guess he's right to a certain extent, what with Mother tethered to my back. But I can't imagine the strawberry blonde having anything to do with the supernatural. She seems too cotton candy sweet. The closest I can imagine her getting to ghosts is passing by Spirit Halloween at the mall.

Mason stands and laughs nervously, his camera dangling from a strap around his neck. He's a whisper of a person, and it's easy to forget that he's been hovering at the outskirts of our conversation.

"I get butterflies too," he says quickly. His voice goes up at the end of each sentence so even the firmest statement sounds like a question. "There's something kind of romantic about abandoned buildings. I've always felt this sort of... I don't know, *love* from Seaside State. More than other buildings. Seaside State is super loving, I can tell."

I roll my eyes at his clear attempt to relate to miss "butter-flies in my stomach" and grab a stick of peppermint gum from the front pocket of my jeans, ripping away the foil. I pop it into my mouth and bite down, hard.

One look at the building and anyone can see he's delusional to think this place is anything but twisted. It isn't love that I feel looking up at the rows of busted out windows, it's the possibility of release. This place is supposed to be haunted, but there's more to it than that. Things disappear here. The building's supposed to be hungry, and I can only hope that what I have to offer whets its appetite.

Mother leans in close, the smell of cloves and dried flowers soaking what little space there is between us. A wave of nausea washes over me as she rests a bony hand on my shoulder, her thumbnail grazing my exposed collarbone. I should be used to it by now. It shouldn't make me squirm the way it does. My cheeks heat with disappointment. I should be so much stronger than this.

"I had to pull a lot of strings to get permission for us to be here," Mason tells us, his chest puffed out, his focus set entirely on the strawberry blonde. "Even if it is only for the night."

"Isn't that all we'll need? You only mentioned one night in your message." I've read Mason's six-paragraph ramble of an invite so many times that I practically have it memorized. In at dusk, out at dawn. There's nothing anywhere in the message about staying for more than twelve hours.

"One night to investigate the hospital and find proof of the paranormal," I add, quoting from the first paragraph.

He slouches his shoulders. "Well, I wanted it to be the whole weekend, but we only got cleared for the night."

I shrug, chewing noisily on my gum.

My teeth sink into my cheek, sending a squirt of blood into my mouth. The gum works to mix the taste across my tongue, and I chomp down on it again and again, releasing bursts of metallic tang. It's sickening. If blood were a chewing gum flavor it would taste like copper and old sheet metal, with a bite of sweetness at the end. The kind of sweet that makes my stomach ache, the kind of sweet that's sick.

The blonde looks over at me, eyebrows raised.

"Sorry," I say, glancing at my shoes. "Hope you don't have misophonia."

"Miso-what?"

"It's when you have a strong aversion to certain sounds. Hate the sound of chewing, that kind of thing."

The girl shakes her head. "No, I was…" Her gaze lingers on my shoulder, where Mother's fingers dig deeper into flesh, causing me to wince. "Never mind."

Words were Mother's obsession, not mine. But ever since she died, I can't help it—I cling to them, same as she did. Mother had an entire room dedicated to the English language, the walls covered in scraps of paper and sticky notes. I cringe, reminding myself that I'll never take it that far. And I'll never have to step foot inside *that* room again.

Mason opens and closes his mouth several times before he finally settles on what to say. "You don't look anything like your picture, Rae."

"I don't update my social media."

I'm better now, I remind myself.

"Well, I meant that you look like a different person in the picture attached to the article. You were a lot thinner and, I don't know, different."

I'm better now.

"The article about the stones is almost three years old. A lot can change in three years." Like Mother being dead, and me being here.

"I'm Gracie, by the way," the girl to my right cuts in, oblivious to my discomfort. "Crazy that we've been here for like ten minutes and haven't even introduced ourselves yet."

A pang rings out in my chest. All that time worrying about how to ask for her name and she's able to bring it up so fluidly, like it's nothing. Like it's easy.

It makes me hate her even more.

"Gracie?" I ask, my brows raised slightly. It's not the name I would have picked for her. It's too soft, too sugary for someone who's clearly hiding fangs.

A gust of wind cuts across the property and Seaside State's windows rattle as if to agree.

"I don't think I've ever met anyone named Gracie before," I say, lip curled. "It's like something a child would name their doll."

Her smile remains tacked in place, but her eyes flash. "Well, I think it's cute. And it's not like *I* chose it." She turns away from me and faces the hospital.

Mother squeezes my shoulder. Her nails dig in, threatening to break skin. THAT WAS RUDE, RAE. WHAT DID I TELL YOU ABOUT MAKING A GOOD IMPRESSION?

Mason glances down at his phone and curses. "We're still waiting on one more person, and they're late."

"I thought you said there were going to be six of us." Gracie frowns.

Mason shuffles his feet. "I was *hoping* for six. I sent over a dozen invites."

"And no one wanted to spend the night inside the infamous Seaside State?" I blow a bubble and pop it with my teeth. "Huge shock there."

"You did," he shoots back.

My skin prickles.

Mother's hand travels from my shoulder to the back of my neck. It's ice cold.

Straighten up. Smile, she instructs.

I run a finger over my bubble gum before pulling it from my mouth. Sure enough, it's stained pink from where I'm bleeding. I crumple it into a tissue and place it in my pocket.

"I've been hooked on this place since I saw the documentary from the sixties," Mason tells us. "You know, the one they filmed only a week before the tragedy. The moment I saw it, I knew I had to film my thesis here. We're gonna retrace the steps the patients took that night, and hopefully with your gifts for the supernatural, we'll get a ton of activity."

He motions enthusiastically, his eyes shining. "It spread from the administrative wing, through the male ward, to the violent patient ward, and so on and so on. The violent patient ward may have been torn down last year, but we'll still drop by. Gotta follow the path it took."

"The fire?" Gracie asks.

"The madness."

I picture him shining a flashlight beneath his chin. He's like a middle school kid telling stories around a campfire.

"You're a senior in college?" I ask him, eyes narrowed.

He flushes crimson. "I look young for my age."

I kick at the concrete. "And I don't look like the 'Stone Girl of the North Shore.'"

Gracie whips her head around, her eyes wide. "Wait, you're *that* girl! Oh my gosh, I *knew* you looked familiar. I think we were in the same math class the year after it happened. You go to Harper Grove, right?"

"I do now, but I was out of school when I was younger." I was what Mother called a "delicate child," the kind that doesn't do well in a classroom surrounded by two dozen other grimy kids. Besides, she never trusted the school nurses.

"Wow, I can't believe it's really you. You're like, low-key famous. Everyone said that you—"

"I know what they said." That I did it. That I wandered

through the woods for weeks beforehand, gathering up the rocks that would bounce off the roof of my family home that night in early spring. They said that I stood with a bucket on the roof of our sunporch, out of view of the street, and dumped them in a steady stream down over the shingles.

Because I was "troubled" or "damaged," or whatever you want to call it. Because I'd watched *Carrie* one too many times.

But no one talks about the fact that our neighbors insist they saw the rocks fall directly from the clouds, or the fact that I was inside with Mother the whole time, curled up against the back of the couch as window after window shattered. Regardless, there's no way I would have had the energy to gather the stones myself.

Oh, Rae, Mother rasps, her cold hand still settled against the nape of my neck. Why do you let that day bother you so much? Weak girl.

"What about you?" I ask Gracie, pointedly ignoring Mother. "I'm guessing you have some sort of story, or you wouldn't have been invited."

Mason perks up. "Gracie's amazing! She—"

"I'm sensitive," she says with a half smile.

"She's psychic," Mason says, waving his arms. "She can communicate with spirits."

"You can talk to ghosts?" I ask, a cold sweat breaking out across my forehead. "Can you see them too?"

"It's complicated." Her gaze lingers on my neck, where Mother's hand grips like a vise.

My heart thunders against my ribs. I think of how she was staring at me earlier, not because of my loud chewing, not because I'm some freak but because of... of... I lean in, keeping my voice hushed. "Can you see her?"

"Who?" she asks, eyes still fixed on Mother.

"Ah! There she is!" Mason cries and Gracie and I turn,

following his sightline down the service road. "The one we've been waiting for."

A girl in a floral print sundress hurries over to where we stand.

"Ana!" he calls out to her, and she gives a small wave in response.

Anathema. The thought is immediate and unintentional. I shake my head, clearing it away.

"Ana knows this building better than anyone," he explains, fiddling with his camera lens and staring almost reverently at the approaching figure.

"A friend of yours?" Gracie asks.

"Y-yes." His eyes dart off to the side. "Well, more like an acquaintance. She cares about Seaside State more than anything, and agreed to help out tonight... almost like a production assistant?"

Gracie cocks an eyebrow. "Is that a question?"

Mason hunches slightly. "Well, Ana's assisting the hospital more than us, I guess. She's here to make sure we don't break anything or set it on fire... again. She cares about the place a lot, and wants to make sure everything goes smoothly tonight."

I couldn't care less about the asylum's glorified babysitter. I need to know if Gracie can really see Mother. And if she can... If she could talk to her, help her come to terms with her passing, then maybe...

I reach for Gracie, but she's completely focused on the girl in the sundress.

Mother chides me, breathing a long string of words onto the back of my neck. PARANOID. DELUSIONAL. NEUROTIC. SILLY RAE. IT'S JUST THE TWO OF US, SAME AS IT'S ALWAYS BEEN.

The girl in the sundress comes up next to where we stand. Her hair is thin and stringy, a nest of tiny threads woven into her scalp. Her eyes are so light that they're practically drained of color. I'm stricken by how out of place she looks, how insubstantial when compared with the presence of the hospital, the imposing strength of it. It's like watching water try to mix with olive oil.

Anathema, I think again, and Mother runs a finger from the base of my neck to the small of my back. I want more than anything to pull my whole spine from my body.

"Apologies for being so late." Despite her disheveled appearance, Ana's voice is silky and mature. She's less a girl and more of a young woman. She might even be in her late twenties. It's difficult to tell.

"No worries," Mason says, looking starstruck. He sticks his hand out and it trembles viciously. "I'm Mason. It's a pleasure to finally meet face-to-face, Ana."

"Pleasure," she says curtly, making no attempt to reach out and return his handshake. His face reddens, and he lowers his hand.

"And you are?" She turns to us.

"Gracie." Gracie's face drains of color as she answers. Her skin breaks out in goose bumps and I wonder if the air here is getting to her. It's at least five degrees cooler in the shadow of the asylum, and she's only wearing a thin cotton t-shirt and a skirt that barely reaches her mid-thigh.

Ana gives her a quick once-over, her expression blank, before turning to me.

"And you?"

"Rae."

She glances back and forth between the two of us. "Skeleton crew, huh?"

Mason's blush deepens. "I really did expect more people, I wasn't exaggerating."

Ana's eyes continue to slowly rake over Gracie and myself, and the intensity in her gaze causes me to shiver. Finally, her eyes soften, and a lazy smile stretches across her face. "This is fine. It'll be easier to keep track of you this way."

"You don't need to come with us," Gracie says quickly, looking green around the edges.

"Yes, I do. It's a matter of safety." She draws out the word safety so it pours from her lips in a susurrus. "I know this building better than anyone. Besides, there isn't anyone else who could accompany you since most people won't come within ten feet of the hospital."

"Because it's haunted?" I ask. *Because it devours?*

"Because it's dangerous. I'm here to protect you as much as I'm here to protect the building. I know its layout like my own face. There are holes in the floor, places where the structural integrity has been compromised. Likely there's asbestos in the walls."

"Should we wear respirators?" Mason asks. "I-I didn't bring any."

Ana shakes her head. "It should be fine. Seaside State is unlike any other building. She's delicate, but sturdy."

The building stares down at us, five stories tall, rows of windows puncturing its side. It certainly doesn't seem delicate. It regards us with cold indifference, the strength of it almost too much to take.

Peeling walls ripple beyond the window frames, and one of the topmost windows is missing in its entirety. The glass is ripped from the pane and the wooden frame is gone. A single white curtain hangs in the gaping hole and is sucked in and blown out again by the wind.

The hair on the back of my neck stands on end.

I think of the room of words. Even though it's gone. I think of the sharp summon of Mother's voice. Even though she's dead.

The white curtain continues its fever fit. It moves in and out of the building, a swift intake of air, a slow exhale. I watch it, completely consumed, until the curtain is drawn back into the frame. It remains hanging, suspended in time. The hospital holds its breath.

I tilt my head, and something shifts behind the fabric. It takes a moment for my eyes to adjust, and for a second, I'm nearly convinced that the curtain is changing color. Flesh tones spread and darken, a slow staining of the veil.

There's someone inside the hospital.

2

GRACIE

The pavement beneath the goth chick's feet splits open. There's a sharp noise, like bones snapping, and my eyes widen as fractures snake out from the soles of her combat boots.

Mason startles at the noise, and I expect her to recoil too. Instead, she's fixated on one of the hospital windows. Even as the fractured pavement dips slightly, she stays rooted in place, her mouth set in a hard line. It's like she hasn't even noticed, she's so focused on whatever she's staring at.

I follow her line of sight, squinting.

Broken window, white curtain, nothing unusual... except for the wrecked pavement.

"R-Rae," Mason says hesitantly. "The pavement..."

She turns on him, snarling. "How could you?!"

Looks like Miss Doom and Gloom has some fight in her. I bite back a smirk and inspect my manicure, leaving the two to hash out whatever the hell set her off. Part of me itches to jump in, but I'm used to observing from the sidelines. It's easier. No matter how well I paint on my expression or put effort into relating to others, there's always a disconnect. I'm playing dress-up in a human suit, pretending I'm like everybody else.

I swallow back the lump in my throat and focus on my nails. They're a deep berry color—more purple than red. Exorcism. My favorite shade of polish. It matches my aura almost exactly, and the rich plum that swirls around my wrists is only half a shade darker than my nails. I take a deep breath. Exorcism is fitting considering what I'm here to do.

The things I see aren't really auras, but that's what I choose to call them. They tell me everything I need to know about a person. They cling to arms and legs and fleshy middles—ribbons of color, physical manifestations of emotion, spoken through opacity and gentle sway. A language that's taken me my entire life to master.

"I didn't come here to be part of some horror movie," the goth chick—Rae—tells Mason. I look up to find her thin arms wrapped around her stomach. She's finally stepped away from the cracked pavement, which branches out in a halo pattern about two feet in diameter. Interesting.

"I'm here because you said you could get me into the hospital," Rae continues. "You said you were serious about this. It may be a joke to you, but it's not to me. It's so important, it's *everything*."

The malum behind her shifts, mirroring her movements. Malums, parasitic creatures that feed off the emotions of the unstable, are my least favorite part of my "second sight." Rae's is twice the size of the ones I normally see, a velvety darkness that deepens as it moves, houseflies dotting the air around it. It's bloated to the point of uselessness.

The thing has clearly been feeding off her for a while. I'm surprised she isn't dead yet.

"This isn't a joke, it's really important to me too!" Mason insists, reaching for her. She jerks away from him and glares. "This documentary is literally gonna set the course for the rest of my life. Did you hear that, Rae? My *life* is on the line here! It's everything to me too!"

Mason's aura hangs like a plastic shower curtain across his shoulders, the color of skim milk. I read what I can in a glance.

Outcast. Loner. Loser. Exactly what I expect to find.

People aren't half as nuanced as they like to believe. Most of the time when I look at a person, beyond the swirls of color, and the clothes and shoes and styled hair, they're nothing but a bunch of clichés.

I'm no exception. Hell, I'm a prime example. My bubblegum exterior, hiding an inky black core. I'm like the lovechild of Malibu Barbie and Hannibal Lecter, charming, and darling, and oh so cute—except for my dark secrets. My tortured past.

It's damn pathetic.

Rae pulls away from Mason. Her aura drips like burnt honey, darkened by the thing on her back.

"I'm not gonna be your punch line," she whimpers, sounding like a wounded animal.

I'm acutely aware of how Ana stands off to the side, watching with the detached interest of a predator. She's like a smudge of dirt at the edge of my vision, a tickle in the back of my throat signaling the onset of an illness. Even thinking about her is enough to make my insides clench.

Everything hinges on my first few minutes inside Seaside State, and I already have Rae's malum to contend with. I can't let anything else distract me. So I ignore the woman in the sundress and focus on the hospital.

Seaside State Hospital for the Insane is the only building I've encountered that has an aura of its own. Most buildings catch emotions like flypaper—bad things stay stained through the wood, and brick, and stone, but when it comes down to it, they're only buildings. Inanimate. Unfeeling and unaware.

Not Seaside State.

Seaside State is conscious. And the building is in pain. It's clear from the shades of red that wrap around it. A blanket of dried rose petals, a deep blush. The color of suffering.

I'm here to exorcise it.

There's a hierarchy to malevolent attachments, and exorcising buildings is my specialty, mostly because it's so damn easy. The things that cling to most buildings manifest as phlegm-like globs that gather in rafters and under floorboards. They're thoughtless parasites created from anger and regret that show their fury through poltergeist-like displays and flickers of memories. Not ghosts, but hauntings in their own way.

They're as annoying as they are easy for me to get rid of. Unlike malums, which are damn near impossible to exorcise. Seaside State seems to be affected by something higher up the food chain than the parasites that latch onto other buildings—something closer to a malum. And if I can get rid of it, if I can cure Seaside State of its sickly aura, then maybe I'll finally be powerful enough to fix things. There's someone I need to exorcise, someone I need to save, and my time is running out.

For all I know, I'm already too late.

I think of *her* and my chest constricts, the sharp pain wrapping like a fist around my heart and squeezing. It's a reminder of how much I've changed because of *her*. She pulled me out of my apathy. She gave me the glorious, grotesque gift of feeling, and everything I've done in the past year has been for her. Out of gratitude, out of guilt. Every exorcism I've performed has been so I can someday be strong enough to cure her. All the empty houses I've stomped inside and cleansed, all the late-night research, hours spent poring over archived volumes in the library; I do it for *her*.

I breathe in deeply to steady myself. I can't let myself get my hopes up—can't think about it as if it's a sure thing. First, I need to help Seaside State.

If we ever manage to get inside.

Rae is still complaining.

She tries hard not to be pretty, with her baggy sweatshirt and greasy hair, but she's appealing in an odd, heavy metal music video sort of way. My mind strays to images of the two of us sharing a bottle of Exorcism polish. I'd paint her toes, and she'd paint my fingers. If it wasn't for the malum attached to her, she'd be attractive. Hell, she'd be hot. But I can't take my eyes off the damn thing on her back.

Still, it's better than Ana, who hangs in the corner of my eye, watching me watch the others.

Rae turns to me, glowering. "What are you staring at?"

Oh, the things I could say.

But her attachment isn't my responsibility, and if her little meltdown just now is any indication, I doubt she'd listen to a word I say even if I tried to explain it to her.

A tight, itchy feeling spreads across my skin, and I pull on every memory I have of *her* to snuff out my discomfort.

I've learned the hard way that people expect certain behavior from me, and who am I to fall short of expectations?

It's better to be buttermilk frosting than some kind of psychic medium. People like it when you're cute and dumb. All sparkle, no substance. People love it when there's sugar in your voice, and your words are light as cotton candy.

When you start talking about malevolent attachments and exorcising buildings, people don't listen. They talk back. They say you're sick, that you need help, that you'll never make it into a good college with a nice sorority if you keep fixating on these dark obsessions. Just ask the aging beauty queen I call Mom— those are her words, not mine.

They say that you've internalized all the trauma from your childhood, all the times you weren't good enough—all the passive aggressions that flew through your McMansion like poison darts. Now that you're nearly grown, it's manifesting in new and ugly ways. My therapist's words, not mine.

No one's ever been interested in *my* words. Except for Mason.

For reasons I still don't understand.

I've never advertised my services as an exorcist, preferring to work jobs based on attachments I happen across organically. A few of my clients have written about me, sure, but nothing that would catch the attention of anyone who operates outside the dregs of the internet.

The blog posts highlighting my abilities make me sound like a child playing dress-up in their mother's clothes.

I haven't done anything to warrant interest or approval from anyone... and I wish that didn't make me *feel*, but it does. It's like a bruise, a radiating pain that I can't find the proper words to define.

Point is, I'm not a local freak show like Rae—the aging beauty queen and her thousands of dollars' worth of therapy made sure of that.

And honestly, it shouldn't matter how Mason found me or why. Exorcising this building is my final test before I take on *her* malum, and Mason's documentary is the perfect excuse to do it. So I need to stay focused.

"Well?" Rae asks, pulling me from the inky darkness in my head. "Why are you staring?"

"You could be pretty if you tried," I tell her, unable to pry my eyes away from the malum.

She rolls her eyes. "Yeah, because 'being pretty' is my number one concern right now. In case you haven't noticed, Mason is trying to screw us over. Or *murder* us."

"I'm not trying to screw you over! And I'm not some psycho killer. I don't know what you're talking about!" Mason cries, his aura dripping like cottage cheese over his shoulders. "All I want is to make a documentary."

Rae turns to face him, the thing on her back twisting with her.

"The guy in the window," she says. "The friend you have waiting to jump out once you start filming. I didn't come here for jump scares. I'm not about that."

"Neither am I," Mason insists, his eyes glassy. "What happens tonight is gonna set the course for the rest of my life. I can't screw this up."

Rae hunches further and the malum on her back swells. My nose wrinkles in disgust at the way it undulates.

Mason blinks back tears, his bottom lip trembling. I'm not sure if it's his spoiled milk aura or his theatrics, but something about him doesn't sit right with me. Rae may be convinced that he has friends waiting to jump us once we get inside the hospital, but the thought of Mason having friends at all is laughable. So is the thought of him taking the initiative to plan something that elaborate.

I doubt he even got permission for us to be here.

The malum on Rae's back continues to press against her, its houseflies hovering in thick clumps around its shoulders.

Still, hers is standard. Nothing like the one attached to Ana.

Ana grabs Rae's arm and leans in close, her thin hair dripping over her shoulders. "Did you see something in the hospital?"

"Not something, *someone*. Up in that window, the one with the white curtain."

I crane my neck toward the spot again, the fabric obscuring the peeling, peach-colored wall that shows in small flashes every time the wind blows. Still nothing. No shadows or black masses or swarms of flies. It doesn't mean that she didn't see something, but whatever it is, it's not going to hang out for too long after being spotted.

Ana turns to Mason, hands carefully knotted in front of her. Her expression remains serene though there's a sharp edge to her voice. "You're the only people allowed in the building, and you're only allowed in under my supervision."

"I didn't bring anyone else here, I swear," Mason says, throwing his arms up.

Rae pulls at the ends of her hair and the malum behind her ripples. "This was a mistake. It's bad enough that we're here alone with some guy who slid into our Instagram DMs."

I fight back a snort. As if Mason could ever be a threat to anyone.

"You guys aren't alone," he says. "Ana's here. The whole reason why she's here is to make sure that we're safe."

Yeah, Ana's here, but she's cloaked in horse flies. Fat, brown horse flies.

A smoky film covers the top half of her body. It looks as if she peeled the wings off thousands of insects and bound them to her silhouette. I've never seen anything like it before.

Usually when malums attach to people, even the ones that wear a guise of flies, it's clear-cut. Parasite, host. No question of where one ends and the other begins. But this is obscene.

The power of a malum can be gauged by the size of its flies, and Ana's... The size and quantity is enough to churn my stomach. They make the houseflies of the thing attached to Rae's back look like child's play. I was already uneasy about being in such close proximity to one of these monsters, let alone two.

Mason's words seem to calm Rae, however, and she relaxes her shoulders. The malum settles behind her, content to keep its distance for now.

They can't always tell that I can see them, and this one seems single-mindedly fixed on Rae. Which is good... for me at least. Less for me to contend with as I deal with Ana and do what I came here to do.

"You know what they say about this place, right?" Mason chirps, perking back up again. "How people see and hear things? Boom! Right there in the window, it's proof!"

He pops the lens cap off his camera and aims it toward the window. It's as if he forgot that he was making a documentary.

"You know what they say about this place, right?" he asks again, zooming in on the window.

"That it's haunted." Rae wraps her arms around her middle again, closing herself off like a coffin.

Mason grins, showing his teeth off like a shark that's caught the scent of blood in the water. "That it's *cursed*. That there's a portal underneath it, that the building is conscious. That it's hungry, that it *feeds*."

"Where did you hear that?" Ana asks, a whisper of a smile tugging at the corners of her mouth.

"Where *haven't* I heard it? After the tragedy of '65, they shut the place down and all kinds of stuff was brought out of here. Occult items, animal bones."

Mason turns to face Rae, his camera still pointed toward the window. "Most hospitals from this era have tunnels underneath so they could transfer bodies from the morgue without freaking out the patients, but when they were clearing this place out, they found a second set of tunnels that just went down. Like, all the way down—without an end. There was a spiral staircase carved out of stone and on the thick slabs, ten, twenty, thirty feet down they found all these altars and items. They never did make it to the bottom. It's known as the endless staircase. It's kind of famous."

"That's a rumor," I scoff. I've stumbled across stories about the staircase while doing research on the building—most of them posted on conspiracy theory websites, printed in flashy typeface with pixelated gifs. *She* tried looking for the staircase the last time she was here, but for all of the tall tales and the detailed accounts of what was supposedly brought out of the tunnels, there's no mention of where they're located.

"Things are supposed to disappear here," Rae says quietly. "I've read stories about the building eating the bad parts of a person. That's why the patients went crazy that night; they were being fed on."

"Anyway," Mason says, turning back to her. "Let's hear what you saw."

Rae glares at him through narrowed eyes. "I told you what I saw."

"Yeah, but we didn't get it on film." He shoves the camera in her face. "Come on, tell us about the figure in the window."

I turn from them to Ana and the buzzing, twisted mess of horse flies dancing around her head. My skin prickles.

"That story doesn't sit well with you, does it?" she asks, her ghost of a smile still pinned in place.

"The endless staircase?" I try to look through the flies and focus on her face, but they swarm in such tight groups that her eyes are almost completely obscured by legs and wings. "It's bullshit. I'm surprised that you're okay with it."

"Why wouldn't I be?" she asks, her voice muffled through the buzzing.

"Mason said you were super protective over this place or some shit."

She shrugs. "Stories like that are the reason security doesn't need to patrol around here. It's the reason why most people stay away."

"Really? Because I'd think stories like that would attract more unwanted attention." I clench my jaw. I can't figure her out. She doesn't strike me as the type who would attract a malum, and while Rae is clearly aware of her attachment, Ana seems oblivious to hers.

"You'll see when we go inside. There's no vandalism at Seaside State. There won't ever be any damage done to her at all, not while I'm around."

The flies crawl across her cheek and I swallow hard to keep from gagging.

"You look like you're going to be sick." She tilts her head slightly. "Is something wrong?"

"I'm fine," I insist through gritted teeth. "Just a little lightheaded."

"This place can be overwhelming for some people." Her smile slips a fraction of an inch.

Mason finishes recording Rae's account of the figure in the window and the two make their way to the foot of the wooden steps leading up to the front door.

"Try not to let it bother you." Ana nudges her way past Mason and Rae and ascends the stairs. She stands above us, in the shadow of the building. It looks as if she's perched between the jaws of a predator.

She reaches into the pocket of her sundress and pulls out a key roughly the size of a fist. Burnt orange oozes from the dried scab of iron, ribbons of oxidation eating away at it.

"Skeleton key for a skeleton crew," she says with a smile that doesn't reach her eyes. "It opens just about every door on the property."

Mason claps his hands together and climbs the staircase, rushing to Ana's side. "Let's get started on this thing."

I take a deep breath. In through the nose, out through the mouth. The smell of the air, the taste of it lingers on my tongue.

The air tastes salty here. The ocean is so close I can almost hear it past the hum of the wind, the muffled traffic, and the deafening silence of the property. I breathe in deeply and savor the persistent taste of the water, and something else in the air, something harsher—the sting of the asylum. Its breath is full of salt.

Salt in the air, and salt in my blood.

Ana unlocks the front door and slips inside, Mason nipping at her heels.

I climb the decaying wooden steps and turn back to where

Rae stands at the foot of the service road. She stays rooted in place, glaring up at the building. The malum at her back sways slowly from left to right like a pendulum. Houseflies shake loose from its silhouette, a trail of buzzing insects left in its wake.

I watch it and silently chew at the inside of my cheek before turning to enter the asylum.

The other two members of the group wait for us just beyond the doorway. Ana leans against a wall while Mason speaks to her in a low, hurried voice. I only catch snippets of what he's saying. "It's almost sunset... nervous... really did think more people would show up."

I have one foot over the threshold when Rae grabs my arm.

"What gives?" I attempt to pull free, but despite her thin frame, her grip is firm.

"We didn't finish our conversation," she says quietly, the shadow at her back pulsing with each word, houseflies drifting in lazy circles. Rae seems to have folded back in on herself after her outburst earlier and I find myself wondering which one is the real her—the wild, wounded fawn or this sad creature unworthy of a name.

She's caught me off guard and I freeze, my eyes wide. For a second, I almost forget the role I'm meant to play.

I take a moment to gather myself then tilt my head to the side, blinking three times in rapid succession. "You want tips on how to be pretty?"

"You can see Mother," Rae says in a low, clipped voice.

"Who?" I ask, genuinely confused.

Her grip tightens. "You were staring over my shoulder for the last fifteen minutes. You looked her right in the face, you can definitely see her."

She thinks it's her mother. The thought sits like a stone inside my stomach. Worse, she's been talking to it—strengthening the attachment. It's a wonder she's not bedridden. She's practically been spoon-feeding it for who knows how long. I might as well be talking to a corpse.

I keep my expression blank. "Yeah, I've been looking at you because you're acting crazy. I don't want to set you off. It's totally not like me to judge someone without knowing them first, but I think you need help."

"Mason said you could see ghosts, that you can communicate with them and you—"

I sigh. "I tried to tell him that's not the case. I can't see ghosts."

"But you can see Mother. My *dead* mother. She's behind me right now, but you don't need me to tell you that, do you?"

"I can't see ghosts," I insist, jerking my arm back.

This isn't what I came here for, and it's not my responsibility to tell her. What's the point of handing out a death sentence? There's no getting rid of the thing; her fate was decided the moment it chose to feed on her.

I know she won't listen to me anyway.

So then why does the thought of her body going cold send a pang through the center of my chest? Why does watching her eyes glisten with concern shred me apart inside?

I wish *she* were here to explain it to me, this rush of feeling... where it comes from, and what it means.

"Are you coming, girls?" Ana's voice leaks out from the depths of the hospital.

"Give us a minute!" Rae calls. Her eyes dig into mine. "Please, I've been dealing with this on my own for so long. I need to know that you can see her too."

I frown. There's no getting around it. She isn't going to let it go until she gets an answer.

I lean in close, ghosting my lips against the shell of her ear. "That thing that's following you around isn't a ghost."

Her response sends ripples of dread through me.

"I know," she says.

3

RAE

Mother digs her fingers into my shoulder and a wave of nausea runs through me. Back when she first attached to me, all I had to do was wrap an arm around my stomach to quell the sick feeling—now, I hug my middle and the ache worsens. I do my best to endure it. It's like Mother used to tell me: pain is the price of family.

THERE'S SOMETHING OFF ABOUT THAT GIRL, she hisses, fingers digging in deeper.

Gracie stands stiffly, as if she's not completely settled in her perfect skin.

"You okay?" she asks. "You're like, really pale."

"I know that Mother isn't a ghost," I repeat, hugging my stomach tighter.

CAREFUL, RAE, Mother rasps, and I take a deep breath as she pulls away, the nausea draining as she loosens her grip.

I wait for Gracie to say something, but she stays silent, her eyes narrowed, and I know I must have said the wrong thing again. Heat rushes to my forehead.

"She's so much more than a ghost," I add, watching her expression, hoping that it softens. "She's larger than life, or I guess, death. Her presence is…" I struggle to find a word that won't offend Mother. "Imposing. Same as when she was alive."

Gracie curls her lip. "That's not…" Her face scrunches up as if she can't decide what to say. With an exasperated huff, she continues, "That's not your mom."

"I think I know my own mother."

"Better than I know the paranormal?"

My body tenses. Gracie already thinks I'm crazy for freaking out earlier, for showing up with a bloody nose, for not introducing myself properly. And now she's saying that… What? That I'm hallucinating? That Mother isn't here with me after all? It's in my head? It can't be in my head; I hear her, I feel her, I know that Mother—

Look at what that girl's done to you. You're all worked up. Mother runs her fingers through my hair, her voice alarmingly tender. She leans in, her lips brushing against my cheek. But you must remember that she's a stranger. She doesn't know a thing about us—does she?

No, she doesn't.

I reach into my pocket and take slow, evenly spaced breaths as I fiddle with the piece of tissue paper that I spit my gum into earlier. The hunk of blood-stained candy shifts from the center of my palm out to the edges and back again, and I release the tension in my neck, my shoulders, my back.

"Um, hello?" Gracie asks, her lips pursed. "Do you know more about the paranormal than me or what?"

"No, but you don't know more about my mother than I do," I snap, pulling my hand from my pocket.

"Believe it or not, I was trying to help you." Gracie turns away, waving her hand dismissively. "Forget it, I shouldn't have bothered."

I said the wrong thing again…

Everything I say is wrong. But at least Gracie's dismissal

doesn't sting as badly as when I mess up around Eliza and her father.

It's not as bad as the added pressure of their perfect home. It's not as bad as their promises of family, and future, and eating "nice dinners" together.

Tears sting the corners of my eyes.

Forget all the words I should have chosen. Forget Gracie. She's already disappearing into the darkened hall beyond the entryway.

All I need to do is focus my energy on Mother, mentally snip the cord that connects us. All I need to do is get inside Seaside State, get to the heart of the building and—

Why would you want to get rid of me, baby? Mother asks. Who will care for you if I'm gone?

"Rae," Ana calls. She's nothing more than a gentle stir through the static of the darkened hall. "Last chance to come in before we leave you behind."

"Coming." I stumble across the threshold and into the hospital. The door creaks shut behind me.

Every window on the first floor has been boarded up, and slivers of light creep in around the corners of the boards, just enough to remind me that there's a world outside this building.

The dark is thick, alive. The shafts of light only work to emphasize the creeping, virus-like quality of the building.

My scalp prickles.

As I inch along after the group, I can't shake the feeling that the hospital has been waiting for us to come inside for a long time.

Up ahead, Mason's talking Ana's ear off about spirit photography and the tragedy of '65.

"And did you know," he continues, his voice high and scratchy. "D-did you know that they never found an official cause for why that first patient went crazy? They weren't off their meds; it wasn't even a violent patient. The violent patient ward, the one they tore down last year, that wasn't even where all this started."

Ana murmurs something about group psychosis and induced delusional disorder.

Gracie keeps pace with them, her kitten heels clicking against the cracked tiles.

I frown. Who the hell wears heels to an abandoned building?

"Is the whole building like this?" Gracie asks. "It looked like there were tons of windows that weren't boarded up when we were outside. I don't get how we're supposed to film anything if we're in the dark the whole time."

"Haven't you been here before?" I point out, still a few paces behind them. "You should already know what the rest of the building is like."

"In case you haven't noticed, there are at least a dozen buildings on the property. I've never been inside this one before. Actually, hang on." She stops abruptly and pulls something from her skirt pocket. A few flicks, and a tiny flame sprouts to life from the palm of her hand. "I have a lighter. I'm not sure how much fluid is left at this point, but it should help for a little while."

"Why do you have a lighter?" She doesn't strike me as the type who smokes, and she didn't smell like cigarettes out on the service road.

"Put that away. The last thing the hospital needs is another fire," Ana snaps. After a moment's hesitation, Gracie tucks the lighter back in her pocket and we continue through the dark.

"I don't even consider this part of Seaside State," Ana adds. "This is the foundation. The hospital's underbelly."

"Reminds me of a basement." Gracie ducks to avoid the various wires that hang from the ceiling, a thick jumble of chords and cables. The air around her swirls as she moves, a blurred figure avoiding blurred shapes. Documents caked with mold cover the floors. They stick to my shoes, feeling more like the remains of dead animals than damp paper, and I kick against the floor to get them off.

Goosebumps bloom along my arms.

This isn't a basement; this is a sleeping predator.

We turn a corner and Ana leads us up a narrow staircase that empties into a pale hallway. It's light and airy, long and narrow. Checkered tiles line the floor, white and red diamonds coated in a thin layer of dust and plaster. The lights that hang overhead have been hollowed out, their bulbs gone, only empty husks of the structures remaining. Eroding oranges and pale cream colors line the hall. The windows are huge, and the hallway is so bright it's almost blinding. The air doesn't smell salty the way it does outside. It smells like old paper, lemon rinds, and sweat.

"Finally, some light!" Gracie exclaims and runs into the center of the hall. She twirls around and around, her fingers grazing the edges of the walls and windows.

THAT GIRL... Mother leans over my shoulder, inspecting Gracie as she twirls.

"What about her?" I whisper, but she doesn't answer.

Gracie stops spinning and stumbles around the hallway, trying to regain her balance. Her hair is tangled and tumbles down over her shoulders. She tosses it back and shakes it out, a cascade of golden flames nipping at the nape of her neck. It's like I'm watching a shampoo commercial.

She looks even more flawless than before, and I keep waffling between envy and anger. I'm not sure if I want to be her or get rid of her.

Ana comes up next to me, the hall so tight that our shoulders touch.

If Gracie seems to come alive inside the hospital—more vibrant, more visible—then Ana disappears. Her paleness blends into the peeling walls, and her shoulder feels more like a gust of wind than part of a body.

Gracie holds her arms out in front of her, her eyes closed as the tips of her fingers brush against the walls. Her face is knotted in concentration.

"This is totally bizarre," she murmurs. "This hallway feels so alive, but I can't get a read on it. No pulse, nothing."

"Seaside State's just a bit shy." Ana steps up next to her and places a hand on the back of her neck. Gracie flinches slightly but doesn't pull away.

I glance over my shoulder to find Mason hovering behind the group, his camera raised slightly, lens whirling as it focuses on where Gracie and Ana stand next to the wall.

"What do you think so far?" he asks.

I almost tell him the truth, that it feels like the walls are closing in, and Seaside State is trying to press into us until we burst open. Instead, I shrug. "It's like this place is alive."

Mason smiles, seemingly pleased with my answer. He inches past me to where Ana stands, and both of them watch Gracie as she tries without success to check the hospital's pulse. Whatever that means.

When I pull back from the group, the walls seem to follow me, leaning in closer, bending slightly, the hint of movement as subtle as the rise and fall of a chest.

"It's a building, not a beast," I remind myself, glancing inside the rooms that branch off the hallway. One mess of peeling paint after another. Viridescent layers, darkening shades of vermillion and cobalt. I can't help but picture the vicious scratch of Mother's handwriting, each of her words transcribed through the coloring.

Shouldn't you stay close to the others? Mother's grip tightens around my waist.

"They won't even notice I'm gone."

It'll be easier to break away from the group now rather than wait until we're deeper inside the hospital.

To get rid of Mother, I need to find the heart of the building.

I combed through countless online forums, read dozens of accounts from people who have successfully fed the hospital. But the closest thing I found to instructions on where and how to get it to eat were "find the heart and be prepared to make an offering." Whet Seaside State's appetite. Reading between the lines, it's not hard to conclude that the building needs blood. And I definitely don't want the others around for that.

Their voices drift back to me. Praise for Gracie, encouragement. "You can do it... We believe in you... I already told you; Seaside State is shy."

I huff. Some psychic she is. First she makes up lies about Mother, then she can't even get a read on the damn hospital. The psychic I saw in Salem a few months back was more help, and probably way more legit, than she is. And she wore a Halloween costume throughout the reading.

At the end of the hall, there's an open door and soft light leaks out over the threshold. It pulls me in.

The light seems opaque, as if I could reach out and grab it, squeeze it until it pops. Until it bleeds. I hurry down the hallway past ruined rooms, across cracked tiles, the whole time wondering if it's really going to be this easy, if the heart of the building could really be so close.

That's what this feels like.

It feels like feeding time.

I take a deep breath and convince myself that I'm ready to make my offering. I'm ready to whet its appetite. A taste of blood and it will suck Mother from my back. A slice across my palm and—

I freeze at the mouth of the room.

The tiles inside are white—shiny, spotless white. They're

clean to the point of being immaculate, as if the room has been scrubbed with surgical precision.

The walls are freshly papered, with lilies of the valley parading across in a horizontal pattern. All the furniture, carefully carved end tables, a gleaming iron bed frame, crisp white sheets—everything is in its proper place. Untouched. Pristine.

While the hallway decays and the other rooms rot, this one sits untouched.

As if it's been perfectly preserved for over fifty years.

The hair on my arms stands on end and Mother pulls back from the doorway, settling by my feet. The way she twists is unnatural, as if she's boneless. Every inch of her, from her prominent collarbones to her bony ankles, is coated in a haze of gray that flickers slightly like white noise on a screen. Watching her thin form contort in such a way sends shivers down my spine.

SOMETHING ISN'T RIGHT HERE, RAE.

Yeah, no kidding.

A light breeze leaks from the room out into the hall. Crisp, cold. As if circulated by an air conditioner. I can almost hear the hum of it trickling from the clean, white room.

I shiver when I realize that I can't be here alone. I don't understand what the hospital is capable of.

It's not capable of anything, I remind myself. *Nothing except feeding. No higher thought, just hunger. It's not sentient.*

But it might as well be. The way it shows off this room, smugly, as if it knows it'll scare me back into line with the others. As if it knows all that gleaming white makes me feel exposed.

"Hey, everyone," I say, my voice thin and breathy. "You need to see this."

They continue to prattle on down the hall. "The building should have a pulse, they always have pulses... I'm certain you'll find it... Gracie, you're very talented, but the building only shows you what it wants to show you."

I spin around, waving my arms desperately above my head. "Get over here! Now!"

Their heads all snap in my direction. Mason readies his camera and they filter over, single file, the hallway seemingly thinner than it was only a few minutes before.

Am I the only one who notices?

It's so much thinner. It's closing in around us.

"What's wrong?" Ana asks, her pale eyes round as dinner plates, but her mouth is set in a thin, straight line.

"See for yourself." I step aside, giving them a full view of the room. "There's something weird going on here. I think I get why there are all those stories about the endless staircase... I don't think they're made up."

They stand in silence for a moment, mouths slightly slack. Gracie frowns and shakes her head.

Mason lowers his camera. "I don't get it. What are we looking for?"

I spin back around and ice shoots through my veins.

The room is in the same state of decay as the rest of the building. No wallpaper. No spotless white. The tiles are cracked and caked with years' worth of dirt and grime. The furniture is gone.

"No," I say, feeling as if the breath has been knocked out of me. "It was clean, it was—"

"Oh Rae, I'm not sure what you think you saw," Ana says gently. "But everything is as it should be."

The way she says it makes my skin prickle.

We pass through several hallways. Each one has a breath, a heartbeat all its own, and I realize that finding the true heart of the building is going to be a lot more difficult than I assumed. All the posts in the forums said that I would know it when I found it—I would be able to feel it. But every inch of Seaside State feels lively. Hungry. Waiting.

I trail behind the rest of the group, forcing myself to keep moving though my legs are heavy as lead.

I know what I saw. I'm not insane—the room was clean.

The others think I'm crazy, I can tell. They don't nag me to catch up and keep pace. They seem comforted by the distance between us, and after my breakdown outside and the incident with the room, I don't blame them.

Mother says that I shouldn't let it bother me. Even though my cheeks burn and my thoughts race, I know she's right. I'm not here for their approval.

Though I'm glad I made the decision to stay with the group for now.

From the outside, the hospital looked intimidating, and on the inside it's even worse. It's labyrinthine, impossibly large. I could wander a single floor for hours and not come to its end. Exit signs hang over doors that are sealed shut. Framed maps that proclaim You Are Here are damaged beyond recognition. The doors that do hang open form a line of ribs, split apart to expose rooms in various bruised shades of purple. Empty bed frames, rubber mattresses, and piles of loose flooring lie in the center of what used to be bustling common areas. A lone wheelchair faces a deserted nurse's station, spiderwebs of cracked glass scarring the ruined partition.

"Where are we going?" Gracie asks, breaking the silence.

"We're following the path of the tragedy of '65," Mason says, adjusting his camera strap.

"But the men's ward is that way." She points a sharp, mani- cured nail back down the hallway.

"How do you know that?" Ana snarls, her voice so full of malice that Mason jumps a little, though she quickly tacks on a grin and lets out a nervous laugh. "I mean, it's difficult even for me to stay oriented in here sometimes."

"I've been here before, remember?" Gracie cocks an eyebrow.

Ana's grin sharpens. "And I have been here many more times than you, yet I still struggle to find my way at times. It's curious that you'd be so well oriented after only visiting a handful of times years ago."

It takes a moment for Gracie to respond, and she drags her teeth along her lower lip, scraping at her lip gloss before finally settling on what to say. "I'm psychic, remember? And I'm getting pretty strong vibes that what's left of the men's ward is back down this hall and to the left."

"We're not going there," Mason says.

"But you said that we were retracing the tragedy."

"Yet," he adds quickly. "We're not going there *yet*. We are retracing the steps, mapping the madness, all that good stuff. We're starting at the beginning."

Gracie arches her brow. "How could you possibly know the exact place where that first patient lost their mind?"

"Mason's more dedicated than you give him credit for," Ana replies lightly. She places a bony hand on his shoulder, steering him away from Gracie, toward the front of the group. "He's really done his research on this place."

This place.

If Mother were still alive, I'd never be allowed here. She'd be too paranoid that it would upset my already "delicate" sensibilities, and heaven forbid I leave the house without her.

As a ghost she couldn't physically keep me away, though she tried, raking her fingers down my back and hissing in my ear. You're not stepping foot in that filthy place.

I tried my best to placate her.

"But Mother," I said gently as we prepared to leave the house this morning. "I thought you would be excited to visit."

AND WHY WOULD YOU THINK THAT?

"Because of the tragedy of '65."

She used to get so passionate about it. Her eyes would sparkle feverishly as she stroked a finger over her collection of newspaper clippings, expression frozen somewhere between reverence and distress. She talked about the tragedy the same way other people discussed old friends. It was almost as if she felt some kind of kinship to it, though whether it was with the patients or hospital remained unclear.

As a ghost, though, she didn't seem to care and it wasn't until I kept pressing with, "Aren't you interested in where everything happened?" that she gave her curt response.

I'M INTERESTED IN KEEPING YOU SAFE.

The "with me" at the end of the sentence went unsaid but hung heavy in the air nonetheless.

If she were still alive, she'd definitely send me to *that* room, her room of words.

The far wall of Mother's word room was comprised entirely of the words that she'd collected and written on scraps of paper. Tiny tomes stuck to the drywall like wanted posters. *Myoclonus. Leucotomy.* DO YOU KNOW THE MEANING OF THIS WORD, RAE?

I push the thought from my head and concentrate on walking. Eliza's father sold the house after Mother died and he was forced to take me in. The wall of words is gone; I never have to go back to *that* room again.

And even though she's plastered to my back, Mother can't tell me what to do anymore. She can't keep me inside or in bed, she can't serve me bitter tea with lunch. *I'm better now.*

We stop a few minutes later at the end of a mint green hallway with large doors painted a similar uncomfortable shade. Even the tiles are green.

My knees go weak and I struggle to stay upright. Seaside State is messing with me again. This can't be real.

Mint was Mother's favorite color. She collected pale green

teacups, lacy gloves, and fabrics. *That* room was painted the same shade as this hallway, the exact same shade.

"Come here, Rae," Mother would say those rare times that I refused to drink my tea or talked back at the dinner table. I'd sit against a wall in the hallway, picking at the plush carpet. I'd sit hunched over and sweating, waiting for the sharp summon of her voice. She'd be seated at her sewing machine in the corner of that room, and it would take all my courage to rise and inch my way over to her.

"Yes, Mother?"

She'd slide a scrap of paper across the table, and I'd inch even closer.

"Do you see this word, Rae? Do you know what it means?"

"No, Mother."

"Learn this word. Be a good girl and learn this word. Put it up on the wall with the rest." The far wall, plastered with paper held up with clear plastic tape. The array of paper pieces looking too much like the peeling paint of the asylum, a shedding second layer.

"You're lucky that I'm teaching you this, Rae," she'd say. "My momma never cared enough to teach me anything. She *left me*. She left me all alone.

"Your Grandma Perry was a selfish woman. She always put herself before me," she'd say. "But everything I do, I do for you, Rae.

"You stop your crying now," she'd say. "Pain is the price of family. Now stand and face the wall."

"But Mother!"

"Stand and face the wall."

The wall of words, peeling like this hospital.

This hallway, green like *that* room.

"So." Mason claps his hands, barely able to contain his excitement. "How much do you guys know about what happened the night of the tragedy?"

He glances back and forth between me and Gracie but doesn't wait for us to answer. "It started with a single patient who somehow managed to get out of their room and run down the hall to the men's ward, where the fire started." We blink back at him.

"And this," Mason continues, gesturing to one of the doors, "is where the madness began."

4

GRACIE

I can't get a read on the damn hospital. The deep, blush-colored pain that oozed from it out on the service road is nowhere to be found inside its halls. They're lifeless. No pulse, no passion. Nothing like the last time I was here with *her*—nothing like the violent patient ward.

I dig my heel into the tile, ignoring the pang of guilt that shoots through my chest.

It's pathetic. I'm acting as if I actually am some airhead teenage girl. I know better than to think about the violent patient ward.

I know better than to think about *her*, as I knew her, before she got possessed.

She drew me in right away, like a fly to honey. Not because of her vibrant laugh, or the way she seemed to rush into things headfirst with an insatiable thirst to know, to experience, to *live* —but because of her pain, and how it contradicted every mask she wore for the world. Pain dripped from her in globs, her aura thick and dark as tar. I was smitten with the idea of *her*, someone who shone so brightly while hiding so much hurt.

Back then, pain was all I cared about. I hunted it down,

sunk my teeth into it until I hit bone. And she had more than enough pain for the both of us.

Now, the memory of her surges through me, akin to a stinging, unseen wound.

I wish we could talk the way we used to. I wish I didn't feel so alone without her.

A breeze blows through an open window at the end of the hall and the sound is unbearably depressing. It's the rattle of wind through a corpse.

A small, sick voice in the back of my head says that I'm not strong enough to exorcise the hospital. And since I'm not strong enough to cure whatever ails the building, I'll never be able to cure a person. I've condemned *her* to death...

"You coming, Gracie?" Mason asks, gesturing toward the room where "the madness began," as he keeps reminding us. "I wanna see if you and Rae feel anything in here."

I shake my head. "I need to establish a connection with the building before I'll be able to feel anything. I'm gonna see if the hospital's pulse is stronger in this hallway."

Even though I already know that it's worse than watered-down; it's nonexistent. Usually by now I'd find evidence of the attachment gumming up the corners of the rooms, clinging to the walls. But there's nothing. The only thing that slightly ebbs my panic is the knowledge that this building isn't like what I've exorcised before. I'll need to approach this differently.

My best bet now is to try another building on the property or, worst-case scenario, drag myself back to the ruins of the violent patient ward and hope I can feel something there. Even if it reminds me too much of *her*.

Rae follows Mason into the room at the end of the hall, and for a moment I'm tempted to call out to her.

I should know better than to try to help her understand the full weight of what she's dealing with. No one ever listens. They deny, they argue, they refuse to believe. Or worse, like in Rae's case—they're attached to the thing in more ways than one. They care about it.

But Rae reminds me so much of *her*. She may oscillate between subdued and combative, but there's a spark in her that I can't help but be drawn to. She's so alive in her misery.

I dig my nails into my palm. I don't feel bad for keeping the truth from Rae. I don't feel bad. If I repeat it enough times, if I ignore the ache in my chest—the hurt that seems to spread, and worsen, and eat at me like a festering wound—then maybe I'll start to believe it.

How would I explain it anyway? What could I possibly say?

That I can't see ghosts, but something worse. Something I'm not even sure I'd believe in if I didn't know for a fact that it was real. I hook my fingers into my ribs, the sharp pain distracting from the hurt in my chest. I steel myself, pushing all thoughts of Rae to the side. I have more urgent things to focus on.

Like how lifeless this building is. It's sterile, manufactured somehow, seeming more like a movie set than something organic.

It shouldn't feel like this.

I take a deep breath and resolve to make a break for it as soon as Ana disappears into the room after Rae and Mason. I kill time looking through the photos I've snapped on my phone, just in case I missed anything. But there aren't any ribbons of color. No dark, glob-like stains. Only waiflike hallways with flaking paint, damp carpeting, and a deflated quality to them that inspires pity. This is the kind of place that's incomplete without its residents, soaked in the pain of all the terrible things that happened here.

My pulse quickens and I wait for Ana to follow after Rae and Mason, but she stays rooted in place, standing next to me in the hall.

I lower my phone, turn to her, and plaster on a fake grin.

"You go on ahead, I wanna see if I can get a reading on this hallway and it might take a while."

"I don't mind waiting." Ana stands watching me, her cloud of flies covering her. The bugs burrow into her hair and kick up dry skin around her jawline.

Mason's voice drifts out from inside the room and it seems so far away, buried within the silence of the hospital.

"Sounds like you're missing something important." I nod my head toward the end of the hall. "I don't want to keep you from the documentary."

"I don't care about the documentary," she says flatly.

Of course not. She's just here to make sure we don't destroy the place.

"I'd like to stay out here with you," she continues. "We have a lot in common."

"Doubt it." I heave a sigh and pretend to snap some more pictures of the hallway. I check my phone before sliding it back into my purse. No bars. The hospital is a dead zone.

"How long are you going to keep that up?" Ana asks, tilting her head to the side, her expression neutral. "What's the point of it?"

A twinge of annoyance runs through my forehead. I told her to go ahead with the others; I told her this was gonna take a while.

"Photos help me get a read on places. Sometimes, when it's difficult for me to see things in person, they'll show up in a photo." I zip my bag shut.

"That's not what I mean." She steps toward me, the flies moving with her. "I'd like very much for us to talk, to get to know each other. I'm sure you'll be interested in what I have to say."

The insects swarm, seeming to multiply with every flick of her wrist, as if she's conducting an orchestra. She flicks it back and forth, again and again. She conjures more and more flies, which she wouldn't be able to do unless...

My mouth goes dry.

"You've been staring at me since I made my introductions," Ana continues, and the horseflies that surround her face twist and morph along with the words. She steadies her hand, seemingly satisfied with the swarm around her.

"No, I haven't." My voice shakes. How did I not see it before? I was so focused on the hospital, so annoyed at its silence that I didn't bother to... I was willing to write Ana off as just another victim of possession, but she...

"Why have you been staring at me?" Ana lets out a small laugh and the flies around her mouth scatter. "Is there something strange that you've noticed, perhaps? Something no one else can see? I wouldn't be surprised considering your *abilities.*"

"You coming?" Mason calls, poking his head around the doorframe. I'm thankful for the interruption. It gives me time to think. "You're missing some really great stuff. It's honestly so cool to be inside one of the patient rooms, you won't believe how awesome it is. And Rae seems super into it. I'm actually having trouble getting her to stay focused on the camera, so if you could help—"

"Give us a minute." Ana pins a smile on and turns toward him. "Gracie and I have a few things to discuss."

He frowns. "But I could really use some help with Rae. She seems distracted and I don't know how to—"

"We'll be right in."

"The sun is going to set in less than—"

"We'll be right in," Ana repeats, a sharp edge to her voice. "Why don't you get some shots with Rae and we'll join you shortly?"

"That's the problem, I can't get her to focus. And the sun is going to set soon... I-I need to get these initial shots out of the way before the sun sets."

"If I'm not concerned, then you shouldn't be either," she snaps, and Mason flinches. "The sun doesn't set for another half an hour; there's plenty of time. Now will you leave me and Gracie to our conversation?"

Mason takes a moment to consider, then nods once before disappearing back around the doorframe.

I try to push past Ana, but she places a hand on my shoulder and the flies that swarm around her fingertips fan out, forming a barrier between us and the end of the hallway.

Mason and Rae seem very far away, and the only thing I can think of is rushing through the cloud and grabbing them, running, leaving the hospital, getting as far away as possible.

This was a mistake.

I'll just have to find some other way to help *her*.

I can't stay here.

The flies gather and I brace myself, taking a step into the cloud. They sting like acid against my skin and I stumble back, my heel catching on the molding carpet.

Ana reaches for me, but I refuse to take her hand—I stand on my own, my knees weak. The flies continue to buzz.

"You shouldn't have tried that," she says lightly, clearly enjoying this.

"What are you?" Little pinpricks of red have begun to pop up on the backs of my arms where the flies touched my skin.

"Don't pretend that you don't know." Her smile stretches wider. The sound of tearing skin pierces through the buzzing. "We're not so different, after all."

A bead of sweat drips down my forehead. There's no way she can know about me. There's nothing about me that would even hint at anything being wrong. I look completely normal.

"I know what you're thinking," she continues. "And you might not show any of the signs, but I can always tell when something doesn't belong."

"I don't know what you're talking about." The sweat drips down over my cheek, tracing the side of my face like a tear.

"This world can be a dangerous place. It can be difficult to survive when you're alone, but luckily, Seaside State found me. And now, I've found you."

Bile tickles the back of my throat.

Her expression darkens. "You're not supposed to be here."

"I was invited here, same as you," I spit, my jaw clenched.

"You know that's not what I mean."

My heart thunders against my ribs, waves of heat shooting up into my forehead, but I refuse to believe that she's implying what I think she is.

She places a hand on my shoulder and a shudder runs through me as the flies weave between her fingers. "You have a secret, something that you can't tell anyone. I've got tons of secrets, and all of them have to do with Seaside State. It's a love affair between me and this building, and when I say that I'll protect her, I mean that I'll protect her. At all costs. You'll be saying things too after tonight. Guess you'll have to wait and see if anyone will believe you."

I pry her hand away and take a step back. "I've seen worse than anything this place can throw at me."

"I don't doubt that you have. It's the kind of girl you are, after all. It's in your blood. It's in your *being*."

She leans in close, and it hits me that she doesn't smell like anything. No windblown coldness. No berries or cream. Nothing. It's like I'm standing next to a ghost.

Her lips brush against my ear. Soft. Urgent.

"I know that you're not really Gracie," she whispers. "You're not what you say you are."

5

RAE

Mother continues to hover over me, chilling the back of my neck, her hands inches from my throat. She steers me into the room after Mason and leans in close, her breath warm against my ear.

You're gonna love this, she says. Stop staring at the floor and take a look.

I glance up.

The room is cerulean. Deep, rich, searing hot. Cerulean blue. The kind of color that girls at school wear to accent a look; bright blue shoes with a black dress, a blue bracelet or bow to contrast a neutral outfit, make it "pop." The color is only bearable in small doses. There's too much of it here. Each wall is the same sticky shade of cerulean, floor to ceiling, ceiling to floor and back again. A never-ending circle of burning color. Enough to sear my skin until it flakes in sheets onto the floor.

I gag.

It's the exact same color as my old room at Mother's house. Same layout too. It's claustrophobic—there's hardly enough space to breathe. It has a narrow entrance like a swan neck, which leads to a cramped rectangle.

One bed.

One window.

Too many walls. Saturated in blue paint.

Mother tugs at my hair, howling with laughter.

It's like we're back home, Rae, she wails. We're home, we're home, we're home.

"Ingress," I whisper. One of the words from *that* room. An entrance. To what, I can't be sure.

I press a hand to my middle as dull pain shoots from my gut up to my throat.

Mason stands back by the doorway and turns to look at me, his camera pressed against his face. "Did you say something, Rae?"

"This is where the patient lost their mind?" I ask quietly, digging my fingers in, bracing myself against the nausea.

Mason nods enthusiastically. "The first one, anyway. I was hoping that you'd be able to sense something, or maybe there would be a spike in activity, and we could get some establishing shots to use in the intro sequence, you know?"

There isn't any furniture in the room except for the metal bed frame. It's all rusting springs and sharp edges. I stand by its side and look to the window for comfort, but the heavy canvas curtain is drawn, and the white of it screams against the walls.

My stomach finally settles, and I drop my arm back to my side.

I can't help but think of the top-floor window and its thin white curtain. I can't help but think of the figure that moved behind it. What color is that room? Does it burn the same as this one?

I shut my eyes and yellow spots dance behind my eyelids, an afterimage of sparks mimicking the patterns in the blue paint.

Mother continues to laugh.

"It's easy to see how someone could lose their mind in

here," I breathe, wishing that the dread drained with the nausea.

"I know what you mean." Mason sounds older when my eyes are closed. "It's like we've stepped into an alternate universe. The real world seems far away. That's the beauty of Seaside State, though—everything out there doesn't matter. None of it. The building doesn't care what kind of person you were before you came here, it doesn't care if you don't have any friends, or spend all your time alone in your room. I wasn't sure who I wanted to be before I learned about..."

He continues to ramble on, but I'm barely listening.

The window must be open; there's a draft on my face, a trickle of wind. The air filters into the room and I wonder why I didn't feel it when I first walked in. I open my eyes, but the curtain isn't moving. It might be too heavy to be swayed by wind, or the air might be coming from somewhere else.

"I really can't thank you enough for accepting my invitation, Rae." Mason's voice cuts back into focus, strangely even, alarmingly deep. "I can't begin to explain how important this is to me."

Every gust of air shrieks its way into the room. My skin tingles and I lower my head. The faintest bleed of blue paint slants in through the black of my hair.

"You okay?" Mason asks.

"Fine."

"Because you're not looking at the camera. I mean, you don't need to look *directly* into the camera, but at least be aware of it. You keep turning your back to it. I get this feeling that you're not really interested, and I really can't afford for you to back out now. We're already inside and if I don't have both of you for the..."

His voice fades again and despite the fact that he keeps talking, it's background noise. He's a smudge at the edge of my vision.

I raise my head and move the curtain to the side. Outside, the property stretches beyond the service road, tall grass unswayed by wind. At the edge of the trees, I notice a shadow, a person, a figure. Their features are blurred, but I can see them outlined against the forest, and if I squint hard enough, tilt my head just the right way... it almost looks like Mother. A younger version of Mother, an older version of me. The same dark hair and skinny frame. The same style of floral dress Mother used to wear when she was still alive.

My body goes rigid.

They even *walk* the same way I do, hunched over slightly, elbows drawn in toward their chest. It's like looking in a warped mirror. Sweat breaks out across my forehead.

Panic pulses down my spine and Mother nags at me, but her voice comes in through a filter, distorted and unintelligible.

There's a faint popping sound... somewhere. Like a gun going off, distant fireworks.

The figure outside raises its hand and static erupts through my head.

White noise.

Pop.

White curtain.

Pop. Pop.

I lift my hand in response, wiggle my fingers the same way they do. Twin gestures as the air pops and whistles, as if pockets of heat are bursting around me, as if the world is on fire —drowning out Mother, drowning out everything.

A voice slices through the low hiss of flames, soft and urgent and very clearly not Mother.

The voice is faint as if buried beneath ash and cinder, and I can't pry my eyes away from the figure.

"You understand why, don't you?" the voice begs, so close, so quiet as if whispered against the shell of my ear. "Come find me."

"Rae!" Mason cries and the static, the voice, the figure all disappear at once. He's next to me, his hand clamped down on my shoulder. When did he get so close?

There's a look of raw panic on his face.

"I'm okay." I pry his fingers off me. "I was just... looking out the window and got distracted."

"I-it's not that," he stutters. "Th-the wall next to you."

My brow furrows, but my skin breaks out in goosebumps as I turn and face the slab of cerulean. There, punched into the wall at eye level, are a series of small holes barely the size of a quarter. White plaster bleeds through the deep blue, and the paint chips around the edges. They're in a perfectly straight line.

"They just appeared," Mason says, voice trembling. "One after another, like they were shot into the wall."

The uniform line of holes bores into me like the eyes of a predator.

The only voice in my head belongs to Mother, the only thing in the window is the white curtain, and beyond it, grass and maple trees. But there's something on the grounds of this hospital, inside it too. I know it—I'm convinced now. With the heat of the cerulean paint causing my cheeks to flush, with holes in the wall, I know it's true.

Haunted isn't the right word. Haunted doesn't begin to describe Seaside State.

This place is wrong, this place is sick, yes—but there's more to it than that.

It's speaking to me.

I can hear its voice, and it should feel wrong, I should be afraid, but instead I'm warm. Instead, I'm burning. Instead, I'm—

"I'm fine," I mumble, my eyes trained on the white curtain.

The window is definitely open. No one else seems to notice, not Mason, not Mother. But I'm noticing. Oh yes, I'm noticing.

The way the curtain trembles slightly. Yes, I can hear it now, the subtle shiver of the fabric against the plaster wall every time the air soaks in and violates it.

The air steeps in and the sound of wind is caught by the blue of the walls and dies there. Flypaper walls. What else do they catch? Hands and feet? Shadow beasts? Wandering the halls. Wandering—

"Rae!" Mason claps his hands in front of my face. "Did you not hear me when I said the wall got shot up by seemingly nothing? I called your name probably a thousand times before you answered me."

I jolt back to reality.

"Sorry." I can't feel the wind anymore. The air inside the little blue room is dense. It's suffocating.

Heat rises to my cheeks. I made a fool of myself. It's like what happened with the white room; the hospital pulled me in and now I look like a fool.

"What's wrong with you?" he asks, his eyes wide.

"I need air." I push past him, stumbling into the hall to find Ana and Gracie staring each other down.

Gracie's mouth is set in a thin line, and she looks green around the edges like she did earlier when we were still outside. But it's not her I'm focused on, it's Ana. Her eyes glisten and her grin is stretched a little too wide. It's cartoonish, terrifying, as if at any moment the corners of her mouth may rip, and something will peel her skin back and climb out.

I freeze, my heart in my throat, but they don't notice me.

Mother leans in close. YOU SHOULD GO BACK INSIDE THE BLUE ROOM. YOU AREN'T SUPPOSED TO SEE THIS.

The hospital shudders around me as if to agree with her, and a knot forms in the pit of my stomach because the hospital knows she's here. It must know what I'm here to do, but it won't show me its heart, it won't help me.

It doesn't want to.

RAE, Mother repeats, her voice sharp and urgent. STOP STARING, YOU'RE GOING TO GET YOURSELF IN TROUBLE.

"You can't tell me what to do anymore, Mother. You're dead." A trail of blood drips from my left nostril and I cover my nose with the sleeve of my hoodie.

I CAN DO WHATEVER I WANT, BABY GIRL, Mother hisses and I'm hit by another wave of nausea.

I wipe the blood from my upper lip and take a step forward, despite the lump in my throat and the way my stomach churns. "So can I."

DON'T.

"Is something wrong?" I call to Ana and Gracie, careful to keep some distance between us.

Ana's face snaps back to normal, and for a moment I wonder if I was imagining the unnatural smile.

Gracie pushes past her and takes slow, calculated steps over to where I stand, her kitten heels clicking against the tile. She stops a few paces in front of me, her back to Ana, and tosses her hair out of her eyes. That's when I notice the fine sheen of sweat across her forehead.

"You look like you've seen a ghost," I say, my stomachache fading. It lasted longer this time. Each time, it lasts longer. And the pain keeps getting worse. I'm hit by a sudden, inexplicable urge to call Eliza and own up to everything I've been feeling in the weeks leading up to the documentary. Would she take me to see a doctor? Would I let her?

"Oh, please," Gracie scoffs. "As if seeing a ghost would bother me. It's kinda my whole *thing*." She glances down at the fresh blood drying against my sleeve. "And you're one to talk, you look like shit."

I flinch.

Her tone is so much harsher than earlier when we argued about Mother. Her eyes are steely, no light in them. They're cruel eyes, beyond that of your typical high school mean girl. It's like I'm speaking to a completely different person.

Then her expression softens, and the cruel mask melts away so quickly it's as if it was never even there.

"I'm sorry," she says, her voice trembling slightly. She slowly stretches out her hand as if trying to prove to a wounded animal that she isn't a threat. "I'm a little on edge; I shouldn't have snapped like that."

Ana stays standing in the center of the hallway a few paces away, her expression blank, her gaze fixed on Gracie.

"Did something happen between you and Ana?" I ask, gently pushing her hand to the side. She startles as our skin makes contact. *Did you see her smile? Did you see how wrong it was? Tell me you saw it too.*

"Did something happen between you and Mason? Why isn't he out here too? He said you were freaking out again and wouldn't look at the camera or something." Gracie rubs at the back of her hand as if she could wipe my touch away. I hate the pang of hurt that runs through me at the sight.

"I thought I saw... My mother told me that... Never mind." Even if I tried to explain the figure I saw, even if she knew what it was, she'd only deny its existence. "But I could have sworn that Ana... Are you sure you're okay?"

Mason finally emerges from the blue room to join her in the center of the hall.

"Ana," he says, looking dazed, his camera swinging from his neck. "I have a couple of things I wanna... ummm... run by you about tonight."

"Everything's fine," Gracie says with a tired looking smile, her hand finally dropped back next to her side. "Don't worry about me. You have enough to deal with as it is."

Ana stands huddled with Mason in the center of the hall, the two of them locked in hurried conversation. They're talking about me, I can tell. They're making fun of me.

Gracie opens her mouth as if to say something, but quickly closes it. She runs a finger along the back of her hand again, then shakes her head. "You're never going to get rid of that thing if you keep feeding it, you know."

"Excuse me?"

"The thing you call Mother. Stop feeding it. It'll only get stronger until there's nothing left of you." She walks over to Mason, avoiding eye contact with Ana. Mason stops mid-sentence and grins at her, though the smile doesn't reach his eyes. He looks exhausted, and I regret everything that happened in the blue room. I know it's my fault he's so stressed. He probably thinks I'm gonna snap in here.

Ana's eyes focus in on me and a chill runs through me.

"Rae, hurry up. We don't want to leave you behind." She smiles and it's nothing like the cartoonish grin I saw before. Again, I wonder if I imagined it. "Come along, this is only the beginning. There's so much more to see."

Mason nods and links arms with her. Even Gracie, despite the undeniable tension between Ana and herself, falls into line with them.

I follow a few paces back.

I'm nothing like them, I think over and over, and every scuff on the tile floor repeats it back to me.

Mason walks in time with Ana, and their feet fall in unison.

I'm nothing like them, and I don't know if I mean Gracie, or Mason, or Ana, or which I feel worse about.

As we continue through the hospital, I look out through the windows, hoping to catch another glimpse of the figure from earlier. I don't tell the others about it, and Mother stays tight-lipped about everything that happened in the blue room.

She stays draped across my shoulders, and I ignore the heaviness inside my chest, the voice inside my head that says Seaside State hungers for me, not Mother. That it wants nothing more than to clamp its jaws down on my neck, and everything up until now—the layout of the rooms, the colors of the paint so similar to home, the figure lurking in the window and on the grounds—it's all connected.

I can almost hear it pleading with me, its voice in the wind that filters in through the cracked windows, in the texture of the peeling paint.

Run.

Leave this place.

Leave *me.*

Gracie's supposed to be psychic, but I don't think she can hear it. I'm the only one.

I shiver.

There are types of parasitic fungi that slowly take over their hosts, replacing the host cells with their own until there's nothing left of the original. Some fungi can even influence the behavior of the insects they inhabit. It's one of Mother's words: *entomopathogenic.* It hung to the left of where I would be forced to stand when she sent me to *that* room. It was written in blue ballpoint pen, the "e" and "n" bleeding into one another. The "e" slowly invading.

I know this place is wrong, like a fungus eating its host. But other things are worse, other things hurt more than plaster and peeling walls. When I refused to drink my tea Mother would—

"Are you ready for the next stop on our tour?" Ana asks and I jump.

She's standing next to me, a lazy smile plastered across her face. I didn't even notice her fall back from the group.

"Which room is next?" I ask, pushing thoughts of Mother and *that* room from my mind.

Her grin stretches wider, and I don't think I imagined what I saw before after all.

I don't think I imagined what happened in the cerulean room either.

It's real. Like the stones that rained down over my childhood home that spring afternoon three years ago. The way the rocks shattered the windows. The way Mother and I huddled against the back of the couch while shards of glass spread across the floor.

"The morgue," Ana says, showing too many teeth.

6

GRACIE

People tell me all the time that I'm a good girl. I have the looks, the grades, the athletic ability. I'm privileged but not entitled, flirty but not a tease. Blonde hair, blue eyes, shy smile. I'm a good girl.

Except all these definitions people stick me with like push-pins are only part of who I am. *What* I am.

I'm pretty, but it's a mask. It's latex pulled tight over rot.

I'm smart, but only when it comes to playing my role.

My whole life is a performance. An illusion. A carefully crafted lie.

It's like how a mortician paints a corpse, pumps it full of chemicals, coats it in wax. In the right lighting, it almost looks alive again.

I'm not good, but I'm not bad either. I'm the muddled in-between.

And I'm dangerous.

~

The room doesn't feel like a morgue.

It's too alive. There's brightness in the margarine-colored walls, an inner light that makes the room glow. Patient documents lay scattered across the floor alongside vials with red plastic caps, their bodies clouded and scratched. They're everywhere, the pinpricks of red, bleeding through the paleness of the room. There's life in the hot flashes of color, even though the hospital feels dead, and Seaside State still refuses to open up to me.

Not that it matters now.

"It's so strange the way the walls are peeling," Rae murmurs, running a finger across the yellow paint chips. "There's green underneath, and white under that. Three layers."

She's right.

The room is skinned alive, all its insides spilling out onto the floor. Epidermis, dermis, and the muscle underneath. The morgue.

I keep glancing over at Rae. Earlier, when she interrupted me and Ana, her eyes were glassy and feverish. And that nosebleed... I shudder, thinking of the blood.

She's getting worse.

I can't stop thinking about the way it felt when her hand touched mine. It was like a shock from live wire, and my skin continued to tingle long after she let go. She felt so alive. It cuts into me to think of someone with that much life snuffed out.

It reminds me of the way *her* light slowly fizzled after she fell prey to her attachment.

I know I shouldn't care, and I know there's nothing I could do even if I wanted to, but I keep tabs on Rae's attachment anyway. I watch and wonder if, when it finally bites into her too deeply, I would be able to help.

Even though you can't even help yourself, I think bitterly. Now that Ana knows what I am, it's even more important that I break from the group as soon as possible. Hell, I need to get off this property altogether. Forget the rest of the grounds and violent patient ward, I need to find some other way to help *her,* because the longer I stay here, the deeper the hole I'm in—and it's only a matter of time before Ana starts shoveling dirt in over me.

She saunters over, a whisper of a smile dancing across her lips.

A handful of her flies stay close, clinging to the wall next to where I stand. If I take a step out of line, if I turn toward the door, they'll descend on me. Biting, stinging like acid. And they're nothing compared to what Ana is capable of.

I have no choice but to play along.

She inches up next to me and places a bony hand on my shoulder. "Have you thought about what I said out in the hall?"

"You don't want to do this here," I warn, glancing sideways to where Rae stands inspecting one of the peeling walls while Mason films her.

"Afraid of what would happen to the others if our conversation were to escalate?" Ana arches a brow while she hooks her fingers deeper into my skin. "Seaside State doesn't care. She wants an answer, and I'm not afraid to get rough if that's what she instructs me to do."

My skin prickles when I think of what she told me before Rae interrupted.

I was right to think that the hospital was masking something—but it's not pain. Even the aura out front is a carefully designed plot to lure people inside.

It's insidious, calculating.

And I'm sure Ana is the least of the sharp and deadly tools at its disposal.

I only have myself to blame for being in this position. I should have gotten a proper read on the building when I was out on the service road; I should have recognized Ana's cloud of flies for what it is. Guilt, like sticky tar, coats my insides. Because it's my own fault that I won't be able to save *her.*

Coming here was a mistake.

I pry Ana's fingers from my shoulder. "I already told you. I'm here for me, I'm not interested in anything else."

"You seem plenty interested in Rae," she says with a smirk. "You haven't taken your eyes off her since our conversation."

Heat rises to my cheeks. "It's like I said before, I'm only keeping an eye on that thing attached to her back."

"Seems out of character for something like you to care about anything other than itself."

"I'm not—I'm not like that anymore."

"Sure you're not," she teases.

I can't help but tense, my hands curling into fists.

"It's no matter. You'll come around eventually." She flicks her wrist, and three more flies join the insects keeping watch over me. "I'm sure I can convince you."

"Doubt it." Once I can figure out a way past her flies, I'm out of here. She talks about the building as if it's conscious, as if it's like her, but that's impossible. The things that attach themselves to buildings are built of raw emotion; they aren't like malums, they aren't sentient. I know that Seaside State is housing something a bit more advanced than the average attachment, but what she's implying can't be possible.

Even after her offer, her invitation, she still hasn't explained exactly what's going on here.

All I know for sure is that Seaside State isn't a normal asylum, and the blush-colored aura that surrounded it out on the service road is only the half of its issues.

Whatever's really going on here, I don't want any part of it. If it wasn't for *her*, I wouldn't have agreed to help with Mason's documentary in the first place. I never wanted to come within spitting distance of the violent patient ward again after what happened the last time. When I was here with *her*. When I... I shake my head, clear the memory.

This whole place leaves a sour taste in my mouth.

It's made worse by the fact that there's no way to get out of here without Ana noticing and trying to retaliate. Now that I know what she is—a malum who's completely devoured her human host, a malum who uses a cloud of flies to manipulate what's essentially a corpse—I know she won't let me go without a fight.

Ana makes her way across the room to where Rae stands, and my skin prickles. She places a hand on the back of Rae's neck and looks over at me, a sick grin spreading across her face.

I'll snap her neck, the grin seems to say. *One step out of line, and I'll break her into pieces.*

"They used to bring dead bodies here?" Rae asks, the malum at her back leaning in close. She attempts to pull back, but Ana's hand stays clamped in place.

She nods and ushers Rae over to a wall in the back of the room. There's a metal frame in the wall, cut into smaller squares that fade back into darkness. Mason hurries after them with his camera at the ready.

I follow, the entourage of flies close by—singing, screaming. Waiting for me to try to run so they can bite, and Ana can have her fun.

"This thing used to have doors and trays," Ana tells us, finally releasing the back of Rae's neck. "Now only the frame is left."

I narrow my eyes, not sure why she's carrying on the charade. Part of me wishes she'd kill Rae already. Slash Mason in half. Let down the façade so there's nothing left for her to threaten me with. She's right, in a way. I shouldn't even care about the others.

I wish I didn't.

"This is where they put the bodies, isn't it?" Rae presses a hand to her stomach as if trying to keep from spewing her lunch, her face pale, though the malum shrinks against her spine. I wonder if she can feel the flies that dart between Ana's fingers, if on some subconscious level she's aware of their wings against her skin.

Ana nods. "These were the cold chambers. They put the bodies in here to slow the decomposition process while they were waiting for autopsy and embalming."

The way Mason looks at her sends ice water running through my veins. The reverence. The blind admiration. All because she's halfway decent-looking and gives him the faintest amount of attention.

If he knew what she really was, he'd shit himself.

"I don't really understand why they bothered, though," Ana continues. "So many of them went into unmarked graves. Well, not completely unmarked. They were numbered at least. Didn't put any names on the stones, though. Their families didn't care how they died, or if they were dead. Some didn't even have families at all. Many people were abandoned here."

A strange expression settles across Rae's face and she opens and closes her mouth a few times, looking like a fish gulping in air, struggling to breathe.

"Can you give me directions to where they used to bury the bodies?" she finally asks. "There has to be a cemetery or some-thing... over at the edge of the property." She glances toward one of the tall windows at the corner of the room. Her aura buzzes, the same color as before but thinner, lighter, like a rain jacket. Something has her keyed up.

"That's not a good idea," Ana says and Mason nods in agreement, hanging on the outskirts of the conversation with wide eyes, like a dog hoping for table scraps.

I wonder what I look like to them, or if they're aware of me at all. Ana's flies still circle my head, but maybe I could slip away while they're distracted. Maybe I could get out of this after all. The flies would burn me, sure. Ana would probably unleash hell on Rae and Mason, but I shouldn't care about that. It isn't my problem. I could get out of here and—

But then I catch Rae's eye and notice the fear—the sharp, glassy panic, and her pinpoint pupils.

The ache in my chest. The things I *feel* when I look at her. It's like a rubber band pulled taut. It's too much.

I can't leave her.

It'll be near impossible to pry Mason away from Ana; he's clearly obsessed with her. Plus, she's stapled to his hip. But maybe I have a chance at saving Rae.

At the very least, I could try.

We could get out of here together.

My heart races at the thought.

"Actually," I say carefully. "Rae has a point."

"I do?" she asks, perplexed.

I take a moment to think about how I'm gonna spin this. Ana won't go along with it, but if I can get Mason on board, she might not have a choice.

I have to assume that she wants to keep playing human for as long as she can. Letting her mask slip would mean the end of whatever long con she's pulling here. Even if she didn't care about killing them, she'd have to explain the bodies since there's ample evidence of her correspondence with Mason. It would be damning for her little tour group to turn up dead.

Unless she doesn't care about playing human and she's just using the others as leverage, keeping them around because she knows I care too much. A chill runs through me. I can't think like this—I need to believe there's a chance.

"It might be worth it to get more footage outside," I begin, willing my voice to remain steady. "Different angles of the property and all that. It doesn't even need to be professional grade or anything. Rae and I could go out and shoot it and meet you guys back here. Like, we could totally record stuff on our phones, and you can splice it in with whatever you've been filming."

Mason shakes his head and my heart drops. "It'll be dark soon. It would be dangerous to split up so close to sunset."

I point toward the window. "Sun's still going strong."

"You'll never be able to find your way back here." He drags his camera strap back and forth across his already red neck. "This place is a labyrinth. It's easy to get turned around. And it's so big there's no telling how long it would take you to find your way back again."

"We'll be fine. I'm really good with directions."

Ana shakes her head and frowns. "I'm afraid I can't allow it. It wouldn't be safe, for you or the hospital."

She locks eyes with me and the flies swirl around my head. I swat at them, the tips of my fingers stinging when I smack one out of the air.

Ana flicks her bony wrist a fraction of an inch, beckoning the remaining flies back to her while the one I hit writhes on the tile floor. She glowers at me before patting Rae on the shoulder, flies swarming between the webs of her fingers.

"Give us a moment, dear," she tells Rae, making her way toward me. "Gracie and I need to have a chat. Mason, why don't you continue the conversation with Rae?"

"But I thought—"

"Continue the conversation with Rae," she repeats, a sharp edge to her voice.

Mason grabs Rae by the arm and pulls her to the opposite end of the room. She shakes free from his grasp but continues to follow him as he starts in again on why leaving would be a terrible idea.

"It's not that I don't trust you, but we came here to make *my* movie," he begins before they move out of earshot and his voice tapers off.

I shift back against one of the cabinets and keep my eyes on Rae, who's now locked in conversation with Mason, her aura slowly morphing back to the color of burnt honey.

Ana leans in close so the others can't hear.

"What were you trying to accomplish with that little outburst? You didn't really think you could just walk out of here, did you?" she whispers, stroking one of her flies with the tip of her pointer finger.

"Did you really think that I would agree to something without knowing the terms? You haven't told me shit about how this whole thing would even work."

She chuckles again. "I'm asking nicely for now. But the clock is ticking, and my patience is wearing thin. Seaside State rarely gives this much time for deliberation; you're lucky she likes you."

Seaside State likes me? It could have fooled me... It's given me nothing but the silent treatment since I got here. And that's not the only thing that's been weighing on me.

I nod toward Rae and Mason. "Why are they here if the point of all this was to get to me?"

She clucks her tongue. "Don't be a narcissist. You're just the cherry on top of the sundae."

"Whatever," I say, pushing past her, but my scalp prickles when I realize what Ana must be keeping the others around for.

She's a malum, after all. She may be puppeting a corpse, but she's not getting any nutrients from it—any unstable emotions it had are long since gone. She needs live bodies to feed. Her swarm of flies must leave the rotting husk she's controlling every so often to find fresh meat. Though I can imagine constantly needing to scrounge for food would get old real fast.

She needs a consistent meal source.

Rae is off the table since she already has her own parasite. She obviously doesn't want to attach to me... given what I am. My guess is that she's targeting Mason. Her corpse has just about run out of juice and it's time to move on to the next one. But she's waiting for my answer before she jumps ship.

You're just the cherry on top of the sundae.

She meant to feed off of Mason this whole time. It wasn't until she saw me on the service road—saw what I am, heard the hospital's whisper in her ear—that she decided to try to draw me into her web.

Rae's collateral damage.

Mason's her next meal.

It all goes back to what Seaside State is, and why Ana's so hellbent on me signing on as a part of her operation.

Out in the hall, she told me that Seaside State is hungry, that there's truth to the stories about this place. It's alive, more a monster than a building. But it can't feed itself, and with fewer and fewer people wandering through its doors each day, it's only a matter of time before it starves.

Ana hunts for it. She brings in runaways, and hitchhikers, and homeless people.

Ana's a servant to Seaside State.

She feeds it.

7

———

RAE

The summer before Mother died, we had mice in our walls. Mother set up traps in the dining room and kitchen, tried for weeks to get rid of the pests on her own before she finally called an exterminator. She'd storm around the house, holding the mousetraps at arm's length between her pointer finger and thumb.

"Filthy, dirty creatures!" she would cry. "Never did like mice. No, your Grandma Perry always ignored them, always let them get into whatever they pleased. But I'm not gonna stand for it. Those filthy things think they can bring sickness into *my* house? Ha! They're the reason you're so ill, baby girl. I guarantee it. I'll show *them!*"

I didn't mind the mice. I only ever saw them when they got caught in Mother's traps, spines collapsed, bodies flattened. The life squeezed out of them.

In a way, I can relate.

It's how I feel every time I open my mouth. Like a mouse in a trap, body squished flat. Intestines squeezed out through my mouth like I'm a tube of toothpaste.

"Sorry for even suggesting we go off on our own," I

mumble, apologizing to Mason for the thousandth time. "I know we need to stick together as long as we're in here. And I know we're here for your movie, but I thought... I don't know. I'm sorry I asked."

Mother runs her fingers through my hair. SILLY GIRL, WHAT WERE YOU TRYING TO ACCOMPLISH?

I'm not even sure. I thought if I could get away from the group, I might still have a chance at finding the heart of the building. I could make my offering and get rid of Mother. I could forget about all the stupid things I've done since coming here, all the things I've said wrong, all the ways I've embarrassed myself. The white room, and the blue room, and the figure that looks too much like Mother. I thought I could run away from it all.

Mason smiles and waves his hand, the one with the camera, moving it back and forth awkwardly. "I already told you, it's fine. I get how being in here can be unnerving if you're not into this kind of thing. It's not like it's been hard to notice how you've been freaking out since we got in here, you know? You're clearly having second thoughts about the documentary."

"It's not that..."

"No seriously, it's okay. You said you're here cause your mom liked this place, right? Well, you're not her."

"That's putting it lightly," I mumble, not even bothering to correct him. Mother didn't like this place; she was obsessed with the tragedy of '65.

"You don't have to worry," Mason continues. "You're not gonna be here much longer. I'm sorry I got all weird on you before, about playing to the camera and all that. Honestly, your freak outs are probably the most interesting thing we've captured since getting here. Though I'll have to review the tapes later, and I'm sure we've captured things that you're not even aware of. But point is, I get it. You're weirded out, it's normal."

"Again, that's not... Never mind. Thanks, Mason."

He seems satisfied and turns his attention to the rows of beakers that line the shelves, zooming the camera in on various sections of the abandoned instruments. It's like I'm not even here. He's completely engrossed in the hospital's dark treasures.

"He didn't care about how upset I was, did he?" I whisper and Mother chuckles as we move back toward the center of the room. "All he cares about is filming his movie."

WHY WOULD HE CARE? NO ONE CARES FOR YOU THE WAY THAT I DO. IT'S THE TWO OF US AGAINST THE WORLD, ALWAYS HAS BEEN.

She's right.

All the defiance I felt earlier, all the resentment melts away. Because I know what she's saying is true. She cares for me.

She may have been harsh when she was alive, but at least she was honest. She always told me exactly what I did wrong. She pointed out when the words I chose were subpar, and what I should have said instead. She was blunt about the sentences I failed to string together, and how important it was for me to learn how to be better.

She was my family.

Eliza always sugarcoats things, speaking to me softly as if I'm a toddler. Her father ignores me altogether and then has the nerve to complain when *I* don't talk to *him*.

They don't care.

But Mother did—she still does.

Tears spring to my eyes and I quickly swat them away.

"I love you, Mother," I whisper. "I'm so sorry for dragging you here with me."

And I *am* sorry. I'm sorry that she felt the need to hang around after her death, I'm sorry for everything that happened the night she died—and everything that didn't. I'm sorry that no matter what happens after this, things will never truly get back to normal.

There is no normal.

There never was.

Somehow, the thought gives me new resolve and I curl my fingers into my palm, making a fist.

So what if Mason doesn't give a shit about how I'm feeling?

I came here for myself.

And for Mother. It will be better for both of us if she's finally put to rest.

The hospital continues to sigh around me, though it gives no sign of where its heart is, or how I can find it. Even though I heard it so clearly while I was in the blue room, even though it told me to come home, I can't help but feel like it wants me gone.

Ana and Gracie walk back over to me, faces pulled taut as a violin string.

Ana locks eyes with me and her expression softens. "Sorry, we didn't mean to exclude you. Where's Mason?"

"Busy." I nod back to where he's flitting like an insect around the cabinets.

Ana chuckles. "He's so predictable. Anyway, I apologize for disregarding your voice."

"I should be the one apologizing to you," I tell her. "I know you can't let us run around here unsupervised. I shouldn't have asked."

Ana chuckles again, a light sound, bells through the dead room. "It's perfectly fine, Rae. I understand wanting to experience as much of the hospital as possible, but you'll have plenty of time to get acquainted with Seaside State. This is only your introduction."

It's as if I'm hit by a blast of cold air and I wrap my arms around my middle. I try to respond but I can't find the words and only manage to open and close my mouth in rapid succession. Ana watches me with a look in her eyes that's halfway between pity and disgust.

You're embarrassing yourself again, Mother chides, her

fingers scraping down my cheeks. She holds tightly to either side of my face, forcing me to look straight ahead.

My first impulse is to jerk free, but I suck in a breath and endure it.

She's doing it because she cares, I remind myself. *I need to be better.*

"It was stupid of me to ask," I tell the girls, finally managing to push the words out.

"Rae..." Gracie says, her voice genuine and warm, which only makes it hurt worse. "It wasn't stupid. You don't need to apologize." She casts a sideways glance toward Ana. "There's actually something I want to talk to you about."

Do you buy that crap? She's making fun of you, Mother reminds me. You never were any good with words.

I push past Gracie, too embarrassed to continue the conversation, and make my way to the opposite side of the room.

"Rae, wait! I need to talk to you." But Ana catches her by the wrist, and she steps back. She doesn't really care.

"Leave me alone," I say and continue to stare straight ahead, Mother's fingers digging into my cheeks.

I take deep breaths and try to center myself, refusing to think about the false sympathy in Gracie's voice or Ana's condescending tone.

None of it matters, not while I'm inside Seaside State.

Not while I'm inside the morgue.

There are shelves lined with beakers and different sized machines with gray knobs. There are areas of the floor with dark-colored stains, the remains of formaldehyde and body fluids, postmortem drippings. The morgue awakens my imagination. Dips in the ceiling, indicative of water damage, become sagging lungs, a bloated stomach. *Corporeal*; another one of Mother's words. It was dead center on the wall of words. That too awake in all its layers.

I lean down and pick up a toe tag. There's a circle of red

material around the metal part where the string is woven through. Red running through the core of this place.

The girls convene around Mason, who straightens up and focuses his camera on them. I watch the group from a distance, and it feels like watching fish swim around a bowl.

Mason and Ana stand on either side of Gracie, both talking to her in low voices, and I feel myself ache from the separateness of it all. It doesn't matter what I say, I'll always be the one looking in through a pane of glass from the outside.

I shake my head.

I have to be better now, I tell myself even as Mother tugs at the ends of my hair, even as my stomach gurgles—from hunger or nausea I can't be sure, and I'm certain now that the hospital won't rid me of her ghost.

I have to be better.

I busy myself at the edge of the room, opening and closing cabinets, rearranging beakers, attempting to read the hurried scrawl on old scraps of paper.

To the left of the cabinets, there's a chunk of wall where the paint has peeled away completely to reveal smooth plaster. I notice it out of the corner of my eye, and it isn't until I turn to face it that I realize...

...this exposed section of wall is roughly my height, roughly my size, roughly my shape. It's completely smooth, clean, and seemingly untouched by the decay that's eroded the rest of the hospital.

A shadow of me.

A silhouette of me against a peeling wall.

My body tenses.

The same hiss of heat I felt in the blue room tugs at the corners of my psyche. The crackle of a fire burning low.

"Rae," the voice from before whispers. Soft, urgent. "Rae, I'm right here. I'm waiting."

So loud. Like it's coming from inside.

My breath comes in shallow gasps, and I pick at the scabs of blood on my sleeve.

If Seaside State refuses to show me its heart, if it refuses to pull Mother from my back, then why does it call to me?

Why is it so loud?

I dig my hand into my pocket and run my fingers over the gum from earlier. Try to calm myself. Try to convince myself that this is like what happened with Gracie, with Ana, with Mason. I know the hospital is taunting me. It doesn't really care.

Then why do I still hear you? Even though the words never leave my mouth, it answers.

"I'm here, come find me," it says. "Come home to me."

Home?

An ache in my chest. A panicked sigh through my veins.

I don't have a home. Not with Eliza and her father. I've never truly belonged anywhere, with anyone.

But still, I pull my hand from my pocket and walk up to the plaster, to the shadow of myself. As I run my fingers around its corners, the splintered paint chips that form a halo around it cause my skin to tingle. It doesn't look like something artificial, and that's what scares me. It looks organic, original to the hospital, like a birthmark. If not a birthmark, something shaved into its side, an opening created to assist with breathing or bleeding or draining fluid.

The fire continues to roar in my ears.

"Rae, I'm right here," the voice urges. Is it louder than before? Clearer?

I stand inches from the plaster, my hand shaking. Mother rears up behind me and even though she doesn't say anything, I can tell that she doesn't approve of this. If she were still alive, she would pull out her dictionary and rattle off a list of infections like a death sentence. If Mother knew what I was hearing, she'd insist I leave.

For all I know, this is another side effect of her attachment, a slow boiling of my brain until I'm too weak to stand, too sick to fight as she continues to hover over me. Punishment until I join her in the afterlife.

But I can't hear Mother; I can barely feel her rough hands on my skin. I hear only static, and a panicked whisper begging me to—

"Find me."

...and I'm not sure if I should listen, but the smooth plaster sits in front of me, a birthmark or a bleeding wound. Exactly my shape and size.

Like this place was meant for me.

Across the morgue, Mason calls my name. Something about moving on to another part of the hospital. I glance over. He stands in the entryway, Ana to his left.

Gracie locks eyes with me and waves me over.

"Rae, come on. We're leaving!" There's panic in her voice, raw and desperate. "I'm sorry I upset you before. Please, don't be mad."

I stare and blink, not sure what to do. Should I stay here, or follow the others?

What exactly is calling me? And where does it want me to go?

"Rae!" Gracie tries again when I don't answer.

"Yes?" I say, looking up at her, my voice strained. How can they not notice my silhouette in the wall?

In a way, I already know why they haven't. Seaside State doesn't want them, it wants me. It's showing me, calling out to me—they aren't a part of this.

"Are you okay?" she asks, one foot already out the door.

Nodding, I pull away from the wall and make my way over to the others.

I look down at my fingers. The tips of them are red. Dribbles of blood slide down and gather in the folds of my knuckles. Dark. Partially dried. All over the hand I laid across the plaster.

Cherry bright. Weeping through the dark, dried blood.

I shut my eyes. I can't feel it on my fingers, but it's there. My fingers, my knuckles are caked in it. Seaside State has left its mark.

WHAT IS IT, RAE BABY? Mother asks, and I realize she can't see it.

If she could, she would have a lot to say about this, wouldn't she? Her baby girl in a morgue. Her baby girl with blood on her hand.

If she were still alive, she wouldn't let me hear the end of it.

IT'S YOUR OWN FAULT, RAE, she'd say. YOU DIDN'T DRINK YOUR TEA AFTER DINNER. YOU DIDN'T FLUSH OUT ALL THE TOXINS IN YOUR STOMACH. YOU LEFT THE HOUSE WITHOUT YOUR MOTHER AND NOW LOOK AT YOU.

I'm sorry, Mother. I'm sorry. I open my eyes and pull my hand up close to my face.

The blood is gone.

It's like it was never there.

Just like the white room and all its sterilized perfection. Just like the breeze in the blue room, and the stones that rained down over my roof in early spring. This wall, this blood is exactly the same.

Andromorphic, Mother would call it. *Aberrant.*

She'd write it out in her thin scrawl on a scrap of paper. An edge torn from a grocery list, or the back of a receipt maybe.

Stick it to the wall.

But, Mother!

Stick it to the wall with the others!

"Come on, Rae," Gracie calls. She waits by the entrance to the morgue, Ana at her side. She twists her body, leaning as far from Ana as the doorway allows.

"Coming!" I call and hurry in their direction, wondering why she's suddenly being so friendly toward me.

"You go on ahead, I'm gonna make sure Rae is okay," Gracie tells Ana as I make it to the door.

Ana frowns slightly. "I can't leave you unattended."

"You won't need to," Gracie insists. "We'll be within view; I just need two minutes with Rae."

Her eyes dig into Ana's and the woman in the sundress opens her mouth to protest but then closes it again.

"Fine," she says and moves to meet Mason in the center of the hall. "But the clock's ticking."

It isn't until she steps back that I notice the look on Gracie's face. She's pale, covered in a fine sheen of sweat—though with her good looks, it seems more like an attractive misting. She picks at her nails and waits until Ana makes it to Mason before leaning into me, as if she's not sure what to say or how to say it.

"If this is about earlier," I say, "I don't need you treating me like some wounded puppy. I know I was wrong, and I tried to apologize, but instead you—"

She clamps her hand down over my mouth. "Keep your voice down, and no matter what you think about what I'm about to say, keep your expression blank. Ana can't know what I'm telling you."

She pulls her hand away and runs a finger over my lips.

"What are you talking about?" I ask.

"We need to leave now. We need to leave, or Ana will kill us."

8

GRACIE

"I'm serious. Ana is going to kill us unless we leave right now." I lean in close to Rae and whisper the words frantically in her ear. It's a shade of the truth, halfway to a lie, but I'm hoping that it will be enough to convince her.

Ana and Mason stand only a few paces in front of us, and Ana keeps looking back to check on me and tap her bony wrist, the flies gathering in her palm. *Clock's ticking...*

But she hasn't sent a fresh batch of insects to keep watch over me, so if I'm going to do something, it needs to be now.

Rae narrows her eyes. "You think I'm dumb. You're trying to turn me into a joke, make me freak out again so you can laugh at me behind my back. I know what you and Ana were talking about earlier."

"Believe me, you have no idea." I tuck my hair behind my ears and keep my expression grave. "I know that you're being affected by this place, way more than I am. I think Mason was right when he pegged you for a psychic."

"I mean, I have been... seeing things." She shifts from one foot to the other, chewing her bottom lip.

"And you can't pretend that you don't feel like something is wrong with Ana."

"Anathema," she mumbles as she rubs the back of her neck, scrubbing at the place where Ana's fingers settled earlier. "She's strange, but that doesn't mean she wants us dead."

"She does, believe me. She's been saying some really weird shit to me since we got here, and I'm done listening to it and pretending it doesn't set off alarm bells."

The malum slides around Rae's neck, resting its head against her collarbone. She rolls her shoulders and it settles into the grove of her clavicle. It shivers as several of its houseflies shake loose from its silhouette and perch along the line of Rae's jaw. It's all I can do not to swat them away.

I jab my kitten heel into the sagging tiles. I'm messing this up, badly. Somehow, I thought it would be easier to convince her to leave with me. But she doesn't know half of what's been going on, and I don't have the time to explain now. I don't know *how* to explain. As it is, Ana keeps casting angry glances back at me, and I know she won't give us much longer to talk.

Or worse, she'll dispatch her horseflies and then I'll really be screwed.

"We need to go now."

The malum slinks down to the base of Rae's feet and she shifts to the side so as not to disturb it. "I can't go anywhere until Mother is gone."

"I already told you, there's no getting rid of—look, there's something wrong with Ana. We can't keep following her, she's not leading us anywhere good. I know where the entrance to the endless staircase is," I lie. "If Seaside State is gonna take our offerings, that's where it's gonna happen."

I look down at my purple nails. Exorcism. I know that I'm not getting what I came here for. I know that it's wrong to give false hope to a dying girl, but if I can't save *her,* I need to save

Rae, with her biting words and gnawing insecurities. She's so endearingly defensive. So alive.

Please, let me have this one thing. Let me feed the ache in my chest, the sickly, human pain until it consumes me completely. Let me feel.

Please, let this broken girl continue to make me feel.

Rae's forehead is knotted in concentration. She curls her fingers into her palms, face drained of color, beads of sweat dripping down from her hairline.

"Are you okay?" I ask as the malum at her back swells. "I know this is a lot to take in, but you look seriously pale."

She looks at me, her eyes wide. I never realized how big they were—liquid brown, so dark they border on black. I could drown in them.

"The heart of the building... it's the endless staircase," she says. "The heart is the staircase."

The heart? What?

I do my best to keep my expression neutral, keep staring at her with the same intensity as before. "Yes. If you want to feed the building, it needs to be on the endless staircase and they're not about to take you there."

"Don't lag behind for too long, girls," Ana calls from down the hall. I twist my head and although she smiles pleasantly, there's a sharpness in her eyes. She stands stiffly, wound tight as if the wrong move will cause her to pounce.

"Tick tock," Ana says, Mason wringing his hands next to her. He hops from one foot to the other as if standing still will allow the linoleum tiles to burn through the bottoms of his shoes.

Rae wraps her arms around her middle.

I shake my head. "Seriously, are you okay?"

"Stomachache," she says, hunching over further. "It happens when I'm nervous, and it'll get worse if you don't tell me what's going on. If you knew that the staircase was the only thing that could get rid of Mother, why didn't you say something sooner?"

"We don't have time for this," I snap.

"What about Mason?" she asks, and I breathe a sigh of relief that she's finally starting to consider it. "If Ana is as dangerous as you say she is, we can't leave him behind."

Mason, with his cottage cheese aura. Mason, who looks at Ana like she's a goddess walking the earth. Mason who's never gonna do anything with his pathetic excuse for a life even if I save it.

"He's deadweight," I say. "And she's gonna come over here soon if you don't make a decision."

"Do you really think it would be alright to leave Mason behind?" The malum peeks out from behind her legs, swirling along the surface of the tile floor.

"He won't believe a word we say no matter what we do. The best way to help him would be to get out of here and bring back help."

She takes a deep breath. "I guess you're right."

"Well?" I ask her. "Are you in?"

She nods, and we run.

9

———

RAE

One evening I hovered next to Mother as she sat at her sewing machine, the bones in her fingers straining against her pale skin as she mended a tablecloth. The machine clicked a soft staccato into the room as that day's word, *longitudinal,* stared down from the far wall, ink smudged slightly at the edges.

"Rae," she said, eyes never leaving her sewing. "Did you learn your word?"

"Yes, Mother."

"Did you stick it on the wall with the rest?"

"Yes, Mother."

She must have noticed the distress in my tone because she clucked her tongue. "Oh, Rae. Don't act as if I'm beating you bloody."

"I-I'm not, Mother."

She sighed, ripping the tablecloth from the jaws of the machine. "Pain is the price of family, sweet girl." She pushed her chair back, the legs scraping against the linoleum tiles. "You may not always like how I choose to raise you, but you don't know how lucky you are. My momma wasn't there for me the way I am for you. She didn't love me the way I love you."

Mother slid an arm around my shoulder, pulling me close to her bosom. "Baby girl, everything I do is for you. You know that, don't you?"

"Of course, Mother." I snuggled close, breathing in the scent of her: cloves and dried flowers.

"I would never leave you the way my momma left me. Because Grandma Perry..." Mother trailed off, releasing me before slumping against the wall of words, the scraps of paper fluttering with the movement. I missed her warmth immediately and hovered above her as she sat with her head bowed for a long while.

When she finally lifted her head, tears were streaking down her cheeks. "She left me, Rae. She left me all alone."

I fell to my knees in front of her and pulled her into a tight embrace. "Oh, Mother, don't cry."

"I miss my momma, Rae," she said between sobs. "Isn't that sick? To miss such a horrible woman? To miss someone who *abandoned* me like she did? You'll never abandon me, will you, Rae?" She pulled away slightly, her eyes boring into mine. "You'll never leave me."

"Never, Mother."

Gracie and I run until my lungs burn, circling down an endless loop of metal stairs, deeper into the belly of the hospital.

Gracie grips my hand for the first half of it, squeezing gently each time Ana screams our names and I can't help but slow down on impulse. She keeps holding my hand even after the screams fade, pulling me forward when I'm not sure if I can take another step. After we get out of earshot, though, after Ana's voice fades into the silence of the hospital, she releases my hand and slows to a walk.

We pause to catch our breaths, leaning against a windowsill in a stairwell.

Mother keeps telling me that this is a bad idea, that I'm going to regret it. I guess that means it was the right decision. My sweatshirt clings to my back and I cough, every breath tasting like a cut.

"Are you okay?" Gracie asks, looking winded but already back to normal aside from her flushed cheeks.

I lift my head and flash her a shaky grin. "I'm out of shape, that's all."

WE BOTH KNOW THAT'S A LIE, Mother rasps. YOU'RE GETTING SICK AGAIN. I TOLD YOU WE SHOULD HAVE STAYED HOME.

My stomach gurgles, a fine sheen of sweat breaking out across my forehead, and I wrap an arm around my middle, terrified that I'm gonna vomit. It's the same feeling I got when Ana placed her hand on the back of my neck earlier. Like I'm gonna cough up everything inside until there's nothing left of me.

Gracie scoots closer to where I stand and lays a hand across my back. "You can throw up if you need to."

I shake my head and shove my hand into my pocket, grasping for the hunk of gum. But my fingers tremble and I fall to my knees, resting my head against the peeling wall. Gracie follows me down, hand still pressed against my spine. She rubs small circles over my back, and I let her. Until the sick feeling fades and we both rise to our feet.

Who knew Gracie could be so nice? It's a little jarring how gentle her touch is, how much care she put into making sure that I'm well. There was something so genuine about the way she comforted me. It makes me feel like I'm seeing her clearly for the first time.

She pulls her hand away. "Better?"

"Yeah."

"Does that happen to you a lot?"

I shuffle my feet and give a noncommittal shrug.

"Does the hospital talk to you too?" I ask her before I think better of it. "I know you're psychic, so you must hear something."

If she can hear the hospital too, we could discuss its messages together, decode its screams.

But instead, she rolls her eyes. "I wish. I wasn't lying when I said I can't even feel its pulse; the whole place is about as energetic as roadkill. Believe me, I have a ton I want to discuss with it but..." She pauses. "Wait, what do you mean 'talk to you too?' It's talked to you?"

I wince. She hasn't heard it. I'm alone in this.

"Maybe we shouldn't have run off. Maybe you're wrong and Ana's just different," I say.

"Oh, she's different all right. She's a psycho killer, and we're lucky we ran when we did."

I try to believe her. Even if it means that we really left Mason behind with a murderer. Guilt tugs at the center of my chest and I draw in a shaky breath, doing my best to suppress it.

"And the entrance to the endless staircase is on the first floor? That's where you said we're going, right?" I check, just to be sure. I asked her when we were running, but we were both so out of breath that I didn't quite catch her answer, and I'm not even sure she heard me to begin with.

She nods, but not before a moment of hesitation.

"What if Ana calls the cops?"

"The hospital's a dead zone—she won't be able to call anyone until she's outside. Besides, I don't think she'd involve anyone else, least of all the police. I doubt Mason actually got permission for us to be here."

"Then we're trespassing?" I ask for clarification.

"Yeah, I guess... Why?"

My stomach clenches violently, and I mutter a string of curse words under my breath.

Rae, Mother warns. Choose your words carefully. Compose yourself.

"My sister will be so mad at me if I get arrested," I mumble, waiting for the ache to pass. It's not as bad as before, more like a sore bruise. But the short amount of time since the last wave of sickness worries me. Does this mean I'll start getting hit by wave after wave? Does this mean that it'll get to a point where the stomachaches won't fade at all?

Gracie's brow furrows. "You live with your sister?"

"Well, half sister. And her father. He's my father too, I guess, it just feels weird to call him that." I pick at the corner of my sleeve, the rust-colored stain from my earlier nosebleed flaking beneath my touch. "He didn't know I existed until last year when Mother died. She always told me that he abandoned us when I was a baby, but I guess he never knew she was pregnant. It's really weird going from not having anyone except Mother to having everyone except for Mother. It feels wrong, like I'm betraying her somehow." I dig my fingers into my sides, heat rising to my cheeks. If I could stuff the words back down my throat, I would.

Oh Rae, why would you share family business with a stranger? Mother grabs me by the chin, her grip tight enough to bruise. I stiffen beneath her touch. You're embarrassing yourself.

She releases my jaw, but the feeling of her fingers pressing into my skin lingers. She's right. I shouldn't have shared anything that personal. I embarrassed myself.

I glance at Gracie, fully expecting her to laugh off my momentary slip.

But instead, she nods solemnly. "That totally sucks. Do you get along with your dad at least?"

I stare at her for a moment, my mouth agape. Mother tries to remind me that there's no way *that girl, that stranger* could be sincere, but her eyes burn into mine and something in me opens up. A warmth spreads from the center of my chest, but it doesn't hurt. It doesn't sting like embarrassment, and I look down at my feet, confused.

"He's okay," I tell my boots. "I don't think he wanted another daughter, though. And my half sister Eliza is great, but I can tell I'm not what she wanted either. I'm too weird, too much, too difficult."

"I'm sorry." Gracie grabs my hand again, and I grip it tightly.

I raise my head. "Don't be. Being in this place helps me appreciate Eliza and her father more. Even though I'm not what they want, maybe they can get used to me. I need to get used to them too, so I kinda get where they're coming from. I know that doesn't really make sense, but I'm not good with words."

Suddenly, all the nights I've spent seated awkwardly at their three-piece dining room set eating in silence seem strangely appealing. It's as if I have a real life waiting for me outside the hospital, a real home and a real family. I can't help but smile to myself. Eliza wouldn't believe any of what I've experienced here if I told her. But she'd be happy that I've made a friend—if I'm even allowed to call Gracie a friend at this point.

Mother sneers. Don't fool yourself into thinking that those two care a lick about you, baby girl. I know you want to get out of this place, but don't you pretend for a second that you have anything waiting for you out there.

"What about your family?" I ask Gracie, refusing to let Mother get inside my head. Even though the effect of her attachment—the ache in the pit of my stomach—continues to linger.

Gracie bites her lower lip, seeming to struggle to find the right words. I understand that struggle too well.

While she tunes out, I scroll through my own list of words. *Lacuna, cicatrize, anagapesis.*

Then she cracks her knuckles as if to jolt herself out of her head and back into reality, snapping back to attention.

"Nothing so tragic," she tells me, her expression blank. "We're normal, super boring. My dad travels a lot for work and my mom tries a little too hard, but it's only because she wants what's best for me." Something about the way she says it makes me think there's more to the story.

"Any siblings?" I ask, wondering how much she's comfortable with sharing. Depending on her answer, I might mention a few things I've been keeping to myself. Things Eliza would blanch at if I told her.

Gracie shakes her head and we stand silently in the stairwell for a few moments.

"If you don't mind me asking," she says, "how did your mother die?"

Heat rushes to my forehead. "Peacefully, in her sleep."

LIAR, Mother hisses, and I wince.

"She died in her sleep," I repeat, a little louder, a little more desperately, to drown out Mother's string of insults—her play-by-play of what happened. *I won't think about that night; I won't think about that night.*

"Well, it's a good thing it was peaceful at least."

I nod. *I won't think about that night.*

"Was she sick or something?" Gracie runs her fingers through her hair, pulling at a few knots that formed while we were running. "I don't mean to pry, and if you don't want to talk about it, let me know."

The clink of ceramic cups. The cabinet underneath the sink. Sugar cubes. Upset stomach and then—

"I don't want to talk about it," I snap, my voice echoing in the empty stairway.

"Sorry."

She suggests we keep moving and I nod curtly. I almost understand why Mason seemed to flit around each room we entered, never standing still long enough to capture a decent shot of the hospital, let alone actually pay attention to what he was filming. Staying still in the hospital makes me feel like I'm eroding, like I'm melting into it somehow. Maybe it's the dust in the air, the saturation of the paint peeling off the walls, but there's a heaviness here. It's all too much to steep in for too long.

Gracie reaches for my hand, and I grab onto it again. Even though she brought up the night Mother died, even though I keep scrolling through every word I said to her. Checking and double checking. Did I say anything that can be taken out of context? Was the meaning clear? Did any of it make sense or am I fooling myself?

Is Mother right after all and I'm stupid to think she'd understand?

We continue down another level, our fingers entwined, and I marvel at the softness of Gracie's skin and the strength of her grasp. I've never known someone so confident, so beautiful, so unaffected by it all. I wonder what it would be like to know her outside of the hospital.

We hurry our pace and continue down another set of metal stairs, our footsteps echoing off the plaster walls, until Gracie stops in her tracks and releases my hand.

My cheeks flush and I find myself wishing she had held my hand for a little longer. I wish I could find the words to ask why she let go.

What has you so flustered? Mother asks, breaking her silence, and my blush deepens.

Gracie points down to where a dead bird lies in the center of the step below us, its belly splayed open.

"That shouldn't be in here," Gracie says. "It's pointed the way we came, so it was trying to find a window or something and get out again."

The gentle twist of its organs, pale purple blending into

pale pink—a pastel nightmare. I crouch down next to it, fascinated by the lack of blood, how the red pools in pockets of skin, sinks below the bones but doesn't stain the floor beneath.

"Rae?" Gracie rests a hand on my shoulder, light as a feather, sending a mild jolt through me. Static electricity. "What are you doing?"

WHAT ARE YOU DOING, RAE? Mother echoes.

"There's hardly any blood," I say quietly, thinking again of the voice I heard and the red that disappeared from my fingers after I pulled them away from the wall.

"Still too much for my taste."

Something about the bird makes my mouth go dry. The hospital has been calling me. Is this what will happen if I answer?

"Are you okay, Rae?" Gracie squeezes my shoulder and I look up at her. Her eyes are wide, and she looks at me the way that Eliza did when I first went to live with her father—like I'm broken, like I'm something to be pitied.

"Yeah. It's really gross, isn't it?"

"It's sad," Gracie says. "I know you probably think I'm this huge badass, but I can't stand the sight of blood. Like, your nose bleed earlier today? It just about *killed* me."

"You should have said something." I rise to my feet and stand next to her.

"Well, I pointed it out, didn't I?" she says with a small smile. "If you tell someone they're dripping blood, usually the go-to move is to clean it up."

"It wasn't dripping, though. It had dried by then."

She shrugs. "It still freaked me out. I hate stuff like that. Like, how fragile everyone is. We have soft skin, and soft veins, and wet, hot blood and nothing to keep everything from spilling out and drowning us."

I can't help but bark out a small laugh.

"What?" she asks, and the look of concern on her face makes me laugh even harder.

"You're completely different than I thought you were," I say once I calm down. "You seem more human this way."

A deep flush colors the apples of her cheeks, and she stares at me owlishly.

"I like it," I add when she fails to respond. "It's refreshing."

Silence settles between us, and we stand over the bird, heads bowed over its twisted body.

"Is it just me or does it look like it's trying to escape?" I ask. Maybe it didn't answer the call after all; maybe it tried to run.

This seems to jolt Gracie out of her thoughts, and she grabs my wrist before pulling me after her. Mother nips at my heels but doesn't say a word.

We start back down the stairs and curve our way around the hospital's spine. I only catch glimpses of each floor. Peach-colored hallways, littered with papers and hollowed-out light fixtures. A wide landing area with windows that stretch the length of the wall, all but one shattered so that only a few shards of glass remain, hanging like loose teeth. A short book-shelf stacked with molding medical textbooks. The air gets damper the farther we descend, tasting like mildew and fermented fruits—which hopefully means we're getting close to the first level.

"You could sense there was something wrong with Ana the same way you can see Mother, right?"

"Right, like that *thing* you call Mother," Gracie says, and I do my best to ignore the bite in her voice. "I knew we had to get away from her because she's..."

"She's haunted too?"

"Not exactly. It's hard to explain."

"If she has an attachment too then we shouldn't be running away from her, we should be helping her." I step in front of Gracie and continue to hurry down the stairs.

"There is no helping her. She—" Gracie seems to debate what to tell me, worrying her teeth along her lower lip before grabbing for my arm, but she only manages to graze my elbow. "Ana isn't like you. She's dangerous. Besides, you haven't had any luck feeding that thing on your back to Seaside State, what makes you think—"

I don't hear the rest of what she says.

My skin prickles. Flashes of heat reach the apples of my cheeks and then drain into numbing cold.

A series of thumps echoes from down the hall. A chorus of sharp noises, falling like a storm against the wooden floors. The noises build in momentum until they're constant, endless. So loud.

Like a rain of stones.

At first, I think the hospital is messing with me again, but then Gracie whips her head around, and I know she hears it too. It's like the holes punched into the wall of the cerulean room.

IT'S LIKE THIS PLACE CAN SEE INSIDE YOUR HEAD. IT'S PUTTING ON A SHOW FOR YOU, Mother rasps, tracing the dip of my collarbones. I shake her off, too shocked to register what she said.

"What the hell is that?" Gracie asks.

The noises swell as if to answer. A rapid flurry of heavy bangs, closer now than before.

Then, a knocking on the wall closest to us, as if someone's rapping their knuckles against the plaster. I jump back, startled.

Mother nuzzles up next to me and her breath lands hot and wet against my cheek. I think of drinking tea while she loads the dishwasher. I think of the night she died and the sound of her fist against—

My eyes widen.

It sounds like the night Mother died.

The afternoon with the stones, and the night Mother died —a chorus of bad memories, ringing out through the hallway.

I tug at the edge of Gracie's shirt, because the stones keep falling, and if we wait too long, we'll be crushed. The knocking keeps getting louder, and it sounds like the stones are getting closer, and the whole hallway seems to quake with the violence of it.

"We need to run!" I cry.

Gracie shakes her head. "We won't be able to outrun it."

Instead, she places her hand against the wall and curls her fingers into the paint.

"What are you doing? We need to go!" The falling rocks, so close now. The sound of Mother's fist against the wall—

I shake my head. It isn't Mother's fist.

Mother isn't the one knocking.

This isn't the night she died.

The windowpanes rattle, and I think of that afternoon in early spring, curled up against the back of the couch with Mother. The windows shattering. The jagged shards of glass and the small cuts they left behind.

"Don't worry," Gracie murmurs. "I can fix this."

She squeezes her eyes shut and claws at the wall, pulling pieces of paint away and letting them drop to her feet. I'm about to tug on her shirt again when I notice the flies on her hands. Blowflies, with fat, shiny bodies the color of an oil spill. They tear through the skin on the back of her knuckles and march single file to the wall.

But that can't be right.

The way her skin puckers and morphs can't be right.

The ripping sound as insects erupt from inside her.

The droning buzz as they cry all together in a swarming mess against the wall.

I back away, Mother screeching in my ear. I KNEW SOME-THING WAS WRONG WITH HER—I KNEW YOU SHOULDN'T HAVE RUN OFF. THIS IS WHY YOU SHOULD ALWAYS LISTEN TO YOUR MOTHER. I KNOW BEST, BABY GIRL. I KNOW TROUBLE WHEN I SEE IT.

The flies continue to buzz, and the rain of stones stops, the noise consumed by the insects.

The knocking fades.

The flies hush.

The hall is dead silent.

Then Gracie takes her hands away from the exposed wall and the flies zip back into the ripped skin of her knuckles. She opens her eyes, and they aren't blue anymore. They're a smoky haze.

No pupils. No irises.

Something about them reminds me of the bald patch of wall that took my shape back in the morgue. And the sticky red that dyed my fingers. And there's something more than that. Something that screams at me from the flat charcoal mist where her eyes used to be, something that drags me back to Mother's dining room table.

The last of the flies crawls back inside her and she flexes her fingers. Her skin closes over the holes, and her hands seem unblemished.

I stare at her, my eyes wide. "What's wrong with you?"

10

GRACIE

This body doesn't belong to me. That's the easiest way to say it, without all the confusing technicalities that come with it. This body isn't mine.

Ana's right; I'm not Gracie. But everything I do is for *her*, for this body—*her* body, for the hope that one day she'll be able to resurface.

I took this body from her, back before I realized the full weight of my actions. I possessed her and suppressed her, and only when I was done, only when I had gotten what I wanted did I realize that I couldn't get out again.

I'm trapped in here.

She's a ripple beneath the skin, a chill in the middle of summer. A voice in my dreams begging me to get out, to give back what's hers.

Lately, I've been feeling her less and less. She's begun to fade deeper into the depths of this body, her consciousness fizzling out.

In the beginning we could think back and forth to each other. She taught me how to perfect my performance, really act like a teenager. I learned so well that the speech patterns have saturated my thoughts, invading my unconscious mind. It's like I'm fluent in a foreign language. All because she wouldn't shut up.

But now I'm lucky if I hear her in my dreams—and the ripple beneath my skin has gotten less and less noticeable. I'm more grounded in this body than ever before.

Her memories pulse through my blood, and in them she's so alive. In them I taste joy, and sorrow, and longing. So much longing. She's infected me, same as I did her—given me the beautiful, horrible gift of feeling.

I know it won't be long before she's gone for good, before there's no saving her. This is my last chance—it may be the only chance I have.

The thing attached to Rae, Ana's cloak of flies, we're the same. We're all shadows, parasites, hungry and desperate things. We're all malums.

I'm one of them.

I'm a monster.

Rae continues to stare at me, eyes wide, lips parted slightly, and I know that I've made a mistake.

I was so caught up in trying to protect her, in trying to make up for all my past mistakes, that I didn't realize we were never in any danger to begin with. I think back to the cracks weaving their way through the pavement beneath Rae's feet. I think of how stressed she must have been, and all the things it could mean.

It wasn't the hospital, and she has no idea.

The skin has closed back over my knuckles, no trace of where the flies broke free. I tell Rae that the hospital was playing tricks. I tell her I don't know what she means when she asks what's wrong with me.

"Nothing's wrong," I insist, the pain in my chest spiking with the lie. "You were seeing things."

"But Mother said she saw it too. Are you sure it wasn't real?" Her voice sounds so small.

"Yeah. Whatever you saw, it was a trick." I really am despicable.

She deflates slightly, and I'm sure I'm in the clear. She thinks that she's made a mistake.

But when I reach for her arm, she recoils.

"Did I give you permission to touch me?" she snaps, rubbing the back of her arm as if I'd burned her.

"I was holding your hand earlier and you were fine with it."

Her cheeks burn red, and she scowls.

I pull my arm back. "I had to get your attention somehow. You were so quiet, and I was afraid that..." That you saw me for what I really am. That no matter what I say, you'll see me as a monster now. A monster that stole Gracie's body and her memories. A monster that got drunk on the taste of human emotion and didn't know how to let go. A greedy, selfish monster that didn't realize what she was doing was wrong until it was too late.

"I thought I saw..." She rubs the back of her neck. "Never mind. Like you said, it was all just a trick."

It's what I want to hear, but it still cuts into me that she's so quick to dismiss her own feelings, her own fears. She's such an enigma. Fierce one minute, insecure the next. Simultaneously closed off and more emotionally open than anyone I've ever met before. It makes my mind reel, and my palms sweat, and my heart pound to the point where it hurts.

She makes me feel so achingly human.

We make it to the bottom of the staircase, walking the rest of the way in silence. Rae keeps space between us, but the farther we walk, the closer she drifts, and there's comfort in her closeness.

Finally, we're back on the first floor, walking down the hall through sheets of peeling cream-colored paint and across dusty red tiles.

The hair on my arms stands on end.

"What's wrong?" Rae asks. "You look sick."

"Something's not right." I look around, and even though the scenery outside the windows suggests that we made it to the ground floor of the building, the air inside Seaside State seems to pulsate. The images beyond the glass panes ripple, looking more like paintings than the real thing. "It doesn't feel like we're on the first floor."

"Because we're not. The windows on the first floor were boarded up and there were all these low-hanging wires."

I point toward the ceiling, where a jumble of wires hangs down from broken-up ceiling tiles. They're not as low as before, but they're the same... to a certain extent. The colors seem off slightly, though it's difficult to tell in the changed light. They're brighter, wrapped in green and yellow plastic instead of... Was it blue before? Red? What the hell did they look like before?

"This has to be the first floor," I say, trying to convince myself more than Rae. Because the longer I stare at the wires, the more my skin prickles. They're wrong. This is wrong.

My malum instincts rear up inside of me, blowflies humming beneath my skin. I'm hit by the urge to peel back my skin and show my true face. The teeth, the claws, the flies. To lose myself to cold indifference and do what needs to be done to protect myself... To protect Rae.

Rae.

I take a deep breath and shake my head. I can't afford another moment like what happened earlier. Rae might have believed that she imagined the flies the first time, but if let them slip again, I won't be able to explain them away.

Or you could tell her the truth. The thought sits like a lump in the back of my throat.

Because if I tell her the truth, she'll hate me. And once I start, I won't be able to stop. I'll have to explain about Ana—and how the thing on her back is killing her. She's strong, she's brave, but I've seen how she cowers in the presence of that thing that's feeding off of her. I don't think she'd be able to handle the truth about her precious "Mother."

She'd be another death on my hands. Another testament to my monstrosity. Like Gracie, and the time I spent in the violent patient ward.

The guilt would be too much.

Guilt, so devastatingly human.

"The hospital is changing," I say instead. "It's messing with us on purpose. There shouldn't be any light down here. There shouldn't be any light at all. The sun should have set by now."

I lay my hand across one of the walls and Rae flinches.

"What are you doing?" she asks.

"I got it to calm down before, so maybe I'll be able to ask it to explain itself."

But I don't feel anything. I hear buzzing—a symphony of flies humming beneath my fingers. Not mine. My flies stay silent.

I turn my head down the hall, half expecting Ana to come around the corner.

But the sound is isolated to where my fingers touch the plaster, and I pull my hand away in disgust. Pinpricks of red sprout across the swirl of my fingerprints, where they were pressed up against the wall.

My body goes numb, frozen by a sudden, terrible thought. There's a reason why Ana was referring to the hospital as a she; there's a reason why she was so insistent on me joining her. There's a reason why this hospital isn't like other buildings.

"Gracie?" Rae asks. "What's going on?"

"I don't think the Seaside State we read about is the same as the Seaside State we're inside now," I say turning to Rae, feeling drained, beaten down, broken.

How could I not see it before? How did I fail to connect the dots?

It's the latest in today's long line of failures.

"There's no way this is a different hospital. It's the same address; it looks the same as the pictures," she says, and I don't have the words to explain.

I dig my fingers into my palm. "It's the same hospital, but it's... evolved. It's not just a hospital anymore, it's more than that. You know how when you're a little kid you hate vegetables but as you get older you don't mind them, even kinda love them?"

Her brow furrows. "That's not exactly the experience I had growing up, but I get what you mean. Still not sure what that has to do with Seaside State, though."

"Appetites change."

"Meaning what?"

"I don't think Seaside State is hungry for the same things anymore. Or, what I mean is that the hospital was never hungry for anything to begin with. None of what we read online has anything to do with the hospital."

I flex my fingers again, hoping that the movement will help me stop feeling so frozen, so useless, so helpless.

We're not inside a building, we're inside a monster.

I don't know how, but we're inside a malum.

A malum disguised as a building.

"We need to keep moving—it's dangerous to be here for this long. Don't tell me you can't feel how wrong it is, how it's sinking its teeth in."

"It feels weird," Rae agrees. "It reminds me of Mother." The malum fans out across the floor as if to agree.

"That's why we need to get out of here as quickly as possible."

"But the endless staircase! But Mother!"

"Appetites change," I say through gritted teeth. I had forgotten the lie I used to lure her away with me. "If the hospital hasn't eaten that thing on your back by now, it's not going to."

She leans against the wall and breathes in. "You don't understand."

The malum drapes itself around her shoulders and she shivers violently.

"She's killing me," she says. "I love her, but she's killing me."

"Staying here is gonna kill you a whole lot faster." I bite my lip and stomp my heel into the tile. I can't explain what's going on without telling her what I did to the real Gracie, and if I do, she sure as hell won't follow me out of the hospital.

"I know how you feel; I came here to get rid of something too." My chest feels bruised.

"But I'm not gonna get rid of it. I underestimated the hospital, and now I'm screwed." Tears sting the corners of my eyes, and I feel the full weight of what I'm saying.

I'm not going to save the real Gracie.

When I came here, it was to exorcise a lesser monster to prove I finally had the power to exorcise myself. It was to die and finally give Gracie her body back. But I can't feel her. And now I'm inside a malum.

Now we're both doomed. Me, and real Gracie. We're both drawing our final breaths. And it's all my fault.

Rae rests a hand on my shoulder and warmth radiates from her fingertips through the sleeve of my t-shirt. "That may be true, but that doesn't mean you can't try, right?"

Her tone is uncharacteristically optimistic, and I stare at her, my eyes wide, my chest aching.

"The only way you'll fail for sure is if you don't try. You can give up, but I'm gonna keep looking for a way to do what I came here to do. Even if the hospital keeps switching the hallways around. Even if Ana catches up. She'll have to kill me if she wants to stop me."

I can't help but be amazed by her. Despite the malum on her back, despite whatever it continues to whisper in her ear, she stands tall. Even though her face is streaked with tears, she stands with her fists clenched and a steely expression on her face.

"You know what else?" she adds. "I know you were lying to me before when you told me you knew where the endless staircase is, and that it's the reason why the hospital hasn't eaten Mother yet."

My heart jumps to my throat.

"I wasn't sure at first," she continues. "But as soon as we got on this floor, I could tell you only ever wanted to make it outside. And I kept following you anyway. At first, I thought it was because I'm stupid. That's what Mother said—that I'm stupid, that I'll follow anyone. But that's not true. There's something about you, Gracie. I didn't see it when we first met, but I think that's because you were hiding."

"Rae..." My pulse races and it's all I can do not to reach out and grab her hand. My mouth tastes like copper, and I want more than anything to tell her what I am and what it means for us. But there is no us—and if, despite it all, everything goes according to plan, I won't be in this body much longer.

"I'd follow you anywhere," she says with a shrug, and it's enough to make my heart burst.

She smiles at me, a small, soft smile, and I realize that I like her. I like her greasy, badly dyed hair. I like her bony elbows, and the way she says my name like she's gasping for air, like it's the only thing that could fill her lungs to the point of bursting.

I like her biting comments, and the way she shrinks back into herself when she feels like she's done something wrong.

I like her.

That's why I want to save her.

That's why I took her with me, and why, even now, I wish I could tell her everything about myself. All the messy, broken pieces that I've kept hidden away for so long.

I reach out to her and—

A door slams somewhere down the hallway and we both jump.

"Is that the hospital again?" she asks. "Or do you think Ana's caught up to us?"

"I don't think it's either."

Tell her, I beg myself. *Please tell her.*

But we have more important things to worry about right now. A series of thumps sounds through the hall. More doors slam and the malum on her back spins madly around her, looking more like a dark tornado than the parasite it is.

"You hear it too, right?" she asks. "I'm not crazy?"

I nod and grab her hand, lacing my fingers through hers. "Let's head into the next hall. It's best that we keep moving."

She nods and we take off, and my heart continues to ache inside my chest.

But I can't tell her, and I let the ache—the *like*—dull to a whisper. Because if I give it room to grow, I'm afraid of what it might turn into.

I won't be in this body long enough to love anyone.

11

RAE

The air in the hallway is thick, saturated, and still. Pale turquoise walls peel to expose cream-colored primer, and light burns through the windows at the end of the hall so that it appears endless, stretching forever into white hot silence.

The thumps behind us die down and we slow to a hurried walk.

Mother hasn't said a word to me since I told Gracie that I'd follow her anywhere. Even as I was saying it, I wished that I could take it back. I'm not sure why, though. For once, I feel like I picked exactly the right words.

We haven't talked about it since then, and there's some relief in that. It's easier to focus on the hospital than what's going on inside my head. The thought of the flies on the back of Gracie's hands, of Mother's dinner table, of me, and her, and everything.

A You Are Here map sits screwed to the wall, but the floor plan is hand drawn, a shaky outline with few details. It makes the floor look so much smaller than it really is.

"Don't let it freak you out," Gracie tells me, eyes trained straight ahead. "The building is fucking with us."

"You're talking about it like it's a person." Part of me hopes that she confirms my suspicions that it *is* alive, that it *does* have a voice. While it hasn't spoken to me since the morgue, that doesn't bother me. I'm more concerned by how it seems to be holding its breath.

Gracie pauses for a moment before responding. "Well, it's like I said before—this is more than a hospital. It might as well be a person. It has a cynical sense of humor, that's for sure. It feels like it's laughing at us. Don't tell me you can't feel it too."

It feels like we're walking on someone's stomach. The soft sagging of the wooden beams, fleshy and organic. The little noises of the place are starting to get to me. The faint echoes. The hum of wind through cracked panes of glass. It's too much.

Before we exit the hallway, I notice writing on the walls near where they empty out into another staircase. We haven't seen any graffiti in the building so far, despite the obvious signs that the hospital has been broken into and explored, and it seems out of place. The words look like they were drawn in black crayon, and from a distance, they're too small to read. Initially, I think they're deep cracks in the plaster, but as we get closer, the words get clearer.

Gracie's gaze stays focused on the end of the hall, but I stop. I stop and stare at the long, pointed letters, the thin lines that make up the shape of them. I read and reread the words, trace their lettering again and again, over and over until Gracie calls for me to catch up. Her voice comes in through a filter.

It looks like Mother's handwriting. That's what's so weird about it. It's the same long, thin penmanship. *Anathema,* another one of Mother's words, is splashed all over the wall, not in the words but in the way they're written. It's the same damaging text.

"Rae!" Gracie calls for me again, and I pry myself away from the wall and the writing.

I walk away, but even in leaving, the words stay stained across my fingertips.

I'll wait for you, scribbled across the walls; *I'll wait, I'll wait, I'll wait.* A heartbeat, a steady flow of blood through the building and across the peeling paint.

Another message from Seaside State.

Rae, I'm right here. Come find me.

And now, *I'll wait.*

Outside the windows, I can't see the trees from this side of the building, only rolling hills. They go on for what seems like miles, fading into the coastline.

Maybe it's the pull of whatever walks here, whatever I saw in the window before we entered, or maybe it's the isolation, the maddened twist of the corridors.

Gracie chews on her lower lip, scraping off a layer of her lip gloss. She notices me staring and stops biting at it, her cheeks reddening.

We enter another cream-colored hallway and walk in silence for a few minutes until it's clear that Gracie's uncomfortable.

"So, what are you going to major in for college?" she asks. "You're a junior too, right? You must be applying to places soon."

When I don't answer right away, her blush deepens and she continues, though it sounds like she's making it up as she goes. "I'm gonna apply to med schools. I'll be a surgeon. Can't you just see me downing a bottle of wine and sewing pieces of raw chicken together?"

"Huh?" I ask, not sure I've heard her correctly. And not just because she can't stand the sight of blood.

"*American Mary*? You've never seen that movie? I mean, it is older, but it's kinda a cult classic."

"It's a movie?" I ask, wondering how any of this is relevant.

She nods as a sheet of paint flakes from the wall and hits

the floor with a soft plop. She stomps through it, the heel of her shoe leaving a puncture wound directly through its center.

"No, I haven't seen it," I say, staring down at the mangled slice of cream. "Why would you think I have?"

The red spreads from her cheeks through her entire face, accentuating the fiery streaks in her strawberry blonde hair. "You seem like the kind of person who'd like dark movies."

"I can't stand horror movies, or anything violent," I say. "Mother drilled it into my head that they were a bad influence. I was only allowed to watch family movies, and even then, Mother was pretty strict. I don't think I saw *The Lion King* until I was twelve because of Mufasa's death scene."

You say that as if it's a bad thing, Mother says as if she can't believe it, but I ignore her until she eventually drifts back along the wall behind me. The light-colored paint muddles in the grayish haze that surrounds her.

"You never watched anything dark on your own?" Gracie asks, her blush beginning to fade.

"One time," I admit quietly. "*Carrie*. I felt so guilty afterward, I thought I would die. I didn't even like the movie that much; it seemed like such a waste of rebellion."

Gracie pauses for a moment before responding, as if she's digesting the information. She keeps her eyes fixed ahead. "We'll have to watch it together at some point... *American Mary*, I mean. It's messed up, but it's really smart and oddly feminist. And the main character is totally me once I go to medical school, minus all the weird black-market shit, and what happens to her at the end of the movie of course."

"Black market? What happens at the end of the movie?" I ask.

"I'm not giving anything away," she says, smirking. "You'll have to wait until we watch it."

My stomach flutters. She's serious about hanging out after this.

"Anyway," she continues. "Since we're clear on what I'm going to school for, we just need to figure out something for you. I feel like you'd be a good psychologist. You seem really analytical and introspective. You should definitely go for psychology."

"Why are we talking about college?"

"It beats thinking about how Ana's probably gonna catch up to us at any moment and how this damn hospital doesn't make any sense. It beats thinking about what a huge mistake it was to come here."

I tilt my head to the side. "Why *did* you come here?"

"Like you said, I'm here to get rid of something."

"What, though?"

"It's personal," she says quickly.

"More personal than trying to exorcise your dead mother?"

She stops walking and turns to face me, her eyes watery as if she's on the verge of tears. "I'd rather talk about college and all the other inconsequential bullshit we have to look forward to when we get out of here. I'd rather pretend that I have some kind of future waiting for me out there."

"I'm not going to college." I stop alongside her and look down at my hands. "I was really sick up until before Mother died. I didn't think I would make it to this point, and even after I got better, it just never crossed my mind. Guess I never got over the thought that I could die at any moment."

She frowns. "Yeah, I remember when the local news did the interview with you about the stone thing, they said you had leukemia or something."

"It wasn't leukemia."

CAREFUL, RAE. Mother digs her fingers into my neck, and I gag. As if on cue, my nausea returns full force like a punch to the gut and I bend forward, my face now only a few feet from the broken, checkered tiles.

Gracie reaches for me, but I shake my head. I fight through the pain until Mother loosens her grip.

"I'm not sure what it was," I tell Gracie. "Mother didn't know either, but she would say things... like I had leukemia, or an eating disorder or whatever. It changed all the time, and the doctors... Well, anyway, it was some stomach thing," I tell her. "I was in third grade the first time it hit. Fourth when it really started to go downhill. I've always had kind of a weak stomach, so it's hard to tell. I can't remember exactly."

"Wow... That's crazy."

"I barely remember it." I shrug, trying to mask how gross it feels to admit it.

My memories of "the sick years" are so abstract they could be dreams. When I think back to grade school I see sets of images, but no words, no sound. White lace. Shaky hands. Red crayon. Nothing concrete.

One of the only clear memories I have is of a nosebleed, and even that is fragmented. I sit cross-legged on the floor. The room is dim; there's only one light bulb, bare, and it flickers, on the verge of going out. A fly sits on my wrist, legs twitching up toward its face, cleaning itself. The blood drips slowly, mixing with the sweat above my lip. I lean over and it drips into my lap and onto the floor. Red. Red. Red. The fly leaves my wrist. My nose continues to bleed.

"It's like that with illness," Gracie says sympathetically. "The high temperatures roast your brain."

I wrinkle my nose and let out a small, nervous laugh. I hope I haven't said too much. I hope that I've chosen the right words. It's more than I've told Eliza, more than I've told anyone, and I'm so terrified that it makes me sound pitiful.

"No, really. Your body is so focused on fighting off infection that there isn't energy left for anything else. It's kinda like the same thing with your attachment. You probably get nauseous cause your body is working so hard trying to fight it off." She leans in closer so that her face engulfs my line of sight. I can't see the hallway behind her, only her.

I feel like I'm seeing her for the first time. Deep in the blue of her eyes, something stirs. There's a pain, an uneasiness.

"Were you sick at some point too?" I ask, because it feels as though I know her, really know her, even though she was a stranger before today.

"Yeah." She stiffens. "Well, no. Kinda, I guess. Well, not me but a friend of mine. We were really close, but I only really got a sense of how bad it was toward the end."

I think of the flies pouring from the backs of her hands. "Did she die?"

Gracie shakes her head. "She's not better yet, but I'm hoping she'll get better soon."

"That's good. Hope is important." I wish she would tell me more about it. After everything I've been through, I want her to know that I understand. But if being isolated for so long has taught me anything, it's that people will speak when they want to. You can't force them. Even if they don't open up right away, it doesn't mean they never will, or that they don't trust you.

It's like how I'll spend hours in Eliza's room with her, sitting propped up in a nest of pillows on her bed while she writes at her desk or paints her nails, cross-legged on the beige carpet. Most of the time I don't say a word, not because I don't think she'd listen, not even because I can't find the right things to say, but because I don't need to. Being around her is enough.

My pulse quickens when I wonder if that's how Gracie feels about me.

We turn down another hall, then another and another.

"There's no end in sight," I say quietly.

"The hallways keep changing," Gracie replies through gritted teeth. "It's not going to let us out."

"I thought we were looking for the endless staircase," I say, trying not to sound too desperate. "Didn't my speech from earlier inspire you to fight against this thing?"

"By going deeper into its stomach?" She raises her eyebrows and I have to remind myself that she's not teasing me. Her reaction doesn't mean that I'm stupid, or that I didn't choose the correct words to express what I needed to say.

"Why not?" I ask, doing my best to sound confident.

"Even if we find it, there's no telling if we'd make it back afterward. Remember that bird from earlier? I know you want to get rid of that thing—your mother. But is that worth dying for?"

"Yes," I say without hesitation.

She frowns, looking down at her nails and chewing her bottom lip.

"Isn't what you need to do worth dying for?" I ask, reaching out to lay a hand across her arm. She looks up once my skin hits hers. There's a flash of longing in her eyes that's gone so quickly I could have imagined it.

She gives a small nod, but her voice is strained when she answers. "Yes, I'm willing to die."

We fall into silence after that, the air between us thick enough to cut. I hunch my shoulders, stealing sideways glances at Gracie, but the expression on her face is impossible to read. I'm not sure what I said wrong. I thought we were making progress.

Mother collapses her skeleton, constricting like a snake around my torso, and I hiss out a breath.

Then, the floor opens up beneath my feet, the hallway coming to such an abrupt end that I stumble, and Gracie has to haul me back by the elbow. There's a deep hole against the wall, chipped tiles breaking off into a rectangular expanse of darkness. A cool breeze wafts up from the opening, and we each bend at the waist to glance inside.

A stone staircase.

My heart skips a beat. Another wave of nausea hits and I press a hand against my stomach.

Gracie looks at me and smiles, though it doesn't reach her eyes.

"The endless staircase," we both say at the same time.

12

GRACIE

My first week inside this body was the most difficult. Back then, the real Gracie screamed almost constantly, crying out from deep inside the mind we shared—the mind I'd forced myself into. At first, I was selfish. I tuned her out. I enjoyed all the earthly delights that had been denied to me up until that point. The warmth, the cold, the feeling of water sliding down my throat on a summer afternoon. Iced tea. Lemonade.

The weeks dragged on and she screamed herself hoarse until I finally acknowledged her. But even then, it was only to shut her up. She's the one who kept challenging me to say more, to explain myself, to help her understand why she was a prisoner in her own body.

Then we'd argue until our late-night screaming matches became late-night chats. And those chats changed everything.

"So, what's your family like?" she asked one night as I sat on her bed, painting her toenails a lemony shade of yellow.

No, I reminded myself, jaw clenching. *They're my toes now. My body, my toes. Mine.*

I had been slipping up lately, thinking of Gracie as the

body's owner rather than an unwanted passenger. It was... frustrating. Like the ache in my chest that occasionally flared. Or the way my pulse spiked every time her voice rang out inside my head. So... frustrating.

"Hey Miss Monster, you with me?"

I blinked, setting the container of polish aside. "What?"

"Your family. You had to come from somewhere." Her voice was light and bright, like wind chimes on a summer day. "Personally, I can't stand my mom sometimes. She's so overbearing, but at least she means well. She cares about me a lot even if she can be a bit harsh."

I wrapped my arms around my knees. Heat rose to my cheeks at the thought of Gracie's mother addressing me as her own, unable to recognize the thing wearing her daughter's skin. A cuckoo in a sparrow's nest. "Your mom seems fine to me."

"What's yours like?"

"My what?" I bite out.

"Your family. The people who raised you."

I hugged my knees tighter. "I wasn't... I don't have family. I'm... alone."

She laughed, but there was no malice in it. "You're not alone, silly. You have me."

That frustrating ache was back in my chest, and I didn't know why. I didn't know why it hurt, why it was so difficult to breathe.

Gracie taught me.

Until I went from holding on for dear life to trying desperately to claw my way back out again.

Until her voice, so bright and clear, dulled to murmurs.

Until the murmurs faded to a thin whisper in my ear.

Until the whisper waned to nothing at all.

～

Isn't what you need to do worth dying for?

Rae and I make our way down the staircase, feeling our way along stone walls slick with condensation. The air seems to swell around us, salty and humid. Alive in a way that's sickening. I hold my phone out in front of me, the light from its flashlight cold against the stone.

Every step feels like a step closer to the bottom of someone's gut, and my eyes narrow when I realize it's the most life I've felt from the hospital since we stood out on the service road.

Even the act it put on earlier wasn't like this. There was something cold and clinical about the strange noises and the way the hallways shifted—it seemed rehearsed; movements devoid of passion.

But this... this is something completely new. Its breathing is heavy, its pulse radiates through the brick and stone, and it truly feels as if we're inside some one, not some thing.

Why is it dropping its defenses now? I wonder. *Why let me catch a glimpse of its face when it worked so hard to keep itself hidden?*

The hair on my arms stands on end.

Because it has us where it wants us.

"My phone is almost out of battery," I warn Rae, still surprised that she convinced me to descend the stairs. "We won't have the flashlight for much longer."

"You have a lighter, don't you? We could use that."

I feel the weight of it in my skirt pocket. "A lighter won't replace a flashlight."

"Then you shouldn't have taken all those selfies earlier," she says, and while her tone isn't exactly mean, there's something off about it. It's too sharp, too abrupt.

I bristle. We were getting along so well. She chose a hell of a time to hop back into defensive mode. "That's not what I was doing. I couldn't read the hospital's aura properly and thought it would show up in photos. And I've never once taken a picture of *myself* since we got here. Like, it's always been the hospital, so I really don't understand..."

I trail off when I notice her chewing her lip, her eyes glassy in the glow of my cell phone light. Wisps of cream saturate her aura, too close to the cottage cheese color that seeps from Mason in a constant spew.

She hangs her head. "I'm sorry, it was supposed to be a joke."

"Oh." Great, now she thinks I'm a bitch. We walk in silence for a few moments until the sound of our shoes against the stone becomes too much. I need to fix this.

Please don't let her hate me.

"I was trying to take its temperature—when I was taking pictures of this place, I mean. Like when we're sick. We have digital thermometers, buildings have photographs. It's like how photos pick up on so much more than real life. Like, if you're tired or sad it always looks so obvious in photos. It's the same for buildings. Normal buildings, at least; I realize now that was never gonna work on Seaside State."

The streaks of white drain from her aura and she lifts her head, glancing over at me. "Did the photos tell you anything about this place?"

I think about it for a moment, unsure of how to explain. How the asylum isn't hurt.

"That Seaside State isn't anything more than a husk," I say finally, eyes trained ahead.

"What's your deal anyway?"

I turn back to her and seeing the look on my face, she immediately apologizes. "I didn't mean for that to sound so rude... I'm not any good with words. I'm sorry."

"You need to stop saying you're sorry all the time."

"Sorry—I mean, I just don't understand you."

I tilt my head to the side, which she takes as a cue to continue.

"You look like a cliché, but you do aura photography and know a shit ton about the occult," she says. "You knew that Ana was trouble, and you can see Mother. You're not freaked out by her either, you just seem... done with it all, like you've been through all of this before and you've officially checked out. I don't understand how someone who looks and sounds one way can be the complete opposite."

I chew my bottom lip and steady myself against the stone wall. It's cool beneath my palm and I take a deep breath, imagining that the relief could travel up through my fingertips. Chill my insides. Numb the heat that spreads from my forehead down into the pit of me. No matter what I say, it'll only raise more questions. And the more time I spend with Rae, the less I look forward to the end.

I told her we were going to watch movies together, hang out after we make it out of here, and for what?

I told her I was going to *college.*

What's the point of saying all that if I'm not going to be in this body much longer?

When I die, and the real Gracie takes back her body—or worse, if she's already dead and I still somehow manage to exorcise myself—none of this will matter.

I'll be gone.

Rae will be left alone and disappointed.

I care too much. I'm too soft to be a monster, too abrasive for a human. Never completely settled in my skin.

"Gracie," she prompts.

I let out a strained laugh and pull away from the wall. We continue to spiral down into the heart of the hospital. "You said you'd follow me anywhere; that's basically saying that you trust me. If you trust me, then it doesn't matter *how* I can do all this, or *why* I know all this. The only thing that matters is that I can, and I do."

"I trust you, but I want to know how you got into this stuff." The malum swirls through the dim passage and falls across the wall behind her. I can tell that it's whispering to her because every so often, she flinches. Still, she's different from when she first entered the hospital. She stands taller, and though she places a hand to her stomach every so often, she doesn't double over like before.

"I want to know you," she says. "The real you. Not this wannabe prom queen bullshit you've been wearing like a mask."

I know the words should make my heart beat faster, but instead my shoulders slump and I blink back tears for all the wrong reasons. Because I stole this body, and I don't deserve a thing she's said to me.

"I want to make it down this staircase without cracking my skull open," I tell her. "It's so dark in here that it really feels like we're in the hospital's stomach."

"When are you going to tell me what you're here to get rid of?" she asks, trying a different approach.

I sigh, wrapping an arm around *my* middle this time in an effort to stop my stomach from hurting. It's not pain, exactly— more of a dull ache. A want. And I can't let myself get trapped by the feeling.

"It's not a ghost, if that's what you're thinking. I'm not like you," I say.

"What are you like, then?"

I stop walking and turn back to face her. "Why do you care?"

"I want to know who I followed into this damn hospital."

"You didn't follow me here; you came because Mason invited you."

"And I left Mason because you begged me to leave with you."

I look down at my nails, the purple looking almost black in the dim light. "If I told you, you'd run right back up those stairs."

"You're being dramatic."

I search her face, count the creases in her forehead, memorize the look of her bottom lip, chapped in a way that looks like peeling paint. She's art. The malum at her back shifts position, eclipsing the left side of her face, but she's still art. And it isn't fair to either of us that we're both destined to die.

She places a hand on my shoulder, and I let her. Maybe it doesn't matter what will happen in the future. Maybe it's okay if I leave this body, if she's sucked dry by the parasite that's feeding off of her, and we both fade into memory. For now, we're partners with a common goal.

We continue down together until the stairs end abruptly at a large wooden door. Light leaks out across the threshold.

I look back up at the spiral steps above us. From the bottom, it looks infinite. Thousands of steps, swirling into black.

"I think this is the bottom." Rae wraps a hand around the knob. "Maybe this means we've gotten to the place where we get rid of Mother. Maybe this is it."

"Rae," I warn, a sick ache in the back of my throat. Something about the door isn't right—the hospital has put its mask back on. "This place isn't like other buildings. You need to be prepared in case what's waiting on the other side isn't what you want."

I don't know who I'm trying to convince, her or myself.

She nods, and even though her hand trembles, she continues to hold the knob tightly.

"Worst-case scenario, I'm stuck with Mother," she says, fighting back tears. "Worst-case scenario, we're not able to find our way back up the stairs again, or the door slams behind us and we're trapped. I'm ready for that. But we made it all the way down here for a reason. It's not for nothing."

I nod despite the lump in the pit of my stomach.

She turns the knob.

13

RAE

"No, no, no, no." I collapse to my knees, feeling as if the wind has been knocked out of me. "It's impossible. The staircase was... No..."

The door empties onto the roof. The *roof*.

Once we walk through the doorway, dazed and hardly able to believe it, it slams shut behind us. I jump, and Gracie tries without success to open it again. She pulls, and kicks, and scratches at it before turning to face me, her shoulders slumped.

"Why would the hospital bring us here?" Gracie murmurs, her eyes wide.

I blink up at her through tears. "The staircase went down. We walked *down* the stairs. This doesn't make sense."

"Seaside State is smarter than we thought."

"It can't be smart, it's a building." Even though I know that's not exactly true. It's alive in its own way. It shifted the position of hallways and slammed doors to mess with us. It *spoke* to me in the morgue and the blue room. It's more than capable of taking us up to the roof.

I rise and make my way to the edge of the flat stretch of tar.

A short brick wall, coming up to just below my chest, surrounds the perimeter and I look past it and over the grounds.

The view from the rooftop is incredible. It's vicious. I look out over the entirety of the property, a series of winding veins and decaying masses, darkened shapes fading into the distance. This building disappears into the haze of early evening, and several other buildings are nothing more than ripples in the heat, indistinguishable from the landscape. The place keeps stretching on into murky shades of violet and softened rose. Somewhere off in the distance the sun is finishing its descent. From where we stand, the night creeps toward us. The sun hangs heavy in the sky, but where we are, it only hints at descent, suspended in shades of red and gold, the sweet light of just before dark.

Everything is cast in amber light. Even the green of the trees is sick, somehow yellowed by the hanging sun. All the while, night edges in, its darkness visible over the far reaches of the property.

"How is this possible?" I ask.

"I told you before, it's not a normal building. It has thoughts, feelings."

"It can't change the laws of physics; it can't stop the sun from setting."

"It can do whatever it wants," Gracie says, digging through her purse. "I could have sworn I had a watch in here. Does your phone still have a charge?"

I pull it from my pocket, tap the screen, and frown. "It's dead."

Gracie shakes her head "And I don't have a watch after all. If we can get some sense of what time it's supposed to be, we can know for sure if any of this is real." She drops her bag against the tar and kicks it. "Leave it to me to bring lip gloss and sunglasses instead of anything useful."

"Have you ever encountered something like this before?" I ask, running through a list of Mother's words. *Abhorrent, resplendent, transcendental*—something that is equal parts awesome and awful.

Gracie shakes her head.

"But you've been to a ton of places like this, haven't you?"

"I've never been anywhere like this before," she says softly. "Most buildings aren't really possessed as much as they're inhabited by... I'm not sure what to call them. But they're lesser malevolent beings, the aftermath of strong emotions or unresolved trauma. In rare cases, when a building has an attachment or is sick, there can be side effects. Hallucinations, bad feelings, that kind of stuff. But that's not what's going on here. I've never been to a place like this; I've never followed a staircase down to find myself up on a roof. To be honest, it's freaking me out."

"How do we get down?"

Gracie grabs my wrist, and her hand is warm as she guides me to the edge of the wall to look over the side of the building. It lies flat, save for the windows that dot its sides, and although there are spaces between the brick, they're not enough to grab onto. Climbing down isn't an option.

"We could jump," Gracie barely whispers.

"We'd die."

"We're gonna die if we stay here. Either Ana will find us, or the hospital will make sure we don't make it out alive. Damn it!" She kicks her heel against the roof. "I should have known it was stupid to go down that staircase. I don't know why I keep expecting things to work out the way I want them to."

I stare out over the grounds. They look infinite, intimidating. And that's not the only thing that's wrong. Even though they don't grow here, even though I didn't see them on the way in, row upon row of oleander trees line the service road leading to the hospital. From this distance, their white petals seem to glow like beacons.

But it's impossible. They're a desert plant—they shouldn't be able to grow in New England.

And the sun should have set by now. The light seems tangible, as if I could reach my hands out and run my fingers through it.

"It's impossible," I murmur.

"Yeah, we've already established that," Gracie says quietly and Mother mutters as if to agree.

"No, not the whole 'being up on the roof' thing. The light. How is this lighting possible? It's like I can see places where the sun has already set even though it's still up in the sky."

Gracie squints. "I don't know what you mean."

"You can't see it?" I ask.

"It's bright," Gracie says after staring for a few moments. "Shades of amber and gold. I don't see any darkness, though, just gold."

"So I'm losing my mind then." I whimper and Mother bites out a laugh as if to agree. Tears prick the corners of my eyes. I thought I was getting better. I thought I had found my own voice; not Mother's, not the sick whispers of the asylum, mine. And now, now I'm—

Gracie grabs me gently by the shoulders, her eyes burning into mine. "No, Rae. You aren't. This place is messing with us..." She trails off as if thinking hard about what to say, and a pang rings out inside my chest. Watching her struggle to find her words feels the same way that her hand felt in mine. "Just because you're the only one who sees it doesn't mean it isn't happening."

"It still hurts that I'm the only one who sees it." I stay focused on the oleanders, their leaves twitching in the wind.

The breeze doesn't make it to where I stand.

I almost miss the air inside Seaside State. The air out here is too salty, too abrasive. It stings my lungs. Another wave of nausea hits me and I wrap my arms around my middle, though I know it's a useless gesture at this point. It won't do a thing to quell my upset stomach.

The oleanders. White flowers, pink too—like water mixed with blood.

"Rae!" Gracie's voice is sharp and urgent.

"I'm fine," I say, continuing to look out over the side of the building. "My stomach's acting up again, but it'll pass soon. I just need to tough it out."

"No, I..." She rushes to my side and grips my wrist tightly, spinning me around. "Look."

She points toward the opposite end of the roof.

I follow her finger to a hatch in the corner of the roof. Ana emerges through it, her white blonde hair looking like a ripple of heat across the tar.

Mason follows closely behind.

They don't look surprised to see us at all, and instinctively, I take a step backward, my spine brushing up against the low brick wall. The only thing between myself and oblivion.

"I knew you'd find your way up here eventually," Ana says with a small smile as the pair exit onto the roof. "We just didn't know you'd get here before us. Apologies for keeping you waiting."

Though her voice remains light, her eyes narrow when they meet Gracie's. There's a sharpness to her movements, an unnaturalness that I didn't notice before. Her steps are jerky, and her shoulders hitch up and fall back down again in rapid succession, as if each joint in her body is attached to an invisible string.

"I-I thought they were going to leave," Mason says, clutching at his flannel shirt. "Oh jeez, I thought I was going to have a heart attack. I seriously would have had a heart attack if they made it out of here without us."

"I told you it would be fine," Ana says, her gaze still focused on Gracie. "Seaside State has ways of dealing with those who wander."

"We didn't mean to come up to the roof," Gracie says carefully. "We meant to leave." She glances toward the hatch at the top of the ladder poking up through the opening. I can see down into the room below—white walls that shine gold in the fading light. "So, if you don't mind, we'll be on our way."

Ana shakes her head. "This isn't how things are going to work, Gracie. You broke the rules by going off on your own, and I'm afraid we don't have a very forgiving hostess."

Gracie's eyes stay focused on the area to the left of Ana's head, as if she can see something I can't.

"I don't want you to do anything we'll both regret," she says, hand raised in front of her, eyes still locked on the thing to Ana's left. "I think it would be best if we talked about this."

"Yes, let's," Ana agrees. "Maybe now you've finally thought up an appropriate answer to my earlier proposal."

Gracie squeezes my hand, the warmth of her skin seeping into my palm before she lets go and starts across the roof.

"What are you doing?" Panic grips my insides. "I thought you said she was dangerous."

She looks back over her shoulder at me, flashing me a shaky smile. "She is, so stay back there and let me take care of it."

"I don't want you to get hurt, though."

She smiles at me, though it doesn't reach her eyes. "I won't, I promise."

She meets Ana in the middle, and I'm left alone.

"What's going on?" I ask Mason as he crosses the roof to lean against the wall next to me.

"Get away from her, Mason," Gracie cries, turning to make her way back to me. But Ana grips her shoulder, mouthing something, and she stops.

Mason looks over the edge of the wall and smiles at the grounds. "It's beautiful down there, don't you think?"

"Not my choice of words but... Look, I'm sorry we ran off without you." My heart is beating so loudly, I feel it in my throat. My breath comes in hurried gasps and I'm not sure why. It's only Mason.

I figure it must be guilt. Because we left him with Ana—we left him in the mouth of a monster and ran off to save ourselves.

"We're back together now, and that's all that matters." He waves his hand dismissively, and I realize that his camera is gone.

Chills run through me. But he's supposed to be making a documentary. Why would he leave his camera somewhere?

I lean in close to him, and he smells like rotted fruit and onions, sweat mixed with citrus. The smell makes me pull back instinctively.

"Are you okay?" I ask. "I told Gracie we shouldn't leave you alone with Ana, but she insisted. You wouldn't believe some of the stuff we've seen since we left you guys. Gracie was telling me that she thinks the hospital might be more than a hospital, if that makes sense. She says it's dangerous. She thinks Ana is too."

"Hm." Mason chuckles, red coloring the apples of his cheeks. "Well, isn't that something."

"What do you think? Is Ana okay to be around? Are you okay—the hospital didn't try to do anything weird to you, did it?"

He smiles a big, floppy grin, blotches of red creeping down his neck and under his collar. "Ana is fine and so am I. Don't worry about us."

"But Gracie said..."

"Gracie and Ana have some things they need to work out." He nods to where they stand in the center of the roof, locked in heated debate.

"Gracie says there's something wrong with Ana." I scoot away from Mason. His smile makes me uneasy, and Mother seems to reach out toward him, like a moth to a flame.

"That's the biggest lie I've ever heard," Mason scoffs. "There's nothing wrong with Ana, or if there is, then there's something wrong with Gracie too. They're the same, after all."

I frown, wondering if it would be okay for me to cross the roof and pull Gracie away from Ana, or if that would only make things worse. "How do you figure?"

"They're related," he says simply, and I gawk at him. "Well, they're kinda like cousins. Gracie is nervous because she knows you're gonna find out about what happened the last time she was here. Ana's trying to tell her that it will be okay as long as she agrees to help the hospital. Once they finish, we can get on with the show."

Gracie's voice repeats in my head.

I used to trespass here all the time freshman year.

This is a big property. I've never been inside this building before.

My focus flickers in and out as I run through everything Gracie has told me about the hospital. Mason's face blurs, splotchy red bleeding into pasty white. Dread forms a tight coil in the pit of my stomach. "What happened the last time she was here? What are you talking about?"

He laughs, the sound coming out strangled. "It would be better if you relaxed and enjoyed the show."

"You mean the documentary?" I ask, feeling small, and dumb, and wanting more than anything to rush to where Gracie stands in the center of the roof, grab her hand, and go. "But you don't have your camera. Did you leave it inside somewhere?"

He smirks, his mottled blush continuing to creep across his pale skin. "I'm not mad at you for running off, you know. Apparently, it's happened before, but it never matters in the end." A fine sheen of sweat has broken out across his forehead, and I take another step back.

"Where's your camera?" I ask again, my heart pounding so hard that I feel it in my forehead, but he doesn't answer.

"How long do you think we were inside for?" he asks instead.

"Where's your *fucking* camera?" My voice reaches a fever pitch, my pulse screaming through my veins. The sick feeling spreads and spreads.

"Answer my question and I'll answer yours," he says lightly, and I realize that he's not stuttering anymore. He's leaned back, relaxed. Everything from his posture to the light behind his eyes looks like it belongs to a completely different person. "How long do you think we were inside the hospital?"

He's up to no good. I can smell it on him, Mother rasps. You've gotten yourself into trouble this time, Rae.

I glance between where Gracie stands next to Ana, and where Mason leans up against the wall next to me, my heartbeat quickening with each passing second.

"We were inside for two, maybe three hours," I tell Mason, who watches me with hungry eyes that gleam in a way I don't trust.

"It felt like an eternity," Mason says dreamily, continuing to look out over the grounds. "It still feels like an eternity."

"I know what you mean," I say over the pounding of my heart. "I'm ready to get out of here."

He lets out a sharp laugh that sends a shiver down my spine.

"You can't leave," he says between cackles. "We haven't even gotten started yet. The sun's about to set."

14

GRACIE

The first time I possessed a person, I was terrified. It wasn't a successful possession. The person fought me off like a bad cold, and then I drifted.

Before this body, there was a lot of drifting—a lot of floating above the trees or creeping along in gutters and around the edges of attics. Feeding, feeding, feeding off sadness and pain and insecurity.

I talked to the real Gracie about that hazy in-between often.

"You must have been lonely," she said once.

I lay on a picnic blanket in her backyard, a book cracked open in my lap. A summer breeze sifted through the trees, and the flower garden at the edge of the yard boasted sunflowers and morning glories. I inhaled floral notes and freshly turned soil, letting the aroma wash over me. So many sensations. So much beauty. So painfully human.

I snapped the book closed and frowned. "It didn't bother me much at the time. I'm used to being alone."

"This must be quite the change for you then."

"Ha, ha," I said dryly, leaning back on my elbows. "Seriously though, when I was... drifting, it's like all I could do was focus on my hunger."

As a malum, all other senses are dulled. Even now, in Gracie's body, the hunger haunts me. Phantom pains that cramp their way through this body. Even now I hunger, even if it's not for human anguish. I'm not sure what would sate my appetite now, only that my insides clench, that I ache, that I want. "The hunger worsens with age."

"How old *are* you? You're not, like, centuries old, right?"

I huffed out a sigh. "What does it matter?"

"It would feel a little weird talking to you like this if you were hundreds of years older than me."

"It's not like I could mark every birthday while blinded by my hunger." I rolled my eyes and ran my fingers through the grass beside my blanket, marveling at how the slightly damp blades brushed against my skin. So many sensations. So much beauty. "But I'm pretty sure I can't be much older than forty."

Gracie barked out a laugh, and heat rushed to my cheeks.

"What?" I snapped.

"You're my mom's age! I'm totally gossiping with someone my mom's age."

"I'd hardly call what we're doing 'gossiping.'"

"Having a vent-sesh, then."

I sighed, rubbing at my temples. "Like I said, I wasn't tracking every birthday; I was too focused on my need to feed. That's what it's like for my kind—hunger, and anger, and nothing else. It was like a constant clawing in the pit of my stomach. All I could focus on was hunger, and wanting, and *lack*."

Gracie hummed in the back of my head. "That must have sucked. I'm sorry you had to live like that."

I slammed my hand down into the ground, tears pricking the corners of my eyes. "Stop trying to empathize with me. I'm

—" The words caught in my throat, and it felt as if there was a glob of wet paper blocking my airway. "I'm killing you."

The summer breeze continued to blow through the trees, a mournful sigh as the silence stretched between us.

"But you don't want to," Gracie finally said, quietly.

"I don't want to." I wished there was some way to fix this, to give it all back. This body, her body. All the wonderful things I'd stolen from her.

Even now, the pit in my stomach stretches wider, and my hunger, though transformed, continues to claw at me.

Ana places a hand on my arm, and I cringe beneath her touch.

"You can't," I tell her.

"I can't what?" she asks, tilting her head. The horseflies that circle her head mirror her movements. They pool on her left cheek, writhing in a mess of wings and legs.

"Whatever you're trying to do, you can't do it," I say instead of calling her out. Hopefully there's still a way to spin this so that Rae and I can get out of here alive. "You already have the body you're in. You can't possess more than one person."

"What *ever* do you mean?"

"I know you're targeting Mason. He's easy prey, but you're not going to be able to take him and keep that husk. And you wouldn't be able to latch onto Rae or feed from her even if you wanted to, since she has her own attachment, so it's better to just let her go."

"You've got it all wrong." She laughs, running her fingers through her hair, tugging at the split ends until several pieces are ripped out from the root.

I steal another glance back at Rae. She stays huddled against the low brick wall, Mason staring out over the grounds next to her. Good. They're across the roof, where Ana can't get to them without going through me. I may be able to save them both after all, even if Rae is the only one who matters.

As long as she's with Mason, as long as she's far away from Ana, she's safe.

Rae locks eyes with me, and I try to flash her a smile, reassure her, but my face won't cooperate. She motions for me, but I shake my head.

"Stay there," I mouth. "We'll get out of here soon."

I turn back to Ana.

"I feed Seaside State," Ana tells me, her mouth set in a straight line. "I feed her, so she takes care of me. You know what that's like, don't you? Isn't that why you crawled inside that body to begin with?"

"What's that supposed to mean?"

"Don't play dumb with me, little girl. You wanted to feel connected to someone—you wanted to feed something other than yourself for once. But it didn't quite work out for you, did it? Well, I found a better type of connection here, and the game's just getting started."

"This isn't a game," I say.

"I know what you think it is: another notch in your belt. Another place you can clear of bad energy in an attempt to make up for what happened when the real Gracie came here, what *you* did in the violent patient ward. But that's not how it works."

"You don't know the first thing about what happened back then," I say, feeling sick to my stomach.

The violent patient ward was torn down last year, but it stays stained across my memory. It's the building where I first laid eyes on the real Gracie. There's no way Ana could know about it; no one else was there when I forced myself down Gracie's throat. No one else was there when I became greedy and reckless and just feeding off of her wasn't enough anymore.

Unless...

My eyes widen, and I look at Ana like I'm seeing her for the first time. "You were there. You were there and you saw what I did. You've been keeping tabs on me."

She shrugs. "Anytime you think you're alone, you probably aren't. Our kind is everywhere, and we're not exactly social creatures. And I don't have to explain the pull of this place— you can feel it for yourself."

I shake my head. "It wasn't like this when the real Gracie was here; it wasn't alive like this. It's changed completely."

Ana scoffs. "Our kind rarely looks beyond our own hunger, so it's unsurprising that you didn't notice. And you really think that human's memories are reliable? It's pathetic how much you lean on your meat suit's perception of the world." The flies circle her mouth. "Anyway, I was curious. You're the reason why I've been able to do what I have with this body. I couldn't handle a full-blown possession, but I've been able to keep this corpse moving once I finished feeding, and it hasn't broken down on me yet."

I clamp my hand down on her wrist and pull her in close. "Keep your voice down."

"How come? You should be proud." She smirks. "You're part of what inspired all this, you know. I lost track of you for a while, but I'm so glad that Mason was able to find you again, even if he had no idea who he had found. I'm so glad that you're able to be here for this."

My body shakes and I keep glancing over at Rae, making sure she's okay. We need to get out of here as soon as we can.

I curse silently. I made the wrong decision again; I made the wrong move. I should have held onto Rae's hand. I should have pushed past Ana and Mason and escaped down the hatch when we had the chance. Even if it means leaving Mason behind again. But no, I had to feel guilty for ditching him the first time. I had to try to fix things.

Guilt is such a human emotion.

It's my fault for swimming through this teenager's thoughts for so long. A most vile game of play pretend.

I should know better by now. There's no talking to my kind. There's no bargaining.

Ana doesn't say anything but continues to smile. The grin rips wider and wider, and her flies swarm.

Heat rises to my cheeks. "It was a mistake. I should never have possessed this body."

"That's because you're weak. I could tell when I first saw you that you didn't have the guts to do what you did. And you've spent so long in that sleeve that it's started to poison the parts of you that are still like me, like us."

"Gracie?" Rae calls to me from across the rooftop and I want more than anything to run to her, but I know Ana would lash out and that would be the beginning of the end. I could take her on if I needed to, but I can't risk the chance that Rae might get caught in the crossfire.

"Don't worry, he can't hurt you," I call back instead. "You're safe over there, so just stay put. I'll be there in a minute."

"Why would I want to hurt her?" Mason asks, his aura clumping around him like wet tissue paper. He turns from the grounds and faces us. "I was worried sick about you guys. I'm so glad you found your way up to the roof. Ana and I were just about going out of our minds."

"I told you we'd find them up here," Ana says. "It's destiny."

"Kismet," Rae says, stuffing her hands in the pockets of her jeans. The malum leans in close and brushes up against her cheek. She tilts her head and says something, but I can't hear it over the buzzing of Ana's flies.

Her smile continues to rip until she jerks her head up toward the sky. A gust of wind howls across the rooftop and her thin hair fans out around her.

"Ah," she breathes. "Mason, are you ready?"

"Of course!" he calls from his place along the wall.

Wait... Mason? What does she mean?

There's no way he can know what she is. Someone as soft as that, someone so weak wouldn't stick around if he knew.

But he grins, and my whole body freezes.

The way he's been looking at Ana. The reverence, the blind admiration. It's not because she was giving him attention, it wasn't because he's some lovesick puppy...

He knows what she is.

And I ignored him, discredited him, and now he's next to Rae. He's next to Rae and there's no way I'll make it across the roof in time.

Ana lowers her head and claps her hands together. "Let's start the show."

15

RAE

I know something is wrong the moment Mason takes off his shoes.

He whistles as he unties the laces and places them neatly at the edge of the roof, careful to arrange the heels so they're perfectly aligned.

The whistling is high-pitched, out of tune, and the hair on the back of my neck bristles.

"What's going on?" I ask, so quietly that there's no way he can hear me. I look to Mother, hoping she'll offer some sort of insight, but she only shakes her head.

I told you something was wrong, but you wouldn't listen. Look at where it's gotten you. All because you didn't listen to your mother.

Ana and Gracie stand on the opposite end of the roof, watching us. Gracie keeps trying to run over to where I stand, but Ana pulls her back again and Gracie flinches as if her touch stings.

Mason continues to whistle as he steps up on the ledge and starts walking slowly along the edge, arms out as if he's on a balance beam. "Don't worry, Rae. I promise I won't fall."

He peels off his flannel and holds it in one outstretched hand like a flag. It billows in the light breeze. The gray shirt he wears underneath it is stained in the armpits.

"Mason," I say, my throat feeling as if it's stuffed with cotton.

He wobbles slightly as he lets go of the shirt and it's taken by the wind. It hovers for a second as if levitating before disappearing over the side of the building.

"It's so easy to let things go." He glances back at me, his eyes completely tuned out. "You'd think it would be more difficult."

"Mason, what are you doing?"

"You'll see," he says, lazy—dreamlike. "Are you ready for the show?"

"Get down from there, it's dangerous." I raise my hand, but it's shaking so hard that it drops back down again.

Mother swirls around my head, screeching.

THIS IS TROUBLE, she cries. WE NEVER SHOULD HAVE COME HERE, RAE!

"Don't worry," Mason chuckles. "I know what I'm doing."

"If you don't get down from there, you'll fall." The wind picks up and my hair whips into my face. The cold bite of salt settles on my tongue.

"I know what I'm doing," he repeats.

Then he stumbles, windmilling his arms, and my pulse spikes as I grab for him, hauling him by the collar of his shirt back onto the roof. He knocks into me as I pull him back, his hand brushing against mine, his skin clammy. His scent hits my nose again—rotted fruit and onions. I try to ignore how my insides crawl as I release him.

Mason regains his footing, facing the ledge again, and I scramble to block him with my arms fanned out and teeth gritted. My heart rabbits against my ribcage, pulse screaming through my veins. I feel it everywhere as I try to anticipate his next move.

If Mason wanted to, he could easily push past me. If he

wanted to, he could take me down with him. My vision blurs again, chest tight as I imagine our bodies twisted on the pavement, swatches of red painting the ground beneath us.

Mason steps forward, his pace even and calm, stopping barely a breath away from where I'm still braced in front of the short brick wall. Every inch of me trembles as he stares down at me with frenzied eyes. "Why do you look so nervous, Rae?"

"I don't want you to hurt yourself," I choke out.

"Hurt myself?" The corner of his mouth twitches, and his shoulders shake as if he's holding back laughter. "You think I'm gonna hurt myself?"

Mason lifts the edge of his shirt to show off the pasty skin of his stomach before running his hands down over his torso, fingers gliding over the expanse of skin. "You think I would hurt this? I would never. This body is so important, Rae. You have no idea how important it is."

He lowers his shirt, and his hand slips into the back pocket of his jeans before he breaks off into a peal of frenzied laughter. "You don't know how afraid I've been to try anything new, to really live. Gosh, I was pathetic. Do you know what a rush it was standing up on that ledge? My heart was beating so fast I thought it would break right through my ribs. Isn't that a hoot?!"

"Mason, I think you need to take a deep breath and calm down."

He pulls something out of his pocket but keeps it hidden behind his back as he watches me with a glazed, feverish expression.

He turns back to look over the grounds, leaning in toward the wind.

"I'm sorry," he says. "Not that it means anything at this point. I had to do what's best for me, look out for number one, you know. It's not that I don't like you. You seem nice enough... So I'm sorry."

"For what?"

"It's the only way." He smiles over his shoulder, twisting at the hips so that looking at his contorted body is enough to give me a stiff neck.

His smile widens, tears springing to the corners of his eyes. He looks like a grotesque marionette as he reveals what he has hidden behind his back with a theatrical flip of his wrist.

It's a thin metal tool with a sharp end and a smooth handle that he grips loosely in his fist. It's something like an ice pick.

My entire body goes rigid.

An orbitoclast. It's an orbitoclast. A tool used for—

"A transorbital lobotomy," he says brightly. "So you see, you don't have to worry about this body of mine, Rae. It won't see any damage. I'll get to the insides cleanly."

My pulse rushes through my ears, my heartbeat deafening as I watch Mason rest the pad of his finger against the sharp end of the tool. "You'll... What..."

A bead of blood wells up, and he giggles—high-pitched, animalistic. "It'll be over so quickly, I bet it won't even hurt." His expression darkens as he tosses the tool from one hand to the other. "I've been hurting for so long, Rae. You can't even imagine how much I've *hurt*. But it's easy to let things go."

"Mason..." I'm frozen in place. No matter how much I will them to, my legs won't move, and all I can do is watch in horror as Mason, silhouetted against the vicious gold of the sky, tilts the orbitoclast toward his face.

And slams it into his eye.

16

GRACIE

Rae's scream is a piercing wail that cuts through the howling wind.

I'm not sure what I'm seeing at first. Mason's shoes sit lined up neatly by the edge of the roof. Rae sits collapsed in on herself and rocks back and forth on her heels, the malum on her back threatening to swallow her completely. Drops of blood are freckled across the surface of the roof, and my eyes scan the surrounding area until they fall on Mason's crumpled form.

"He—he had an orbitoclast. An *orbitoclast*," Rae screeches, her voice raw with panic. "Mother's word. Mother's word—orbitoclast... It's like an ice pick. It's like an ice pick and I couldn't stop him. He's dead."

The wind picks up and repeats it. *He's dead, he's dead, he's dead.*

I run to her as quickly as I can, ignoring the way Ana's flies swarm, biting into me like acid, but I barely feel them. All that matters is getting to Rae.

"We need to get out of here now," I call to her, and she shivers.

I never realized how skinny she is, all bones and angles,

with skin so thin I can practically see the skeleton showing through.

Her hair whips forward and obscures her face until she's a mess of wild hair and muffled screams. She drops to her knees and is silent, finally, after an eternity of screaming. Her hair is still tangled in the wind, thrashing like a dark flame. It engulfs and burns away her features. The malum at her back spirals up like smoke.

Candle girl, I think.

I skid to a stop next to Mason's corpse, curled on its side. Even in death, his aura clings to him in a milky film, reminiscent of pool scum. I take a deep breath and flip the body so it faces me, cringing back against the sight of the long metal tool shoved to the hilt inside the corner of his left eye near his nasal cavity.

A small trickle of blood runs down his cheek beneath the tool, so red against his now chalky complexation. If it weren't for the blood, and the tool—*orbitoclast,* I think numbly—he looks as if he could be sleeping.

I turn from the body, my gaze raking over his abandoned shoes, worn down Converse that look so sad, so deflated, as if they're the ones who died, before flicking to Ana.

She stands at the far end of the roof, doubled over laughing.

A pang of guilt shoots through me. Shame, a tightness in my chest that makes it hard to breathe.

Guilt, so horrifyingly human. If I had paid attention, if I had noticed the signs, then maybe I could have stopped this. Maybe I could have broken whatever hold Ana had over him, told him the truth.

Bile tickles the back of my throat again. I killed him. I killed another person. I did the opposite of what I came here to do.

But then Rae grabs my hand. Her palms are slick with sweat, and her forehead glistens like the pool of Mason's blood. We stand on the roof of the building, and in the fierce wind it's like Ana isn't hovering in the background cackling, her flies covering her like a second skin.

"You girls just about finished?"

I yelp and release Rae's hand, turning to find Ana standing inches away from us.

The flies cover her completely and it takes me a second to realize what she's doing. It's not until Rae starts crying and the flies gather in the dips of Ana's collarbone that I see her fingers sinking in. She's ripping at herself.

Ana digs her pointer finger and thumb into the fleshy center of her cheek. Her nails puncture the skin and bright red teardrops slip down over her chin.

The sound of flesh tearing.

Of Rae crying.

Of Ana giggling as she rips the skin off her jawbone.

She takes another step forward, her expression calm. She opens her mouth, but I don't give her time to say anything, I jump at her.

"That tickles!" She howls with laughter as I kick her in the stomach, stumbling before straightening up and cracking her neck.

I feel along the tarmac and find a jagged piece of metal among the debris. I hold it in front of me like a knife.

"Oh, that's cute." Ana continues to laugh, blood and spittle flying from her ruined jaw.

Even when I sink the metal into her shoulder, she keeps on laughing. No matter how hard I kick, no matter how deep I dig the metal, Ana remains unfazed.

"Get the fuck out of here!" I scream at Rae, and she jumps as if it stings.

She hurries to the hatch that Ana and Mason crawled up through, glances back once, and disappears into the depths of the hospital.

"What are you trying to prove?" Ana asks. "I've been nothing but cordial toward you and you pull this."

"You killed that poor boy!"

"Technically he killed himself." She smirks. "Bet you regret leaving him behind when you took off, huh? Not that it mattered in the end; all paths lead back to me."

We grunt and roll. Kick, bite, slice. She tears at my shoulder and I elbow her in the nose. It cracks to the side, splintering apart at the base and dangles within the loose skin.

She scoots back along the concrete and stares up at me, grinning. "You're stronger than you look."

The flies gather in her nostrils and on the backs of her hands, soaking up the blood, clotting the wounds.

"I'm strong too," she says, but remains on the ground as the flies continue their work.

I turn to leave, but a cloud of flies rushes up in front of me and I stumble back. Ana grabs onto the edge of my shirt and uses it to pull herself up.

"Seaside State won't let you go until she gets what she wants."

I steal another glance toward the hatch, then turn back to her. While I'm glad that Rae's no longer on the roof, I'm not comfortable leaving her alone inside Seaside State for too long. There's no telling if the roof has shifted, if it's pulled her deep into its winding hallways. I need to settle this as quickly as possible so I can find her.

But there's no way to get through the flies. Not by force, anyway.

"Fine," I say, lowering my arm. "We can discuss the terms."

Ana laughs, her mess of a nose swinging with each breath. "You already know what I'm asking for."

"But why?" I ask. "What do you expect me to do exactly?"

"We're shorthanded around here," she says, as if it's obvious. "I need more people to hunt on behalf of the hospital."

"And Mason? Is that what feeding time looks like?"

"I wouldn't worry about him, he's not exactly around anymore. If you want to talk terms, let's talk terms. You feed the hospital; she feeds you. It's that simple."

"I hate to disappoint you, but I'm leaving this body," I explain. "I won't be around to help feed your precious hospital, and I'm gonna get the girl who this body belongs to as far away from all this as possible before I say goodbye for good."

"The girl you stole that body from is dead."

The back of my neck prickles. "I can feel her."

"No, you can't." Horseflies crawl from her nostrils and she shoves her nose back into place with a sickening crack. "Our kind has a special set of skills, but it differs from beast to beast. You can see auras, those smudges of color. Pretty useless, if you ask me. But me? I know things. I can always tell what a person wants. I know you wanted to cure the hospital before you knew what she was. I know that when you realized what she was, your plans changed. You wanted to feed yourself to her. But that's your mistake. She isn't without reason, without intelligence. She's not a slave to her hunger, and she's not going to eat you in a gluttonous rage."

"I'll find another way to leave this body." I crouch low to the ground and wrap my fingers around a chunk of concrete before rising to my feet again.

Ana doesn't notice; she's not focused on me. She's too busy ranting, waving her arms as her flies do what they can to hold her face together.

"No, you won't," she says. "And even if you managed to leave the husk, you'd just be leaving the flesh behind. The girl is dead —you killed her a while ago and now you're swimming around in her corpse. And no matter how hungry Seaside State gets, she won't touch you. There's no point in holding out for something that will never happen, and there's no point in pretending that you're not a murderer."

Ana slinks closer and tilts her head to the side. "To be honest, I don't know what the hospital sees in you."

My fist tightens around the concrete, its rough edges digging into my palm. Ana's warm breath fans across my face, her eyes glimmering, and a shudder runs through every inch of my body. I pull my arm back and slam the concrete into her temple. It connects with a nauseating crunch and she collapses in a spray of blood. Warm, like her breath.

I drop the concrete and take off after Rae.

"Please be down there, please be okay," I mutter as I descend the ladder that leans against the lip of the hatch. My feet hit the floor and I turn to find Rae standing in the far corner of the room.

"You're bleeding," she says, her eyes wide, and I look down to find my t-shirt splattered with red.

"It's not mine." I look up at where the sky peeks through the open hatch and point toward the opening. "We need to find a way to barricade it."

"But if it's her blood, doesn't that mean that you…"

"I didn't kill her, I just knocked her out. She's gonna come to at any moment. I know what she is and she's fast, she's strong— trust me when I say we want to throw as much as we can between her and us."

Rae nods once and helps me secure wooden beams and pieces of piping beneath the hatch. I can only hope that they hold.

Rae sits against the wall, her knees drawn up under her chin, her eyes closed as I finish the barricade. It's like the weight of what happened on the roof hit her all at once, and she's just now processing it. I understand, I do. But we don't have time. We need to get moving.

"Are you okay?" I ask, and she opens her eyes a crack as I crouch down, level with her face.

"What was that?" she asks.

Above us, Ana—or the thing that calls itself Ana—hurls itself against the hatch, the wood splintering with every new attack. I can't help but smile. If the hospital were so hell-bent on Ana getting to us, wouldn't it help her get through the hatch?

Still, each crunch of bones hitting wood sends a fresh wave of panic through me.

I grab Rae by the wrist and pull her up. "We need to go; the door won't hold for much longer."

"What is she?" Rae asks again, the malum circling her head like a vulture, houseflies trailing behind it.

"I'll tell you once we're somewhere safe."

She shakes her head. "Tell me now. I'm not going anywhere with you until you do."

"I won't get a chance to tell you anything unless we move." I run my fingers over the back of her hand and do my best to flash her a reassuring smile. "You trusted me before; I need you to trust me again. I'm not going to let anything happen to you."

But she stays rooted in place, and I can't avoid it any longer.

"She's a... She's not human, she's a monster."

Her eyes widen. "What does that mean? What kind of monster?"

"The dangerous kind." I tug on her hand. "Now come on."

She hesitates for a moment but eventually allows me to guide her out through the room.

The walls are so bright that even the parts cast in shadow glow like lightning bugs. It's an organic color—the color of a paper cut, the color of surgery. I look away and guide Rae out of the room and into the hallway. Her body trembles but she keeps moving, and I'm struck again by how brave she's been through this, how strong.

Something doesn't sit right with me about the room, though—the dark red paint causes a shiver to run up my spine. Goosebumps rise across both my arms and Ana continues to throw herself against the hatch in the ceiling. She growls and the sound radiates out, a low rumble through the empty chambers of the hospital.

17

RAE

Mother never let me watch scary movies; she wouldn't even let me watch the news because she thought it was too violent. The most violence I ever saw splashed across a screen was when I watched *Carrie*, and all of that was carefully choreographed, rehearsed, red dye in corn syrup. I've never seen another person bleed.

Until today.

Until Mason stabbed an orbitoclast through his eye, and Ana tore her face apart.

I stop mid-step and pull Gracie back next to me.

"What are you doing?" she asks, exasperated. Her hair, slick with sweat, clings to her forehead. "We need to keep going."

I shake my head. "Not until you explain what's going on. It'll be easier to win against that thing if we both know what we're up against."

"There is no winning against her, there's only getting the hell out of here and hoping she doesn't follow."

"We already tried that, remember? And the hospital led us right back to her. If we're gonna beat this, we need to be on the same page. You can't expect me to hold it together if I have no idea what we're up against."

Gracie sighs. "I told you what she is."

"No, you didn't. You said she was a monster but that's so vague, and cryptic, and doesn't explain anything."

I wait for her to respond, but instead she drags her teeth along her bottom lip, scraping away what remains of her lip gloss.

"Well," I ask. "What is she?"

She kicks her kitten heel against the tile. "She sucks."

I throw my arms up. "Oh, come on!"

"No, really. She does! The kind of monster she is doesn't have a name, at least not to humans. Maybe they did a long time ago and it's been forgotten. They call themselves malums —they're kind of like supernatural parasites. They feed off of negative emotion and pain."

"Like the hospital." And Mother. An ache echoes through me, through my bones, the meat beneath my skin. I sway against it.

She nods. "Usually, they attach to a person, suck them dry, and then move on to the next one. But Ana has managed to keep control of the corpse after the soul inside has passed away."

My stomach clenches and a fresh wave of nausea washes over me. "You mean that girl is dead?"

Gracie takes a deep breath. "Whoever had that body before the creature took hold is long gone; only a shade of her remains. You can't see it, but there's a cloud of flies around Ana, and the flies are what's controlling the body now that the soul is gone. The flies are Ana. And I think, though I'm not certain how it works, that Ana is somehow attached to the hospital, that they're feeding each other."

"I saw flies crawl out of your hands."

She glances down at her nails. "I don't know why you saw

that. But if you're aware of your mother, maybe you pick up on other things."

"You said it yourself—my mother isn't really haunting me. She's like Ana." The words fall from my mouth like a stone, like a death sentence, and I'm left chilled to the bone. All the time spent sitting across from Eliza at the dinner table, all that time sitting across from her father in the living room, refusing to confide in them—to talk about *that* night, and *that* room, and the wall of words, all because Mother told me not to.

All the times I rolled over, played possum, let her leave footprints up and down my spine... It was all for nothing.

Mother is gone. Only a shadow remains.

"This whole time I thought I was listening to a ghost," I say quietly. "I was so afraid of killing you again, and you aren't even her."

You don't really believe that, do you Rae? Mother asks, draping an arm over my shoulder. We know each other so well. are you really going to listen to what this stranger has to say? She's not like us, Rae. She doesn't understand you the way I do. No one will ever understand—

I clamp my hands down over my ears and grit my teeth. "Will you shut up already?"

"Is it yelling at you?' Gracie mouths, and I nod.

Mother pulls away from me and hovers a few feet back. I don't appreciate being spoken to that way.

I pull my hands away from my ears and straighten my spine, attention focused on Gracie. "She looks just like her, sounds just like her. And she knows things—she knows everything. It's like she can see inside my head."

"They take different forms," Gracie explains. "They morph and bend depending on the victim. Whatever will placate you, whatever will keep you from fighting them."

I shake my head. "I've been fighting it. The whole reason

why I came here was to get rid of it. Feed it to the portal or whatever's supposed to be in the basement of this place. Kill it."

"That doesn't mean that it…" Gracie sighs and rubs between her eyes. "What was your relationship with your mother like?"

I'm your best friend. Your only friend.

"I don't know how that's relevant."

No one in this world cares about you more than I do.

I swipe my hands through Mother, and she screeches. She falls to the floor and spreads out across the tiles, looking less like a ghost and more like a monster.

"She was my best friend," I tell Gracie. "My only friend. She took care of me when I was sick, she taught me words and their definitions, and how to appreciate language. Her own mother left when she was really young, so she made it her life's purpose to never leave me." Tears spring to my eyes and I swat them away with the back of my hand. "Sometimes I felt as though we were marooned on an island. We were so far away from everyone and everything. Sometimes I felt like she was the only one who would ever understand me. We were so connected, so in sync that it hurt. It hurt…"

"Did you love your mother?" Gracie asks, her voice soft and low.

Of course you love me, she whispers from my feet.

"I had to." I think of all the nights I spent bent over the toilet bowl puking, all the times my nose bled after dinner. I think of Mother brushing my hair before I went to bed at night and singing to me softly while I sweat between the covers.

Gracie's expression slowly shifts. "Things between you and your mom were kind of messed up, weren't they?" she asks. "That's why it chose her form, because you don't know how to say no to her."

"I say no to her all the time!"

"That thing attached to your back is huge, Rae. Which

means that it's been gorging itself on you, which means it's been with you for a while, right? At least six months?"

"A year... It's been a year since my mother died." The night that Mother died, as I stood over her corpse, the ghost—what Gracie calls a malum—tore from her mouth in a cloud of dust. It rushed me, grabbing onto my shoulder, and told me that she wouldn't leave. She'd never leave.

Gracie's bottom lip trembles, and she stares at me as if I'm a shattered mirror. She stares at me as if I might cut her if she gets too close. "How have you not lost your mind?"

"Is that what happens when they feed on people? Do they turn them crazy?" I think of the figure I've been seeing, so much like Mother and myself. And the voice I've been hearing —the blood on my fingers that wasn't really there. I've been used to the physical side effects of the attachment for a while now, but not the effects it's had on my mind.

I thought it was the hospital. I thought Seaside State was crying out for me, but maybe it's my mind short circuiting, boiling inside my skull. All because of Mother. All because of this... parasitic thing.

"If it's really been with you for almost a year, then yeah. You shouldn't be able to form complete sentences."

"What exactly does it do to the... the hosts?" I ask, my mouth dry. "Will I end up like Ana? Will she control my body after I die?"

RAE! Mother screeches, wrapping her arms around my shoulders, covering my back completely.

Gracie shakes her head. "Ana is unique. Usually, when a malum attaches, it eats the host alive and discards the husk."

My pulse quickens and Mother attempts to huddle in close, but I swat at her, tear through her, my heartbeat in my throat. "How do I get rid of it?"

"You don't," she says solemnly. "Unless it willingly chooses to leave you, there is no way. It's..." She takes a deep breath, her voice shaking. "It's the reason why I came here. I knew whatever was attached to the hospital was more formidable than other buildings. I thought if I could exorcise it, I could exorcise a person. But I can't. I was an idiot; there's no way to get rid of a malum."

Mother draws in a sharp breath and falls away from my back, settling at my feet where she swells over the dusty tiles. She's sulking. Even knowing what she is, I can't help but think of her as Mother.

Mother who held a hand to my forehead. And a cup to my lips. And who kept the heavy curtains drawn in the heat of day, shutting out everything that wasn't us, that wasn't mother and daughter, patient and makeshift nurse.

"Rae?" Gracie asks and tears leak down over my cheeks, leaving a bite of salt in their wake.

"What's the point of being able to see them if you can't fight them?"

"I've been asking myself the same thing," she says quietly. "The things that I get rid of, they're not like what's attached to you. They're smaller, less powerful, easier to expel. It's like the difference between a head cold and pneumonia. You can't drown out a lung infection with over-the-counter cough syrup. I can't exorcise a person."

"Why not try?" I ask. The light in the hallway shifts, and the grounds beyond the windows darken. Dusty shades of orange and canary yellow tumble in through the panes of glass.

"It's too dangerous. You could wind up brain-dead, or worse."

Mother wraps her arms around my ankles. I know I should be angry. I know I should hate the thing, but a part of me is relieved. It isn't really Mother. I don't need to feel bad for killing it.

If I can kill it.

"If what you've told me is true, I'm gonna wind up brain-dead anyway. It's worth a try," I tell Gracie.

Gracie goes silent for a moment, and I instinctively reach out my hand and rest it on hers. "Let's just try to find a way out," she says.

We turn down several hallways, and although they look familiar, they're in the wrong place. Halls that were on the first floor are now on the top floor, and we can't find a way down to the floor below. We walk the length of the hall, back and forth, check in all the rooms.

"Nothing?" Gracie asks, waiting in the doorway to one of the rooms while I check it out. She straggles the threshold so that the hospital won't shift as she inspects the rooms.

"It can still shift, and you'll be cut in half."

"No, it wants me. It's not gonna murder me." She peeks her head in the room, but it doesn't have anything to offer us. A green vinyl mattress on the floor, a picture of a hot-air balloon plastered on the wall. No staircase. I go to the window and stare out over the grounds. It's too far up for me to jump. Besides, there are bars on the window. I walk back to where Gracie stands.

The sun doesn't seem to have moved; the light is still a ground up clementine shimmer through the windows. We've been searching for at least a half hour. It should be dark by now, but we drift on in suspended animation through orange and gold.

We walk in silence for a few more minutes until she points in front of us, her finger shaking. She grins, though the smile is unsteady.

"I recognize that room," she says. "We walked past it earlier on our way to the morgue."

I look through the doorway, and the pale blue of the paint is familiar but...

"The hospital's changed again," I say, a pit forming in my

stomach. "That room should be floors beneath us; it shouldn't be up here."

"Maybe the halls finally shifted in our favor and we're farther down than we think."

I shake my head, my stomach clenching.

It's on the wrong floor... I lean against the wall to keep from fainting.

The room is on the wrong floor. The hospital is continuing to play games with us, and the farther we go, the more hopeless it seems. There's no getting out of here. It won't let us.

Gracie reaches for me. "Are you okay, Rae? Is it your stomach again?"

"I'm lightheaded," I say, struggling to push the words out. Mother settles across my shoulders, clamped around me like a vise. Spots dance in front of my eyes and I stumble.

"Maybe you should sit down."

I shake my head. "This is normal. It happens—"

"When you get nervous."

"Yeah." That's not it at all. I don't know how much longer I can keep pretending that it's fine. I don't know why I bother either. Especially if Mother isn't Mother. And even if she was, I'm here to get rid of her. There's no loyalty anymore, no more wishing away the past.

"Nothing to be nervous about," Gracie says, resting her hand lightly on my arm. "We're going to get out of here together."

I draw in a shaky breath, Mother dripping down to my feet before darting out behind me, stretching long as a shadow at sunset. "Honestly, this isn't normal. I haven't felt like this in over a year. Remember how I told you I used to be really sick as a kid?"

She doesn't want to hear you complain about that, Mother warns, still keeping her distance. That's family business.

"And you're not my family," I say through gritted teeth.

Does the fact that I'm not your mother really change things that much? she asks.

"Of course it does!"

Mother clucks her tongue. After everything we've been through together. After everything we've done to each other. I know all of your secrets, and I still love you, I'm still here for you. I'll always be here. Why do you think I haven't killed you yet?

A shiver travels up my spine.

Mother slinks farther back along the tiles and a wave of nausea hits me like a punch to the gut. I wrap my arms around my middle, swallowing hard. "I'm really not okay right now."

"Is there anything I can do?" Gracie asks.

"Mother used to give me tea," I say numbly.

"Well, I doubt we'll find any tea here." She smiles. "I don't think you'd want it even if we did."

I dig my fingers into my sides, hoping the nausea will pass. "You don't know how right you are."

"Is that thing on your back still yelling at you?"

I shake my head. "She's upset that I called her out for not being my mother. But I think she figured I'd realize it sooner or later. She was quieter than usual after we started walking together, after you started telling me things."

The light drains from the hallway and the temperature drops. Orange bleeds into red, which is drawn out into a soft, festering purple. We hit a dead end and turn around to find that the hallway has been replaced with a long, rectangular room. Pale blue, vicious in the bruised light.

I draw in a sharp breath, my heart jumping to my throat. Gracie only shakes her head in disappointment.

"Guess we have no choice," she says, reaching for my hand again as we cross the threshold together.

The room sheds its skin. Long strips of pale blue hang from

the walls, and the plaster beneath, the puss and bruises of this building, claw their way to the surface. There is a pink chair at the center of the room, a cassette player perched on the seat, and a white sheet draped tenderly across one of its shoulders. Stray ceiling tiles lie molding at its feet. One of the walls is slanted and comprised entirely of panes of glass.

Light pours into the room and illuminates the piles of debris so they look like they're burning.

Despite the warmth in the room, a patchy layer of ice coats the floor.

My stomach clenches and Mother continues to drift behind me like a trail of smoke.

18

GRACIE

My kind has no history, no legacy, no place in human society—not even among the myths and legends of this world. There is no word for us, no definition that has been given to us beyond that which we've given ourselves. We're volatile, so when we meet others of our kind, it's all claws and teeth. Anything we may learn from one another is lost to bloodied knuckles and black eyes.

Our unstable chemistry.

Our unsavory biology.

Our wrongness, like the world is allergic to what we represent.

The malums that attach and feed seem so distant that I wonder if we're truly related. Or if we're cousins only in the sense that we feed off humans.

I'm taken back to when real Gracie asked about my family, and I stuttered out a half response, arms curled tight around myself.

"You're not alone, silly," she said. "You have me."

"And what happens once I'm done killing you?" I choked out past the near-constant ache bruising the center of my chest.

The silence between us was thick, almost alive in its own right.

"Is that why you took my body?" she asked. "Because you were lonely?"

I startled, knocking the bottle of yellow nail polish on its side. I scrambled to pick it up before it spilled, hands shaking and pulse hammering in my veins. "Before this body, I didn't know what lonely meant. All I knew was hunger."

"I don't think that's true," Gracie said, her voice soft and melodic. "From what you've told me, it sounds like your kind is very lonely. You can't rely on each other, you barely communicate, and you're so blinded by your hunger that when you do run into something like you, you get so damn territorial that it almost always ends in a physical fight. Anyone would be lonely under those conditions."

She was right, of course; it just took me too long to realize it.

I've only ever met one other of my kind before today—someone who possessed a body with all of my rage and none of my shame. We didn't talk, we only fought, and by the end of it they were running off clutching a dislocated arm, and my face was swollen from the blows. A passing present from my only family. Nothing discussed, nothing learned.

Ana's the first to talk to me, to offer me a family beyond this body and Gracie's fading consciousness. Maybe it's because the desire to fight is so ingrained in me. Maybe that's why I'm not willing to accept the offer.

The icy room is littered with water-damaged photos and old cassette tapes.

I stand to the side, arms crossed over my chest as Rae prowls around the room. "There's nothing in here," I say. "We should try to find an exit and keep moving."

"The hospital brought us here for a reason." Rae bends at the waist to pick up a stack of photos, quickly leafing through the images.

"Rae..." I don't know if the shivers that wrack my body are from the cold or the fever with which she rifles through the photos.

"There has to be a reason," she mutters to herself. "There has to be something here."

Wind filters in through hairline fractures in the window-panes, a high-pitched whine cutting through the room, and I glance out over the grounds. There's a perfect view of the front of the hospital, but the glass is warped in a way that makes it look like an abstract painting. All harsh strokes of color and formless blobs.

Suddenly, there's a sharp intake of breath, and I twist to find Rae holding a photo gingerly by her thumb and forefinger, eyes wide. She bites down hard on her bottom lip. Enough to make it bleed. Red stains the white of her teeth. Red snakes its way through the pink of her lips.

I cross the room to where she stands, all too aware of where Ana's blood has dried to a brown crust across my shirt. My skin crawls.

Rae holds the photo out to me, but her hand is shaking too hard for me to see the image. After a few seconds she lets go, the malum at her back swelling, causing her to curl in on herself as the photo flutters to the ground.

"Mother is saying—" She stumbles back. "No, Mother. Please, stop!"

The malum at her back covers her almost completely, a black veil cutting her off from me, from everything, dozens of houseflies swarming around her head.

"No!" she cries, slamming her palms against her ears, the flies weaving in and out between her fingers. "No, I can't accept it."

She falls to her knees, and I crouch down next to her. I lift her chin and she drops her hands, staring out at me from within the mess of flies. Her eyes are wide and frantic.

"Rae, please," I say. "You're scaring me."

"The photo... I saw... and Mother... She used to say all the time how her mother abandoned her. My Grandma Perry. I thought she meant that she left the house... but this..." She crooks a finger toward where the photo lies face down, ceiling tiles strewn around it like sacrificial offerings.

I reach my hand through the cloud of flies, ignoring how they sting my hand, and wipe the tears from her cheeks. The malum recedes slightly and the flies clump around it.

I take Rae's hand and help her stand, and only when I'm sure she won't fall over do I bend and pick up the photo, turning it right side up so I can see the image.

In it is a skinny woman in a hospital gown sat upon a table. The photo is black and white, but it's clear that her dark hair is matted, and her eyes stare unseeingly at something beyond the camera.

She's the spitting image of Rae. A little older, her cheekbones a fraction more angular, but close enough that she could be her older sister, or maybe—

"It's my Grandma Perry," she says quietly, pulling at her pinkie nail and chewing her bottom lip as the malum undulates behind her. "I kept seeing this figure—out on the grounds, inside the hospital. I think... I think it's my Grandma Perry."

As if on cue, the cassette player on the chair clicks on and whirls loudly for a few moments before a grainy voice filters through the room.

"I'll tell you exactly why I did it." The voice is soft and sounds so much like Rae, only more mature, more weathered. "There's something wrong with this place. It's been eating away at everyone inside it, and the only way to stop it is to kill it. That's what I was trying to do when I set the fire. I didn't mean to hurt anyone; I didn't mean to hurt them. I didn't, I didn't, but ohhh it's eating away at us. I can feel it under my skin." There's a series of low moans and a sound like nails down a chalkboard.

"Mrs. Perry," a deeper, male voice cuts in. "Mrs. Perry, are you alright?"

Rae winds her hair around her fingers, tangling it through her hands. Small strands are tugged out at the roots and fall at her feet, joining the ice that coats the floor. They slice across the coldness.

"You're okay, Rae," I whisper soothingly and smooth her hair back, but she's trembling so hard I fear she'll snap in two.

"I didn't mean to hurt anyone," Mrs. Perry, Rae's grand-mother, repeats, her voice grainy as it stretches through time. "But I don't mind a little hurt when it's for the right reason. These folks here, they're as much family as I'm ever gonna have anymore. And pain is the price of family."

19

RAE

My bones freeze, my lip trembles. *Pain is the price of family.*

Mother used to tell me that all the time when I was little, when I was sick and would rely on her for everything. She'd stay home from work for days and days. Feed me soup, keep a cool cloth on my forehead.

"Your fingernails are turning blue," she'd say and rub my hands until the blood began to circulate again. It exhausted her. She never got a moment to herself, but when I would apologize, when I would cry for how much pain I was putting her through, she'd bring a finger up to my lips and hush me.

"Pain is the price of family," she'd say, and wrap her arms around my shoulders. "I'd do anything to keep you here with me."

That's the reason why I didn't protest when she wouldn't let me go farther than the backyard when I went outside to play. That's the reason why it didn't bother me that she wouldn't let me have a phone or other freedoms that many girls my age are readily given. It hurt, it pained me, but that doesn't matter. *Pain is the price of family.*

I shudder.

I list off a bunch of Mother's words, silently recite them to myself. *Batrachotoxin. Brodifacoum. Strychnine.* I think of the way Mother used to rip pages from the dictionary, quickly, and without mercy. The way her hand shook when she wrote. The sharp, dangerous curve of her penmanship.

I can't find the words. Mother would know what to say. She had a word for everything. She spent hours poring over dictionaries so that she was never caught without the right sentence on the tip of her tongue.

Mother found her dictionaries in library discard bins, she found them roadside the night before trash day. She started to collect them shortly after I turned five. The dictionaries came before the words, before *that* room.

Then she started with the sticky notes, placing them on pieces of furniture and the blank walls of our living room. After the sticky notes came the days when she'd fixate over the fact that Eliza's father—my father—left her. And my grandmother left her. How everyone left.

"He abandoned me," she said one morning over breakfast. "Your good-for-nothing daddy. He was so much like my momma, that man. Your Grandma Perry left me too. You'll never abandon me, will you, Rae?"

I sat at the kitchen counter and looked at the word she had stuck to the fridge that day. *Catharsis.* The "t" and "h" practically stitched together. I couldn't steady myself or get rid of the sick feeling in my gut.

She kept saying, "Everyone I love always leaves, always leaves, always leaves…"

Again, and again, and again.

I can't get out of the icy room fast enough, my grandmother's words still echoing in my ears as all the pieces slide into place.

The tragedy of '65, Mother's obsession, all the clippings that she kept detailing the fire.

The fire my grandmother set.

Because she was a patient here. And the hospital was hurting them—her and her friends, the other patients.

Seaside State has a vendetta against me, against my family. That's why it's been taunting me, that's why it wants me so badly.

All because of what my grandmother did.

Gracie and I hurry through the hospital, changing our path as the hallways shift.

"We need to stay one step ahead of Seaside State," Gracie says. "As it is, I'm surprised it hasn't brought Ana to attack us again."

"Maybe it has other things in mind." The hospital seems to be losing its grip on reality. There are too many windows in the walls now, and they seem to multiply the farther we walk, creeping their way up the walls and onto the ceiling until it's nothing but glass on all sides, the thinnest slices of peeling paint between them. We're surrounded on all sides by thick, warped glass looking out onto the inky twilight of the grounds and into patient rooms with green plastic mattresses laid out like bodies on the floor.

Until the glass seems to slip over the floor too, and stepping over it, we can see the floor beneath ours. Down to halls the color of blood, flaking like a sunburn. My stomach flips.

"So your grandma really torched this place?" Gracie asks, keeping her pace hurried.

"At least I know why this place is messing with me now. It's giving me a headache." In another few feet the windows shift again, and when I glance back over my shoulder, it's as if they were never even there. Everything is back in its rightful place. So quickly, like a rubber band snapping. The suddenness of the change is enough to send me reeling.

Seaside State continues to add and subtract rooms and entryways, seemingly at random.

There are some new additions to the halls too. Various murals are painted over what used to be neutral paint. Bright colors and smiling animals. I grimace. Rabbits shouldn't smile; turtles shouldn't have teeth.

We slow to a jog, then to a walk, and then stop and lean up against a wall, struggling to catch our breaths.

Gracie jumps away from it.

"Did you feel something?" I ask her, and she nods.

"It's hot to the touch. And look…"

I step away from the wall to stand next to her and turn.

Ward 8 Welcomes You is painted on the wall in red paint, the color of a fire engine. Ward 11, Ward 13. I make a list inside my head.

"That's new," I murmur.

"We should keep going," she says.

We turn a corner and come to a mural that takes up the entire wall. It's painted in bright, bold colors. Geometric blocks of blue, red, and yellow make up the background. The foreground consists of a faceless man embracing a female figure that has peeled halfway off the wall. The man's face is distorted and looks like a pumpkin that's been stepped on. I can't make out any of the female figure's features; she's peeled away almost entirety to reveal pale pink and the cream-colored wall underneath.

"Hello, lovely." Gracie barely whispers the words. They come out like an exhale, a hum of wind. Hello. Lovely.

"What?" I ask.

"Hello, lovely. It's written on the wall." Gracie points. The tip of her finger droops and her hand hangs limp at the wrist.

I look, and there it is: Mother's handwriting. Again. Or maybe it's my grandmother's. I wonder if handwriting is hereditary, if all the women in my family have such damaging penmanship. The sharp staccato of the words is harsh against a naked corkboard that sits screwed into the wall. The words are small and delicate despite the violence of the script.

"It's terrifying," she says in a whisper.

"You have no idea," I say back.

The light slices across the text.

Beneath the corkboard there are more words; six words, written over and over again.

Pain is the price of family. Pain is the price of family. Pain is the price of family.

It's written in the same black crayon as the writing in the hallway from earlier, except bits of certain letters have flaked away. The p's are cut off at the bottoms, and the e's and a's are near impossible to tell apart. The contrast between the two sets of writing is startling, especially since they seem to be paired together. One person's response to another's message. Both in Mother's, or Grandmother's, or the maternal line of the Perry family's hurried scrawl.

"Ugh," Gracie gasps. "What's that smell?"

It smells rotten, a mix of eggs and expired mayonnaise. Through the rotten smell there's an earthy musk, and beneath that the faintest hints of garlic. It smells primal.

"Maybe it's Ana," I suggest. "From what you told me, malums sound a hell of a lot like demons. And aren't demons supposed to stink?"

"I'd know if it was Ana," Gracie says flatly.

It's just me and Gracie and dozens of flies. They coat the walls in a film, a constantly moving sheet of wings and legs.

Gracie doesn't seem to notice. She doesn't react when we pass them, and I'm not about to tell her about them. For all I know it's another side effect of Mother's attachment, another curse my grandmother left for me, another piece of evidence that my mind is slipping.

It's the blood on my hand all over again. The flies erupting from the back of Gracie's hand.

I keep hoping that I'll blink and they'll disappear, but the farther we move down the hallway, the thicker the clumps of flies become.

Footsteps sound off behind us and I twist around, but all I see is Mother gently swaying at my back.

They aren't human. The thought cuts through me. The footsteps don't sound man-made; there's no way they can be. It's a lighter tread.

It's a pack of predators. The thought chills me. I look over my shoulder again, but there isn't anything there. The only thing out of place is the flicker of a shadow across the corner of the wall, a phantom predator or invented terror.

"I hate how quiet it is in here," Gracie says, shivering.

"What do you mean it's quiet?"

"That it's quiet? Like, it's dead silent in here."

"Don't you hear the footsteps?" I ask. They're getting closer, along with the faint sound of panting.

"The only thing I can hear is the..." She looks over to where the flies coat the wall then shakes her head. "No, never mind."

"What? Tell me." If she can see the flies too then that means...

"I... It doesn't matter. It's okay. Let's keep walking." She's been chewing her pinkie finger and when she finally stops biting it and removes it from her mouth, it's stained red. She's chewed off her purple nail polish in its entirety and bitten the tip of her finger open.

I frown. "I thought you couldn't stand the sight of blood."

"Hmm?" she asks, licking the blood off her pinkie. She examines the tip of her mangled nail, then spits on it. The saliva mixes with the drops of blood that are still escaping through the wound. She rolls it between her thumb and forefinger. I wish I could put a Band-Aid on it. I can't take the way it's open, especially since she keeps dragging her hands all over the walls. It'll get infected.

The blood trickles down her finger and settles at the base of her wrist.

"You're bleeding."

She frowns. "No, I'm not."

"You bit through your pinkie finger," I say.

"Excuse me?" She holds up her hand and I grimace. Her pinkie nail is still intact. The blood is gone.

"But it was just there. I just watched you peel off the top layer."

"You watched me bite off my nail?"

"I... I thought I did."

She holds a hand to my forehead. "You're burning up."

"You think I was hallucinating?" If the flies aren't real after all, then maybe my grandmother didn't... No, she did, she did and that's why the hospital hates me.

"I think the hospital is a lot smarter than we've given it credit for; it will do anything to pick us apart and make us feel like we're losing our minds. It makes it easier for it to... well."

"Maybe it's Mother. I think she's made me see things before... or I've seen things because of her. She hasn't spoken to me since I snapped at her earlier, and I've been getting worse the longer she's hung around."

I think I know Mother when she's close, when we're together, but separation is our antiseptic, a slow IV drip to wash her away, drown her out, like scrubbing out a stain. It chills the highways of my skin. She's not the same now that I realize that I've been on my own for almost a year.

I think about Mother and my stomach churns. I think about her, and I don't want to leave the hospital if I can't find a way to be rid of her for good. Even though it *isn't* her, and that makes it hurt worse. Because I'll never be able to ask her about my grandmother, and what made her hold so tightly onto me. So tight I suffocated.

Because I love Mother. I love her. And it rips me up inside.

I want to tell Gracie what was happening to me, and why Mother died, why I thought I was haunted.

But I can't find the words for it. I don't know where to begin.

Back when she was alive, Mother always wanted me to stay close to her. I could never leave her side. I didn't mind it when I was younger, but once I started school, it began to wear on me.

I was eight years old, and she told me I couldn't sign up for cheerleading.

"I can't drive you to every practice, Rae. I'm busy," she said. "I'm a busy woman. And what about me, don't you love me? You want to leave me alone even longer than you already do. The house is already empty enough with you away at school all day."

She tried to guilt me. I remember it, faintly, like I'm hearing it through a filter. Her words funnel through to me.

"You don't have to, my friend's mom can drive," I told her, the guilt searing a hole through my gut.

"You think I'd trust some stranger to drive my baby girl around?" She sighed dramatically. "You don't know how lucky you are, Rae. My momma was never there growing up, she left when I was so small. I didn't have her to watch out for me like this."

"Please, Mother."

"It's not a good idea," she said, and I gave up after a few more minutes of back-and-forth. This wasn't the first time I had tried to join a club or do a school activity. Every few weeks I came to her with another question, thinking that if I found the right activity, she'd let me be a part of it.

Two weeks later I asked her about a program that my school was running where I could learn a foreign language.

"It meets before school, early, so you won't lose any time with me. I'd usually be sleeping anyway," I told her. I was hopeful that this would be well received.

"Why?" she had asked.

"I want to learn Spanish," I said.

"Why?" she repeated.

"I think it would be fun."

She shook her head. "It's time for dinner."

She started giving me the pills shortly after I asked about the Spanish lessons. I had been having nightmares. The first few nights, Mother would rush into my room and smooth my hair back until I calmed down and went back to sleep.

Then she started coming in with pill bottles. I'd wake up in the middle of the night screaming and Mother would run to my bedside, pill bottle in hand.

"What's the matter, love?" she asked.

"I had a bad dream."

She wouldn't say anything in response, and would instead shake a few pills into her open palm and hold them in front of my face. When I asked her what they were she shook her head and placed one in my mouth. She didn't leave until she was sure I swallowed it. There were all kinds of pills at first. Little round tablets and gel-filled capsules. Reds and whites and yellows. Then she switched to aspirin and herbal tea.

One aspirin followed by two cups of tea after dinner.

I always thought she was poisoning me, making me sick to keep me home. But there was never any proof, never any certainty. Only the small puncture wounds in the medication and the sour taste.

These don't taste like aspirin, Mother.

You get headaches if you don't take them.

They taste funny.

You get headaches if you don't take them. I love you, Rae. Take your pills, they're good for you. They're good for you...

And the tea, the bitter tea...

I knew deep down what she was doing, I knew something was wrong. I didn't get sick until after Mother started giving me pills to help my night terrors.

It makes sense now that I think about it. I started making friends in grade school and getting invited on playdates. Mother didn't like that.

She loved me too much to let me go.

Munchausen, another one of Mother's words. Munchausen syndrome by proxy. Her definition. She was keeping me sick to keep me home. She was keeping me home because she didn't want to be alone. All the medicine I didn't need, all the bitter tasting tea, all the time I spent home in bed, and in the doctor's office. She enjoyed every minute of it.

It made her happy to see me suffer.

And that's why I killed her.

20

———

GRACIE

Ever since I entered this body, people have been telling me to be a good girl. Be a good girl and smile for the camera. Be a good girl and take the compliment. Be a good girl and keep your pretty little mouth shut.

Be a good girl.

Even though it's been repeated countless times, I'm still not sure what it means. It seems to me that being a good girl doesn't have very much to do with being good at all.

It's about being compliant.

Even before I entered this body, I was never good at doing what I was supposed to. I could fake it and fake it well. I would float around and eat, suck the pain and the crazy from the hearts of men, and women, and dogs and birds, but never be full.

When I first got stuck in this body, all I could focus on was the pain. Tension headaches, and toothaches, and the way a human's skin burns if they stay out in the sun too long.

But the more time I spend here, the more I focus on the beautiful things—things I didn't even know existed until I sunk into this skin.

The smell of a freshly mowed lawn, and summer air, and the sound of laughter in a crowded hallway; how movie theaters smell like imitation butter and old upholstery.

The joys of spaghetti and meatballs.

If it wasn't so wrong, I doubt I'd want to leave this behind.

I squeeze my eyes shut and try to feel the real Gracie, hear her, hear anything. But there's only me. Only this body I stole, and I wonder, not for the first time, if I'm already too late.

I keep thinking about what Ana said, how Seaside State protects her in exchange for fresh blood. But what use does our kind have for protection? We're such solitary creatures, with no natural enemies except ourselves. No notoriety, so humans are none the wiser. I keep thinking about how I asked the wrong questions during our exchange.

"You're being really quiet over there," Rae says. "Are you feeling okay?"

"I could ask you the same thing. You've been dead silent."

Rae frowns. She opens and closes her mouth a few times as if she wants to say something but can't find the words. The malum huddles in but she swats it back with a flick of her wrist, and to my surprise, it drifts back until it trails behind us like car exhaust.

"You beat it back," I say with admiration.

"Yeah, I'm trying to be more... in charge, I guess. Seaside State didn't eat her, so I might as well get used to it. Try to shift the power dynamic. For as long as I can remember, she's been the one who's been in charge. I don't think I realized how bad it was when I was younger, cause when you're little that's the way it's supposed to be. But then I got older and it got worse, and I... Sorry," she says, color rising to her cheeks. "I'm rambling."

"What did I say earlier about apologizing? Besides, I like

seeing you put that thing in its place." I flash her a weak smile and while her eyes initially light up, she seems to realize that something's not right and her expression darkens.

"Are you okay?" she asks.

"Don't worry about it. You've got enough on your plate without all my shit too."

"You can talk to me if something is wrong, though. I'm not gonna judge you or think it's weird or anything. Because honestly, what's weirder than Mother? Or my grandmother being a patient here? What's weirder than Seaside State?" She lets out a laugh but cuts it short when she realizes I'm not joining in, and her eyes burn into mine. Dark and serious. "We're in this together. We protect each other."

"Don't use that word."

"What word?" Her brow furrows.

"Protect," I mumble. "I hate that word."

"Why?" she asks, frowning. "Isn't that what we're doing? I'm sorry... I said the wrong thing again. I always say the wrong thing."

I shake my head. "It's not you, it's me. Why would you think it's you?"

"It's always me. I never say... Forget it. We have more important things to worry about right now."

"For all I know, we might be digested by this place before we make it to the first floor." Rae is the only one Seaside State would be digesting, and that's assuming the paranoia it's pumping her full of is enough to get past the malum already attached to her back. "Tell me."

She gazes absently out the window for a moment, the malum continuing to trail at her heels. "Do you ever wish you were more than yourself?"

"You mean like that thing feeding off of you," I quip.

She lowers her head. "Never mind."

I flinch. "No. I'm sorry. I'm kind of a bitch."

"Kind of?" she asks, a harsh edge to her voice.

"I'm not very good with people."

"I don't believe that for a second."

"Why not?"

"You're so... You're the popular type. The kind of person who has a bunch of friends, who everyone falls in love with cause you're so pretty and you know it and... and I'm sorry."

"Stop apologizing. It's a fair assumption."

"But it's still an assumption. And I hate assumptions."

I nod. "You'd rather people get to know you. I get that."

She shakes her head. "No one knows me. My mother was the only person who did and now that she's dead, I'm alone."

"I wish I had that kind of relationship with someone."

"No, you don't."

I hesitate before answering, unsure if I should push the subject.

"I want someone to love me like that," I say tentatively.

Tears well up in Rae's eyes.

"It wasn't love," she says quietly, then hurries ahead of me.

I rush after her, tugging on the sleeve of her hoodie.

"Don't touch me!" she snaps.

I release her but stay next to her. "I know you want to get rid of her, I know things were tense between you but..."

"If you tack a 'but' onto the end of that sentence, then you don't get it. There is no but, and tense doesn't begin to cover it. I didn't leave the house because of her, I didn't have friends because of her. I barely went to school. She was the only person I had, and she was my best friend, but I didn't have a choice. I was alone and she was there. She was the *only* one there. And when she died, I felt so guilty because I was relieved. I was happy. I was devastated, but I was also over-fucking-joyed. There's no way to make you understand because *I* don't understand and I was there—I was the one who felt it."

Heat rises to my face, and I bite the inside of my cheek. "I'm sorry, Rae. I didn't realize."

"She's gone, but she's still here. She's still following me around and yelling at me and telling me I'm stupid and that everything I say is wrong, and how can I not believe her? She's the only one who really knows me."

"Rae..."

"I know, it's a malum or a demon or whatever, it's not really her. But it sounds like her, it knows about *everything.*"

I look at her for a long time, focusing on the places where the malum fuses to her skin. I'll never get used to the way my kind looks. Even in its bloated state, even after feeding on Rae for close to a year, it still looks as if I could blow on it and it would dissipate into a cloud of houseflies.

I wish it were that easy. But I look at Rae, at the dark bags under her eyes, at the blue veins that show through her skin and I realize that if I don't do it now, I never will.

What's the use of waiting anyway? We may not make it out of here.

"I'll try to help you," I say, not giving myself a chance to back out.

She blinks up at me through the tears. "You will?"

"Yes, right now." I place my hands on either side of her forehead. "But I need to remind you that it's dangerous... I've only ever exorcised buildings, and the things that latch onto inanimate places aren't like malums; they're weaker. If this goes wrong—"

"I know the risks," she says quietly. "I told you earlier, I'm willing to die for my goal. Either I get rid of Mother, or I don't have to deal with the attachment anymore regardless. I'll be happy with the outcome either way."

"Don't say that." I shut my eyes and feel the warmth of her skin, the slow lull of her breathing.

I pull at the inside of her mind, snipping the threads that bind them together.

I see Mother through Rae's eyes—this sigh of a woman, with her frizzy hair and flowered blouses. The smile that never quite reaches her eyes. Eyes that glisten without joy, without warmth. Eyes that hint at horrors beyond my comprehension.

I step up to her, this shadow of the woman Rae grew up with, her cheeks red, her teeth coffee stained and crooked.

"You need to go. You're not this woman—you're not anything at all."

The woman peels apart and the malum seeps out, dark gray and formless, floating above the deflated pile of skin.

"And what does that make you?" the malum counters. "You're not that body you're residing in—you're not human."

My breath catches and I wade inside Rae's mind, pressing my fingers to her forehead as if I could leave my fingerprints like kisses across her skin.

I can't do this, it's too difficult. I can't—

"Yes, you can," Rae's voice echoes through her head and a soft warmth surrounds my body until I feel her pressed up next to me. "We can do it."

I take a deep breath and concentrate. I face the malum hand in hand with Rae, her palm burning in mine.

"Baby girl, come on now," the malum pleads, its voice sickly sweet. "You don't want to hurt me."

"Pain is the price of family," Rae deadpans, and the malum hisses. I feel her hand shake in mine, and as she distracts the malum, my fingers work to erase the connection, snip the thread, and snuff it out. But the process is painstakingly slow, and every time I feel as if the connection has snapped loose, there's another sinew-like cord tangling them up together.

"You're not my mother," Rae says, the slight tremble in her voice the only evidence that she's distressed. "My mother died a year ago."

"And you'll be joining her soon." The malum's voice turns low and gravelly as it drops any pretense of being Rae's mother. It swells to twice its size and towers over where we stand. It tilts to the side and laughter ricochets like broken glass through the void as it focuses its attention on me.

"And you'd better back off before I stir the girl's organs, slurp them up and discard the shell," the creature purrs, and Rae squeezes my hand tighter, but her presence swells, filling every corner of her mind.

"You are not my mother," she grits from between her teeth. "And you are not welcome here. Get out!"

At Rae's command, the creature trembles, the remaining cords snapping in rapid succession, and I give her one final push. I push with all my strength and the malum slips back inside Rae's mother's skin, loose cheeks flapping in the wind, lips swollen and puckered.

"After a while you get high off the memories," it rasps. "The feelings. The taste. And it's enough to make you forget what you are. It feels comfortable beneath the skin. I so did enjoy wearing your mother."

Rae screams again and I push out, the tips of my fingers flexing through the darkness.

The malum smiles, revealing rows of coffee-stained teeth. It smiles, then screams.

And then it's gone.

21

RAE

A part of me always knew what Mother was doing—not in any firm way, but I had a feeling that something was wrong. I had a feeling she was poisoning me. But it didn't make any sense, because she loved me so much—she loved me too much to let me go. And in a sick way, I couldn't blame her for that.

Until I could.

Until lying in bed felt like a death sentence. And the cold sweats, the stomachaches, the bloody noses all felt like betrayal. All the times she combed my hair or sang to me suddenly weren't enough to make up for all the pain she put me through.

The night that Mother died, I made her tea from the oleander leaves—the same bundle of dried petals and stems that she'd fed to me for the better half of my life. I never meant to kill her, only to upset her stomach, only to have her rely on me for a change. In a way, I thought it would bring us closer together. It was my way of showing her that I understood, that I didn't hate her. I could never hate her.

But I made too much, or maybe she was weak, or maybe this was what she had coming.

She couldn't get out of bed and banged on the wall between our bedrooms all night.

Frantically, at first. Then just one or two thumps every few minutes. She never cried out for me, she never made a sound outside of the banging, the rap of her knuckles against plaster.

And even as tears filled my eyes, even as the thumps got fewer and farther between, I forced myself to ignore her.

And in the morning, she was dead.

Gracie pulls the malum from my back and it feels like she's ripped off a Band-Aid. The absence digs into me with all the sharpness of an ice pick. I've been so focused on freedom for so long that I didn't bother to think of what it would mean to actually get it.

It's emptiness.

It's numbness.

It's like losing a limb.

"Are you okay?" she asks, crouched down next to me, her face inches from mine.

"Fine. Dizzy." I stand, holding onto the wall for support, and run my hands along my spine. "She's really gone?"

"You tell me."

The momentary shock of it fades and a warmth washes over me. She's gone, extracted like an abscessed tooth.

There's pain, yes. There's an emptiness, but there's comfort in it. There's silence. I feel like I shed my skin.

"You did it," I say, tears streaming down my face.

"*We* did it. You gave the final push. I've never seen a connection break so quickly. Seriously, though, are you feeling okay? I know that regardless of what happened between you, you and your mother were close."

"It wasn't really my mother," I say more for my benefit than for hers. "My mother died a year ago."

"But now you're alone."

"I have my sister and I have my father." My lips tingle when I say it, when I call them my family. But they are now—they're my family. My only family. And in a way, so is Gracie. I want to tell her that I'll never truly be alone as long as I have her, as long as we're in this together. But instead I smile. "Now I'm myself again."

Gracie stumbles slightly and I catch her under the arm.

"Are you okay?" I ask.

"Fine. Dizzy," she says with a grin, and once she steadies herself, she grabs my hand and we walk down the hall.

"We may still be stuck in here, but something tells me it won't be for much longer. It's almost over."

"I hope you're right," she says.

"What happened the first time you were here?" I ask, my fingers laced through hers. "Does it have to do with what you came here to get rid of?"

She tries to jerk her hand away, but I hold firm.

"How do you know about that?" she asks.

"Mason said something about it while we were up on the roof. He said it has something to do with why you and Ana were at each other's throats." I didn't think it would be right to bring it up before now, but with Mother finally gone, I feel like I can think clearly for the first time in almost a year.

Gracie keeps her eyes lowered. "If I told you, you wouldn't like me anymore."

"I'll tell you my secret if you tell me yours," I offer.

"What secrets could you possibly have, sweet Rae?" she asks, and although her voice is light and teasing, it takes everything I have not to let them dig into me.

Of course she doesn't think I have secrets, I think bitterly. *I'm not interesting enough for secrets.*

"The night my mother died…" I can't bring myself to finish the sentence. "Look, I understand what it's like to keep a secret, and it's awful. And I don't want anything to come between us after we get out of here."

We take careful steps, avoiding shards of broken glass.

"If I tell you about the first time I was here, there won't be any us after all this is over." She draws in a shaky breath and lets it out again. "I've hurt people. I've killed them."

"I killed my mother." I don't mean to blurt it out, but the second I say it, I feel like a weight's been lifted. No matter her reaction, I'm finally free.

To my surprise, she grips my hand tighter and looks over at me with sympathy. "That must have been very difficult for you. I know that you loved your mother."

"You don't seem surprised."

"I thought you killed her; it really isn't a huge shock."

My limbs go numb, and flashes of heat shoot up into my forehead. "You thought that I killed her?"

She nods. "The way you would talk about her, and the things I saw when I exorcised the malum—when *we* exorcised it—I knew something must have happened."

Tears spring to my eyes. "And you don't hate me?"

She gives my hand a squeeze. "Your mother was an awful woman. I can't hate you for doing what you needed to do to protect yourself."

"I could never hate you for what happened the first time you were here, whatever it is."

Her expression darkens and she slips her hand out of mine. "I already told you, I'm not gonna talk about it."

"Why not? I told you that I killed my mother; nothing can be worse than that."

"It's a long story."

"I have time. *We* have time."

We pause at the edge of a doorway and she takes a deep breath. "I'll tell you once we get out of here. Over lunch."

"Like a date?" I ask, my cheeks burning.

"Like a date," she confirms, just as red as I am.

"Yeah?" I ask, unable to hide my grin. "You do know that lunch is one of the least romantic meals there is, don't you?"

She smirks and leans in closer. "Who said anything about romance." She brushes a strand of hair back from my face.

My heart thunders against my ribs and I part my lips in anticipation, but she pulls away. She stumbles back, her eyes wide, knees shaking.

"What's wrong?" I follow her gaze to the doorway at the end of the hall.

It's Ana.

And Mason.

22

GRACIE

"Mason?" Rae's face drains of color and she takes a cautious step toward where he stands in the doorway.

It takes me a moment to notice, but his arms stretch a little too long, his head lolls to the side. His skin is pale and chalky.

"Wait," I say, grabbing her arm. She stops and allows me to pull her back.

He walks up next to Ana and she wraps an arm around his waist.

"What's happening?" I whisper.

"I made it home," Mason says, a shroud of flies now hovering lazily where his aura used to be. There aren't as many as around Ana, and they're thinner, smaller—fruit flies. The flies of a fledgling.

My stomach churns.

She changed him.

"And I came home before him," Ana adds, leaning in closer to the thing wearing Mason's face. "And now it's your turn."

"I already gave you my answer," I tell her, jaw clenched.

"But we need you to come home." Ana takes a step forward,

her limbs bending unnaturally, the horseflies swarming around her.

Rae shivers with every mention of "home" and I wrap a protective arm around her. "I won't let you near her."

Mason lets out a laugh, the sound high-pitched, like the wail of a siren. "We don't care about her, we want you."

Ana clucks her tongue. "Now, now, Mason. Who's to say we can't be interested in both?" Her predatory gaze settles on Rae. "After all, Rae seems to have finally gotten rid of her attachment. She's back on the menu."

"Mason," I beg. "Look at what Ana did to you. You don't need to listen to a word she says. I can help you; I know I can find a way to get you back to the way you were if you trust me enough to let me try."

"Why would I want to go back to the way I was? You're acting like I had no say in what happened." He looks to Ana who smirks.

"It was consensual," she insists, tracing his jawline. "He practically begged me to do it."

"What is 'it,' exactly?" Rae asks, stepping out from behind my arm. She continues to hold onto me but looks Ana directly in the eyes, with only the slightest twinge of fear.

Ana smiles a slow, queasy grin. "Ask Gracie. She knows."

I shake my head. "I've never seen anything like this before." Though that's not entirely true, if the evidence of my kind littered through the asylum is any indication. Mason isn't the first person she's done this to, and he won't be the last.

Because whatever she's done, there's no maintaining it. I clench my fist. "What you're attempting to do is impossible; it won't last."

Ana scoffs. "Just because you lack the imagination to do it doesn't mean it can't be done."

Rae's tightens her grip on my hand and looks over at me with wide, watery eyes. "What's she talking about?"

"She changed Mason; she made him like her."

"Seaside State gave him the gift," she corrects, smoothing back Mason's hair. "She's hungrier now than ever before and needs more friends on the outside, more bodies to collect her meat and kindling. I promised Mason he would live eternal if he served as waiter."

"Except you won't," I say. "Whatever she's done to you won't last. Once you outlive your usefulness, she'll get rid of you and move on to her next victim."

"Shut up! I love the hospital," he says, his voice throaty and damp. "I loved her ever since I first read about the tragedy, the first time she got a taste for flesh. She was the only thing in my life that mattered. I can't tell you how many hours I spent reading about her, dreaming about her. I could hardly eat, I was so lovesick. Then Ana found me in the forums."

"I didn't even have to convince him, really," Ana says. "Usually, it's a much more difficult sell. And no one has ever made it this far before."

"That isn't true, Mason! You aren't special, she's done this before. You're not the first one to—"

"He *is* special. No one has been willing to give up everything for the one they love."

"But I was," the thing wearing Mason's face says brightly.

Ana nods. "Usually, I don't go about it like this. Usually, it's enough to bring a few potential meals to the party, and Seaside State takes her pick of the litter. Then the lucky one transitions softly. But there were only two of you this time, and out of the three one was already a meal for another. Gracie... Well, Gracie already serves a different purpose, so he had to take matters into his own hands. Feed the hospital so that I could guarantee his transformation. Such a brave boy, such a wonderful addition to the family."

"You can't honestly be okay with this," I cry, turning to Mason. "She murdered you!"

Ana smirks. "Technically he killed himself."

"She saved me!" he howls. "You don't know what it's like because you're so beautiful, and everyone loves you. Because you've never had to struggle. But I'm always sitting alone at lunch, I'm always spending my weekends locked inside my room playing RPGs and wishing that pretty girls like you would so much as look at me. And what about after I graduate, huh? I go work some shitty part-time job, and live in some shitty apartment, with shitty roommates, buried under bills until I die? Now, I have a purpose. Now, I'm important."

Ana clucks her tongue. "*Were*, Mason. You *were* always sitting alone. But not anymore."

The thing wearing Mason's skin smiles. "Not anymore."

"Besides," Ana continues, "you don't need to feel jealous of her. She's only borrowing that body—she's not really that beautiful. Can you see it now? The lack of aura, the lack of flies? That girl is a cold, windblown thing. Ancient and aching. Just like us."

Rae frowns. "What do you mean?"

Ana howls with laughter. "You mean she hasn't told you? Gracie is dead. You've been running around the hospital with the thing that currently inhabits her body. She's the same as your dearly departed mother, or rather the creature that wore her face. Only Gracie here managed to possess and destroy her victim. She's a parasite, just like us."

Rae slips her hand from mine and stares at me quizzically. And it's the lack of outright mistrust that cuts me to my core. "What are they talking about?"

"Did you ask her about the first time she was here?" Mason asks, and Rae takes cautious steps away from me, her eyes wide.

Mason takes the opportunity to grab her, his elongated arms locking her tightly to his chest.

She lets out a muffled cry.

"One of us, one of us," Ana sings. "We accept her, we accept her."

"One of us," Mason echoes, and tears drip down Rae's cheeks when she finally understands.

"You were in on it?" she asks, struggling against Mason's hold. "You were one of them the whole time?"

"No!" I cry. "I'm like them, but I didn't want to be a part of any of this. I only ever wanted to protect you."

I rush at Mason, but Ana steps out in front of him.

"Let her go," I beg.

"We've tried asking nicely, and I really don't want to get rough about it, but you've forced my hand."

"Stop," I say, feeling the nails in my left hand grow and sharpen at the ends. The backs of my knuckles rip and my flies dance out across the skin. I'll slit their throats if I have to—no one else is dying because of me.

"What do you care, anyway?" Ana asks, stretching her smile wider so her teeth glow, ferociously white behind her chapped lips. "You're one of us. She's food."

"I might be one of you," I spit from between gritted teeth. "But she's not food."

My nails finish elongating and I silently apologize to Gracie for what I'm putting her body through. Even if I'm the only one in here anymore. It's the least I can do for her.

"Tell you what," Ana continues. "We're all civilized here, we're all understanding. Gracie, we want you to be part of the family, but what good will that be if you resent us? I'll give you a choice."

I hold my left hand behind my back, eyes locked on Rae—trying to communicate in a glance, trying to tell her that it will be okay, and I'll rip them to shreds soon.

"What's my choice?" I take cautious steps forward, glancing between Ana and Mason, trying to decide which one to go after first.

"You could refuse to join us, and we feed this girl to Seaside State before forcefully recruiting you—or killing you. Honestly, at that point it might be better just to kill you." Ana shrugs. "Or, you agree to join us, and we let her go. You feed the hospital; she lives. Everyone's happy."

"Gracie..." Rae kicks against Mason, squirming in his grasp, but it's no use. He's too strong.

"It's okay," I say, continuing my advance. "I'm not going to let anything happen to you."

I stop in front of Ana, and her cloud of flies hovers around her head like a devilish crown. Her mouth snaps back into a straight line, her teeth disappearing behind cracked lips.

I take a deep breath. "I hope I don't regret this."

She sticks out her hand, a long bony thing attached to a thin wrist. "You'll be joining us?"

"Not a chance."

I pull my hand from behind my back and lunge at her throat. My pinkie nail sinks into the soft flesh beneath her jaw and she jerks back, sending a spray of dark liquid squirting through the air.

She rushes at me, unfazed, and digs her fingers between my ribs. I cry out, reaching for Rae as I fall to the ground, my elongated nails shrinking back to normal size, my hand falling limp. The flies drop to the floor next to me.

I lie splayed on the floor and Ana rests her foot on my temple, the heel of her shoe digging into my skull.

Red distorts my vision.

"That was very stupid of you," she says, clucking her tongue. "You all but signed that girl's death sentence."

Mason jerks Rae back, pulling her down the hallway, and all I can do is watch helplessly as she's dragged away.

23

RAE

This is all wrong. It wasn't supposed to end like this. I'm alone for the first time in almost a year—truly alone, and it doesn't matter.

Mother's gone, and it doesn't matter.

My stomachaches are gone, and I'm going to die anyway.

Mason dragged me through the hospital, pulling me by my arm, my wrist, my shoulder blades, until he deposited me in a room and shut the door. I hit my head against the wall and spent who knows how long knocked out and aching until I came to again.

The room looks exactly like *that* room, complete with Mother's wall of words. Paint peels from the pale walls, a festering green, like an open sore.

My name. Repeated over and over again. Dripping red.

I'm so focused on my name that I don't notice the figure at first. It lies curled up in the corner, its thin fingers digging into the wall behind it. I take cautious steps forward, all too aware of how the figure's hair drips like an oil slick.

They roll to face me, and I moan.

It's me.

My exact copy lies sobbing on the floor, white froth pouring from her mouth. Her eyes are bloodshot, a careful line of red dripping from her nose, pooling beneath her. There's too much of it.

I reach for her, and she tries without success to lift her head. It lolls to the side and her face falls into the blood with a dull slap.

"But you aren't real," I say, keeping my voice hushed. "None of that was real; it was all a result of Mother. It was all an echo of my grandmother."

Except this isn't the first time I've seen or heard her.

I remember being in elementary school, when Mother first started shoving pills down my throat, and seeing her hover lazily at the edge of my vision.

I remember the day that the stones fell on the roof and hearing her call to me over the sound of shattering windowpanes.

I realize now that voice, the one that begged me to find her, she was never a hallucination, never a side effect brought on by mother's attachment, or my grandmother haunting the fringes of my mind. Never Seaside State.

She was always me.

I was trying to help myself; I was trying to wake myself up and make myself recognize how Mother was killing me... realize my family's connection to the hospital. But I didn't realize anything until it was already too late.

"I'm so sorry," I whimper. "I'm so sorry I couldn't help you."

She moves her lips and tries to speak, but all that comes out is a faint gurgle.

"I didn't find you soon enough."

A dull headache blooms in the back of my head. I think about Mother, and herbal tea, and oleander leaves.

I crawl to her, my fingers scraping against the ruined tile. Now that I'm close, it's clear that we're not exactly the same. She's a shadow of me—a shimmer, like the silhouette of my form against the wall in the morgue. She has my face, and my clothes, but she's a whisper. A gust of wind. All my features tacked onto something fragile. Her skin is sticky with sweat as I lift her into my lap, and she rests her slick red palms against my cheeks. They're cold and waxy.

"I waited too long. I let her ruin me." I let her poison me, let her continue to haunt me long after she was gone, and she's still stuck between my bones, under my skin, in my blood. She's a toxin my liver can't filter out, a pain that refuses to heal.

"I had to wait for Gracie to save me, and even then..." Thinking of Gracie makes me feel sick to my stomach.

My mirror image shakes her head, and through the foam, through the blood and spittle, she pushes out the words. "No, you saved yourself. You finally saved yourself."

I pull her in close, hold her against my chest as she sinks into me and disappears.

"But I was too late," I whimper, my vision distorting before I collapse.

Oleander petals bloom around me in a kaleidoscope of color. I dip my fingers into the pool of blood, reading it in braille, committing it to memory even as it fades.

My name stares down at me and I gaze up through the halos of color, through the oleander petals, my breath coming in short, uneven gasps.

I spent so long letting Mother feed off me, and now Seaside State has taken her place. Mother's feeding was like a weight pressing down on me, a pressure that increased so slowly over time that I acclimated to the pain. Her teeth were gentle as they dragged against my jugular, and I didn't feel a thing as she sank in and started tearing out chunks.

Seaside State is different.

It chews into me with a ferocity that sets my nerves alight. It's as if my entire body is dotted with puncture wounds, but instead of bleeding out, I'm letting Seaside State in through the wounds in my skin. It seeps into me, taunting me with memories of everything I've had to suffer through, taunting with the promise that it was all for nothing.

I'm going to die alone on the floor of an asylum, so deeply buried inside this ruined building that no one will likely ever find my body. I'll never be able to go home. To Eliza. To father. To the promise of nice dinners together.

Mother continues to haunt me, and she'll remain with me as I die here.

What can I do? I think helplessly. *I'm no match for one of those things.*

That steady rain of stones, the culmination of so much violence. I close my eyes and see them falling, hear them pound relentlessly against the roof of my house.

But they weren't the first thing.

No.

There was Mother's garden, the flowers uprooted again and again.

There were knocks on the walls, and hairline fractures in the door of the medicine cabinet.

Flowers, and fractures, and stones.

So many stones.

When I'd get stressed, when I'd get scared, when Mother insisted on pills and an early bedtime. When there was no way out.

Flowers pulled up by their roots.

Sheets of glass cut clean down the middle.

The stones.

What if it wasn't paranormal at all?

What if it was me?

I hover in that hazy twilight between sleep and wakefulness.

"I can't fall asleep," I mumble. "If I do, I won't wake up again."

My eyelids droop. I think of the stones.

That afternoon replays slowly, like stitches ripping open. One by one.

"I'm feeling better today, Mother," I said, my chin propped up on the dining room table. "Maybe we could go to the mall later, get some pretzels and window-shop."

Mother frowned deeply.

The kettle on the stove screamed, hot steam hissing from its spout.

"It's time for your tea, Rae."

I scrunched my nose. "I don't want tea, I want to go to the mall."

She poured the liquid into a large mug and set the bag to steep.

"It's time for your tea," she repeated, but I had already left the table and made my way into the living room.

Mother stormed after me, pulling me up roughly by the arm. "We're not going anywhere today, Rae baby. It's time for your tea."

"Mother, you're hurting me." I squirmed within her grasp and kicked hard in every direction, but her grip only tightened.

She yanked, attempting to pull me back into the kitchen.

"No!" I screamed, and then the stones began to fall.

I conjure up how that felt. The pain, the horror, the dread. I concentrate the last of my energy on the door, on the thought that somewhere in the depths of Seaside State, Gracie waits for me. Gracie needs me. Even though she's one of them... My insides clench at the thought, and it aches so badly, I fear I'll break.

But she's *not* like them. She's not.

If I tell you about the first time I was here, there won't be any us after all this is over.

I've hurt people, I've killed them.

Gracie tried to warn me. Though uneasiness still sloshes through my gut, I cling to the fact that she tried, in her own way, to share her truth.

The pain I feel, the pain I focus on only works to strengthen me, and I double down on it.

The door bursts open.

I stare at it, my forehead slick with sweat.

It worked. All it took was a push, a little effort and a lot of pain, but I opened it. With my mind.

Of course it worked.

I should have recognized this part of myself sooner. I should have used it. Beyond what I did with the stones, beyond those rare moments when a plate would shatter, or a cabinet would slam shut. Moments that I thought I had dreamed. I should have defended myself.

But even though there's a sense of loss, of regret, those aren't the words I cling to.

There's only one word.

Power.

And it's mine.

I crawl along the floor and out into the hall. It's easier to breathe, but I'm still weak, still unsteady on my feet.

"I'm coming. Please hold on," I whisper, hoping that Gracie can hear.

24

GRACIE

It's over. I lie curled around myself on the dirty floor of the hospital. Slowly, my vision clears, Ana leaves, and the hospital seems to lean in, mocking me.

Everything that I survived here was for nothing. I couldn't save the original Gracie. I couldn't save Rae, and now I can't even save myself. I'm stranded inside this body, a lonely island of a girl. No, not even a girl. A shadow living in a husk. A malum with no way to leave.

I sit up and lean against one of the peeling walls, dizzy and broken.

Mason enters after a long time and stands above me, watching silently.

"You should have joined us," he says finally, after an eternity of silence. "We could have been a family."

"Like you aren't going to force me to hunt for the hospital anyway."

He shrugs. "It's that or die."

"I've been trying to die for years."

"Because you killed that girl you're living in," he says, shaking his head as if it doesn't make any sense. "I don't get why you're so torn up about that. From what I read, it didn't seem like she was happy—which I'm assuming is the reason you were able to get inside her in the first place. Ana told me that when it comes to feeding, we only go after easy prey. Sick, demented, destroyed." He giggles suddenly and holds a hand to his mouth as if he's surprised at the sound.

He throws his head back and grins, the smile ripping across his face. "Fuck, it feels good to finally be free of all that. It feels so good to finally *be* something."

"A monster," I spit.

"A necessary part of the food chain. We eat the sick and they die. We clear the world of its broken. One day, we'll be the only ones left."

"And then what will you feed on?"

His expression brightens and he leans in close to me, smelling like wind after a storm. "Oh, that's right. Since you made it inside a body, you don't have to feed off the negativity anymore. It's part of the reason why Seaside State has been so interested in you. It's not a normal thing, you know—full-blown possessions. She was lucky to get inside the hospital, but a living thing, a cat or dog, let alone a human... that's practically unheard of."

I frown, a headache blooming in the center of my forehead.

Mason cackles, the sound mirroring the crackle of a flame. He laughs so hard that he doubles over, grips his sides as dark tears swell around the corners of his eyes. They well up, inky and muddled.

"It's like me, isn't it?" I say, ice water chilling my veins. "Only instead of possessing a human, she possessed a building... and now she can't find her way out again."

"She doesn't want to get out again. She doesn't understand why you want to get out of that body. Maybe one day you'll be strong enough to talk to her yourself, and you can explain."

"How did you even find me?" I ask. "I know Ana was watching, but she lost track after a while, and I was so careful not to draw attention to myself."

"You really are an idiot," he says, his eyes clouding. "I had no idea it was you when I reached out—I got lucky."

The headache explodes through my head and sends pulses of pain down into my face.

"Now, I'm offering you an opportunity to settle into the fold. The girl whose body you stole is gone; you killed her a long time back. There's nothing left for you out there amongst the meat and kindling. Come and be with your own kind again. Walk with us."

Rae. I still have Rae.

He chuckles as if he can read my mind. "That girl won't be around much longer. Seaside State is about to finish its meal. Besides, you think she wants anything to do with you, a murderer, an otherworldly creature? A parasite? The same as her dearly departed mother?"

"I care about her," I say quietly. "And even though we've only just met, I want to get to know her. I want to be part of her life even if it's only for a little while. Is that so wrong?"

"Well, you certainly won't be in her life much longer," Mason cackles. "Your journey ends with you and Seaside State, tangled together and lovesick. Either you join us and feed it, or it feeds from you."

"It can't feed from me, you idiot. We don't eat our own kind. And Ana is only insistent on me joining the cause so she can stop having to turn people like you every time one of her creations drops dead. She'd be using me to replace you, how do you not get that?"

Rae, please hold on a little longer. Please let there still be time to save you.

"Don't look so glum." He rushes me, digging his elongated fingernails into my back. I bite into his neck and jerk my head back. His flesh rips easily, peeling away like old paper. Blood spurts into my mouth and I spit it onto the floor. The metallic taste remains, and red drips down over my chin.

He howls in pain and collapses before I kick him in the stomach. But then he grabs my ankle and pulls me down to join him.

"That was a dirty trick," he hisses.

"And getting me here was a trick too. We're liars and parasites, right? It's what we do."

His smile stretches wider until the corners of his mouth rip, and careful lines of blood drip down over his chin.

"Why would you want this, Mason?" I ask. "What could she possibly have promised you that would have been worth it?"

"I already told you; I had nothing left for me out there."

"And what—you thought you could reach out with some glowing message about how 'talented' and 'special' I am, and I'd come running?"

Mason peels away another strip of skin from his left cheek, his top row of teeth completely exposed.

"Do I wear the skin, or does the skin wear me?" he asks, his tongue flicking along his chapped bottom lip.

"Where's Rae?" I cry. "What did you do to her?"

"Did you know that there's a type of fungus that feeds off microscopic or minute animals? They're called carnivorous fungi. They have this trapping mechanism—some have multiple, both active and passive. Passive traps are ones they set and forget, kinda like when you put a slow cooker on. Active traps, well, others do the work there. You see, Seaside State has both active and passive traps." He runs a claw through the clumped remains of his hair. "Ana and myself are active. We leave the grounds to scout; we bring promising morsels back for it to judge and devour. Or really *she* does right now, but I'll be going out into the field soon too, making myself useful. We're different from you. We're different from the others like us too."

Cold sweat breaks out across my forehead when I realize what he means. "You hunt in packs."

"We hunt with *purpose*. Now," he says, raising a leg up on an overturned wastebasket. "Back to the difference between passive and active traps. You see, most of our kind—people like you, Gracie—can hunt their own food. They're able to wander around the world and slurp and suck and gorge themselves. But Seaside State got an idea, a way to break the mold. A way to be better. Before she was a hospital, she was one of us. But only feeding on one person at a time can be so limiting. Why not ten or twenty? Why not a whole slaughterhouse full?"

The picture of Rae's grandmother flickers behind my eyes, the gravelly drawl of her voice scratching through my ears. *There's something wrong with this place... it's eating away at us. I can feel it under my skin.* "Seaside State... back when this place was active..."

Blood spurts from the place where Mason's top lip used to be, so dark it borders on black. "It was a buffet. It was an all-you-can-eat, glorious spread of fine, tormented cuisine. Much like how you possessed that body, she possessed this building. And she ate, and she ate until—"

"Until the patients couldn't take it anymore. Until the tragedy of '65." Until Rae's grandmother fought back.

"It's been harder for her to find food since then. She's practically emaciated. I'm not sure how Ana found her, but they struck a deal and now we make sure she's well-fed. And she leaves plenty for us too."

"Is that what you did with Rae? You offered her up to the hospital like some kind of palate cleanser between meals?"

"I haven't done anything. Seaside State is doing all the work for me. It's still not too late to join us, you know. Feed the hospital and she will feed you."

"I'm sick of you and Ana trying to recruit me. If Seaside State wants me so badly, she can speak for herself."

"She only speaks to Ana."

"Isn't that convenient…"

"Well?" he asks. "This is your last chance."

I pretend to think about it for a moment, all the while focused on how Mason struts about the hallway, all too pleased with his new form. There's no way I'm selling my soul to this thing, if I even have a soul. If there's any chance at redemption for me after what I've done, I'm not going to find it dragging bodies into this black hole.

"Only if you let Rae go," I tell him.

He clucks his tongue. "Come now, you're smarter than that."

"Mason!" We both turn to find Ana standing at the entrance to the hallway. She stands hunched over in the doorway, her thin hair hanging like a veil over her shoulders with light bleeding through it.

She straightens up and walks over, her pace hurried.

"What's wrong?" Mason asks, tilting his long neck to the side so his head hangs lopsided, like the victim of a hangman's noose.

"There's a problem. It's the girl."

"Rae!" I cry, but they both ignore me.

"Seaside State says there's been a—"

"You can communicate with the hospital?" I ask, frowning. I figured it was a lie she told Mason to keep him complacent.

"She's not the only one," Mason says sharply. "Or, at least I'll be able to once I get the hang of things. For now, she only talks to Ana."

"Then how do you know that Seaside State is talking at all? Ana could be making it up so that you feed her."

"Once I get stronger, I'll be able to hear her too. Right now I'm a fledgling, but once I feed—"

"Is that what she's been telling you? You said it yourself; our kind are liars and parasites. What makes you think she's being up front with you about any of this? For all you know, she could be lying to feed herself and Seaside State isn't even sentient, it's just a sad old building."

"I know what you're trying to do and it's not gonna work. I'm not an idiot."

"No, you're not. It's not like you'd gouge your own eye out on the word of someone you've never met."

Ana stands between us but doesn't do anything to intervene. A slow, lazy smile spreads across her face and her eyes take on a glazed, feverish light. She's enjoying our banter.

My heart hammers and I glance between her and Mason. Mason, missing chunks of skin, and spurting black fluid, and looking at Ana with the lost stare of a lovesick puppy.

Whatever she came in to tell him takes a back seat to our argument.

I notice my opening, a chance to get Mason fired up—to make him turn on her, although it's slim. I don't even need him to straight-out attack her, I just need to instill some doubt. Once they're distracted, I can run for it.

"You know who you remind me of, Mason?" I ask. "One of those people who goes into chat rooms filled with people claiming to be vampires or werewolves and offers themselves up, only to find that your new supernatural pal is just a weird kid in a cloak partying in their mother's basement."

"I think you're jealous because I was chosen, because Seaside State saw the potential in me."

"You said it yourself, Ana found you in a forum. It could have been anyone."

"That's not true, I'm special!"

"We're all 'special,' that doesn't mean shit." I steal a glance at Ana, and she watches with a bemused look on her face. "I used to think that everyone was a cliché—that no matter what people tried to do, it could all be boiled down to a few character traits. But I realize now that it's the opposite. We're not all clichés, we're all unique. And that's exactly what makes us the same as everybody else."

"Except for one thing, dipshit. You're not human! None of us are!"

"You used to be. You could have wound up food as easily as anyone else, except that Ana needed dumb and malleable recruits. She knew that she could use you and you wouldn't question any of it because you're too dumb to—"

"I hate to interrupt," Ana says calmly. "But time is of the essence."

"What's wrong?" Mason asks.

"Rae escaped from that room you put her in."

"So? The hospital will finish her off regardless."

"Seaside State is having some... digestive issues at the moment. She asked that I come get you, so that you could help."

"What does she need me to do?" Mason asks, practically salivating.

Ana tilts her head as if listening to some unseen speaker. "She says to meet Rae in the morgue and take care of it."

"What about her?" he asks, tilting his head toward where I stand.

"Leave her to me."

25

RAE

The floors are crusted with flies. Dead and curled in on themselves, belly-up. They crunch beneath my feet like autumn leaves. They lie sprinkled across the dirty tile floors, punctures of color in an otherwise white hall.

I open doors and windows as I pass them, and I feel the hospital strain against me. It isn't happy. Without Mother at my back, it's silent.

I stop in front of one of the mirrors, and my reflection looks so strange, warped somehow within the glass. There are so many shades of gold all swirling together, slicing my face in two.

The hospital does its best to keep me from Gracie. I open doors only to find solid walls behind them. I turn corners only to find myself in the exact hallway I meant to exit, tracing my steps back through the trails of dead flies.

"You're not gonna stop me," I shout. "I'm going to find Gracie, and we're gonna finish what my grandmother started, and you're gonna rot!"

A pang rings out inside my chest when I think of Gracie.

Ana and Mason said she was one of them, and she didn't deny it.

But then I think of how she attacked Ana, how she reached for me as I was dragged away, and I press forward through the trails of flies and the hospital's shifting halls. No matter what it does to deter me, I don't let it hold me back. The air crackles with electricity, seemingly a small shift away from breaking apart completely.

It's scared.

It's dead, and it knows it.

I come to the end of the hall and open the door to reveal the morgue, now on the wrong floor, its paint two shades darker than before. Everything sits in its proper place: the cabinets, the tables, the beakers and vials—only now they look like predators, huddling in the corners of the room. Vague shapes, shades darker than before. So much darker.

A shiver travels up my spine. "Nice try."

I spin around only to find that the hallway has shortened to a length of about five feet. I'm boxed in. The morgue is the only option.

"Fine," I breathe and take a step inside.

"It's about time you got here." I look up to find Mason standing in the center of the morgue, looking every bit as gruesome as before.

I take a deep breath in and let it out again. The room is cast in hues of orange and gold, sickly yellow over trembling copper. I can't pinpoint the source of the light; it seems to stream in through the walls, through the vents in the ceilings, ribbons of brightness tumbling in every direction. The air is so thick I could reach out and grab it, pull it apart like taffy.

The silhouette of me is still against the wall next to the cabinets.

Only now it's an opening the size of a crawlspace.

It's quiet here; no wind, no echoes, not even the hum of flies through the walls. I stand suspended in golden light, an insect trapped in amber.

Mason's long arms hang next to him, his head bowed, his fingers knotted elegantly in front of him. He's a few feet away and slightly blurred by the haze, but I can see the shape of him.

My stomach clenches.

I walk up to where he stands and stop in front of him, close enough to hear him breathe, but there is no breath. His chest rises and falls, but I can't hear a sound. There's a dark stain on the right arm of his flannel and he smells like honeycomb.

"You're not gonna grab me again, are you?" I ask, trying to sound brave despite the fact that my heart is in my throat. It occurs to me that I could throw him across the room, use the same force I used to escape the room he locked me in… but I'm stiff from fear, unable to so much as twitch my fingers without them shaking. Tears prick the corners of my eyes. How can I still be so weak?

He shakes his head.

"I've been waiting," he says, his voice a deep rumble, that moment between lightning strikes. I hear it in my head, buried deep inside the gray matter. "Seaside State said I would find you here. She's told me you've been causing a lot of trouble."

"So this is why the hospital was so damn insistent that I come inside this room. Well, whatever it sent you here to do, it's not going to stop me. I'm a lot stronger than I thought, and I'm more than happy to test out my new skill on you." My heart hammers against my ribs as I bluff. I doubt I could so much as hover a stick right now.

"Such big words from such a little girl," Mason says. "If you're looking for Gracie, you won't find her. And you won't like what you find even if you do. She's joined our happy family. So you can give it up and let Seaside State do the rest. I promise the death will be quick, just like falling asleep."

"Gracie would never go along with any of this."

"Gracie isn't even her real name. She doesn't have a name, only what she stole from that poor girl she took that body from."

"That doesn't matter," I say, though tears spring to my eyes. "Even if what you're saying is true, I don't care. I killed my own mother; I can't judge her for killing someone by accident." Even though Mother was an accident too. Even though the knowledge of what I did still festers beneath my skin, and it will remain there for the rest of my life. There's no escaping what I've done; there's only living with it.

I imagine it's the same for Gracie.

Mason advances toward me until we're inches apart. Up close, the stain on his sleeve looks like dried blood and I grimace.

"I know what you're thinking," he says, chipping at the stain with his pinkie nail. "And no, it's not Gracie's. As much as I would love to entertain you with stories of how we gutted her, lying takes effort, and effort would be wasted on you. After all, you're only a meal."

"If the hospital wants to devour me so badly, then why hasn't it done it by now?" I shoot back.

"Maybe we could sit and talk," he suggests and gestures to the row of cabinets to our left. He lifts himself up onto the counter with ease. "I know you don't trust me, but I think you'd be interested in what I have to say."

My eyes drift back and forth between the entrance to the morgue and where Mason sits.

He laughs a guttural, throaty laugh. "She isn't going to let you out of the morgue, so don't even think about it."

"If the hospital is so powerful then how did I get out of that room?"

"That's the thing, Rae. I don't fucking know." He crosses his legs and throws his head back. "And honestly, I don't care. Seaside State sent me to take care of you, so here I am. I'm not gonna question it. I'm making myself useful, and if Gracie knows what's good for her, she will too. Which, speaking of Gracie, we should really sit down and talk, yeah?"

"Fine," I say through clenched teeth.

I wander over to Mason and with a bit more difficulty manage to pull myself up onto the counter to sit next to him. We sit directly across from the cold chambers, the rows where corpses slept.

He chuckles and picks off tiny flakes of dried blood, tossing them to the side. They're rust-colored snowflakes. They form a small pile on the floor.

"Now," he says. "This is what I wanted to talk to you about." He rolls up his sleeve to reveal a long, thin slice that runs from the top of his arm all the way down to the wrist.

"What am I looking at?" I ask, my heart thundering against my ribs.

"How I got to be the way I am. How I became one of them."

"I thought you changed when you lobotomized yourself..."

"That was only part of it," Mason confirms. "Did you know that the cells in the brain can stay alive for hours after death? All the neurons and pathways and shit flicker out slowly, like dying stars. So after I prepared this body for what was to come, Ana did the rest. With blood and flies. When Ana bleeds, there are flies in the blood, and the flies carry the gift. All you need to do is drink the blood before you die, plant the flies, and hope they take root." He waves the arm with the scab. "She had to open me up afterward to make sure they took root in me, and she had to bleed more into the wound, add more flies, and so on, and so on. Point is, this shit didn't come easy."

"Why would you want it at all?" I ask.

"Why don't you?" He stretches out his hand and flexes his fingers. "I'm supposed to feed you to the hospital—I *should* feed you to the hospital. But I like you, Rae. You're not stuck up like the girls at my college, and you weren't a total bitch to me when we first met out there. Which is a low bar, sure, but you couldn't imagine how entitled some girls are, how they get off on treating nice guys like shit. But you're not like that, and I want to spend some time with you before this place guts you like a fish." He smiles, almost shyly, though the charm is lost to the haze of his bloodshot eyes. "Hope you don't mind."

My eyes widen and it occurs to me that there's a way to get through Seaside State, a way to escape this room and make it to Gracie. But I'm not sure if I'm strong enough to do what needs to be done. Mother always said that I was weak, that I needed someone there to guide me, correct me, do everything for me. She kept me from choices, from using my voice for so long that—

"Come on, you're not gonna be stuck up now, are you?" Mason scowls. "I'm trying to be nice."

Even though he stretched out through his transformation, he isn't much taller than I am, and while seated, our heads are almost level.

"You know how Ana helped you transform?" I begin tentatively.

He nods.

"Can you help someone become... close with Seaside State?" My mouth tastes like cotton, and I swallow a few times to try to clear the taste, but it only makes it worse. "I know you're new to this, but you know the process and I'm sure you're just as strong as Ana."

"I am, aren't I?" he says with a grin. "Ana did say that she needs more of us around here, and Seaside State is having trouble digesting you."

I think of the bloodstained wad of gum in my pocket as he runs his fingers back and forth across my wrist. My veins stick out blue against his touch. Even though his touch is gentle, he applies pressure as he moves his fingers. It's overwhelming.

I lean my head against his shoulder, doing my best not to

cringe at the feeling of his body against me. The warmth radiates through the fabric of his shirt. He feels the way that blood moves through veins—slow, steady. Constant. So different from before, and I wonder how long I'll have to keep this up. Keep him distracted. Keep him from trying to turn me.

I lean back and let him continue to tug his fingers across my veins. They stretch against the skin. They're full to the point of bursting. Full of so much blood.

"Did Ana tell you the real reason behind the tragedy of '65?" he asks. "What really happened, and why we're so excited for the opportunity to help Seaside State? I can tell you about it if you want."

"I'd like that very much," I say, my heart pounding. "Gracie told me that you're these parasitic things and I guess... Is Seaside State like that too?" Sweat breaks out across my forehead and I wonder how long I'll have to pretend, how hard I'll have to fight to survive.

"Exactly."

He pulls me closer to him.

He's so warm.

He's burning.

"Our kind feeds off negative energy. Seaside State used to live off the patients who were brought here. She did this for years and years until the fire. After the fire happened and the place was shut down, she couldn't find food anymore. Every once in a while, there would be an urban explorer or a bunch of college kids looking for something freaky to do, but she couldn't latch on, and she couldn't keep them inside long enough for a full meal. She slept for a long time—she hibernated. Then Ana found her, and the rest is history. We feed her and she feeds us."

I think about it and a shiver passes through me. My grandmother setting fire to this place after being fed upon for who knows how long. Who knows how much it addled her brain before she found the strength to fight back.

Seaside State tried to make a meal for herself, but instead of burning it, it wound up burning her.

And at what cost? My grandmother didn't die in the fire—I know that much from the recording—but based on what Mother told me, I don't think she was ever released. I wish I had paid more attention when Mother would ramble about her abandonment. I wish Grandmother's decisions weren't still haunting us now.

"You have no idea how shitty it is to almost be destroyed by your own meal," Mason says, releasing my hand. He twists his arm so that the cut from before hovers beneath my lips. "Here's what's going to happen. I'm gonna open this back up, and you're going to drink from it. It'll change you."

"Change me into what?" I ask and chew my bottom lip, all of a sudden not sure if I should continue with this or try to make a run for it.

He laughs. "Something better."

I'm aching all over. I ache for the asylum; I ache for Gracie and the maternal side of my family and the ghostly version of myself who tried to warn me about all of this.

When I woke up this morning, when Eliza and I each had a bowl of cereal and did the crossword puzzle, when we drove down the winding roads leading to this place, I wouldn't have guessed I would end up here.

Mother may be gone, but I'm just as trapped as I was before.

My eyes keep darting to the other end of the morgue, to the hallway beyond it. The soft pastel colors peeling, peeling, peeling.

"I'll tell you what, Rae," Mason continues. "I'll let you in on the secret once you're a part of the family. There's a whole recipe, you see. It has to do with the time of day, the position of certain things, the things we bring in offering to the hospital."

"Like a sacrifice?" I ask.

He claps his hands together. "Exactly!" He takes a deep breath. "I wish I could have been here when the fire started, so I could have stopped it. Even if it meant I wouldn't be given this opportunity. Once you become part of the family and get to know the hospital, you'll realize how she didn't deserve it."

I wish I could have been here when the fire started too, so I could watch the building burn. I wish I could have held my grandmother's hand when she lit the match and placed a palm against the hospital wall while the hallway filled with smoke. And as I choked, I could have told Seaside State that she deserved it. She deserved to burn for feeding off the patients who came here to get better. She deserved to burn for treating them like livestock, like an all-you-can-eat buffet, when they were so helpless.

I hate malums. I hate how they latch onto the weak and turn them into lifeless husks.

"You said that Gracie is like you?" I ask, a lump forming in the back of my throat.

"Sort of. She was born that way, though, not made or transformed like me."

I clench my jaw.

Even if Gracie is a malum like Mason, like Ana, like the hospital—she isn't like them. She got rid of Mother; she set me free.

She doesn't care that I killed Mother, because she killed the girl whose body she stole, and in a way that makes me feel closer to her. Because we understand each other. Because there aren't any secrets between us anymore, and I won't be afraid to speak with her about what happened in my house when I was growing up—what happened to me.

It must be lonely to be what she is. To not have a face or a name of your own. To not feel like you have a place to belong in the world. To not have any evidence that you're real.

Mason tucks a stray strand of hair behind my ear.

"What are you thinking about?" he asks.

"What's going to happen when I become like you?" I lie.

He touches my cheek and I cringe. "If you want to become like us, you need to drink." He runs a fingernail along the slice in his arm and red beads bubble up against the skin.

Haematophagy, the consumption of blood. Mother wrote that word on a sticky note once too, like *anathema*, over and over again. She'd go through phases. Sometimes the sticky notes were neon yellow and stuck up on the bathroom wall. Sometimes the sticky notes were blue and left on the counter in the kitchen. *Haematophagy* was pink and, unlike anathema, the definition was written beneath the word.

"Gives you a better appreciation for the pink paper," Mother had said. "Pink, almost like blood, but not quite."

Haematophagy. I repeat it inside my head, sounding out each segment of the word.

"Rae?" I turn to find Gracie standing in front of the cold chambers, next to the entrance to the pastel hallway.

26

RAE

Gracie's t-shirt is splattered with red. Rust, and ruby, and watercolor shades of pink butterfly out across her chest. A fine spray of color reaches up her neck and frames her face like a vase. The hem of her skirt is torn, and her left heel is missing, but she stands tall and smiles when our eyes meet.

"Is that really you or is Seaside State messing with me?" she asks.

"I was gonna ask you the same thing."

Her hair seems to glow in the golden light of the morgue, like the inside of a kerosene lamp. Even bloody and battered, she looks like home.

Her fingers are wrapped around the metal frame. They're cut open, her pinkie looking as if it's gone through a deli slicer, and there are little puncture wounds in the asylum floor from where she's bled on it. The red of her blood mixes with the red of the test-tube caps.

"Are you okay?" she asks.

I pull away from Mason and slide down off the counter. "I am now."

I run to her, and she wraps an arm around me, her other hand still clamped down on the outline of the cold chambers.

She turns her head, burying her face in my hair. "I thought they killed you. I thought I let you get killed. I wouldn't have been able to live with myself if you died because of me."

"I'm fine," I breathe. I want to tell her about the girl with my face, and how I've been slowly unpacking all the baggage that Mother left me with. I want to wrap myself around her and fling our bodies through the narrow windows of the morgue, and roll with her out on the lawn, and lie in the tall grass out by the service road and trace the contours of her face.

Her shoulders heave and I push her hair back, tilting her chin toward me. Her mascara trails down over her cheeks and her eyes are puffy and red.

"How much of that blood is yours?" I ask, my heart dropping to my stomach. I try to pull away from her in case I might be crushing something—causing some sort of unseen damage —but she shakes her head.

Mason breathes heavily, his eyes darting between me and Gracie. Blood continues to drip down the length of his arm and into the creases of his clenched fist. "What did you do to Ana?"

Gracie looks down at the blood splatter that covers the front of her shirt. "You're a smart guy, figure it out."

The color drains from Mason's face and his hand trembles as he pulls at the edges of his shirt. He looks more like the boy we met out front on the service road, uncertain and shaking. Sounds like him too, and it gives me a sick sort of satisfaction that his transformation couldn't completely erase the person he was before. "I bet you're bluffing. A-Ana won't stand for this— she'll come and finish you off, just you wait."

Gracie's eyes never leave Mason as she rubs small circles into my back. *Stay calm,* the motions say. *We'll get through this together.*

I notice how Gracie's knuckles on the hand that grips the

cold chambers are all but shredded. Blood in various stages of coagulation hangs onto the skin, looking more like bad Halloween makeup than an actual wound.

"That looks really bad," I say to her.

"This is nothing," she says lightly. "You should see what I did to Ana."

"How did you find me?" I ask her. "Seaside State keeps shifting the hallways; it took everything I had to make it this far."

Mason sits frozen on top of the counter, his eyes wide and his expression strained. He pulls his fingers through the air as if he's trying to read the room in braille, but grunts in frustration and lowers his palms after a few moments.

Seaside State won't speak to him, I realize. *He's trying to call out to Ana, to the hospital, to anyone at all, but he can't get through.*

"I couldn't let him hurt you," Gracie says and tightens her grip on the metal frame. "The hospital tried to keep me out. I tore through a wall to get here; it kept cutting off all my direct paths. And honestly, it's taking everything I have in me to stay here right now."

"It's trying to push you out?"

She nods. "It's not gonna work, though. I'm stronger now that I'm with you."

Her knuckles burn red, and she bleeds red, and continues to stare at Mason.

He swats at the air one last time and curses, throwing his head back and shaking out his hair.

"I don't understand what you want from me!" he cries, eyes raised to the ceiling. "I've done everything you've asked for, please give me a sign that you're listening!"

Gracie stops rubbing my back and hooks her arm around my waist, gently, as if she thinks her touch is enough to scar me.

"Rae," she says when it becomes clear that Mason isn't an immediate threat. "I'm sorry I didn't tell you the truth about what I am. I was afraid because the whole reason I came here in the first place was to kill myself."

Even though she keeps her eyes forward, I can tell that tears are welling up behind them. Her bottom lip trembles.

"Gracie..."

"All this started in the violent patient ward across the property," she says, eyes still trained on Mason. "It got torn down last year, but back when it was standing, Gracie used to go there with her friends. They would drink and tell ghost stories and try to scare each other. The group was different every time they came, but she was always a part of it. People were drawn to her. She had this way of making everyone in the group feel important, and if someone was sitting off to the side or seemed to be having a bad time, she would always make an effort to help them feel included. She was loud, and funny, and beautiful. And she was so unhappy. I could smell it radiating off her, this thick scent of despair. It's like when people bake cookies and the smell fills the room. It smelled so good to me. I knew I wanted her."

"Gracie, you don't have to explain." I cast a nervous look toward Mason, but he's busy bargaining with the hospital.

"Give me a chance," he says, dragging his hands along the sides of the cabinets. "I can prove myself to you."

I look back at Gracie. "I already know that you killed her, you don't need to explain if it hurts to remember."

"Please, let me do this." She takes a deep breath before continuing. "I watched her for weeks. When she wasn't visiting the violent patient ward, I would fantasize about her and how all that sorrow would taste. I think that's why it went so wrong. I starved myself lusting after her pain and when I finally went to attach to her, I took it too far. I wedged inside her body, this body. I had tried to possess people before, but it never lasted—and honestly, it felt weird and wrong. It never stuck. Until I got inside this body.

"At first it was wonderful, but I could still hear her in the back of the head we shared, screaming. I told myself, 'Just one more day, just one more day.' I told myself that I could leave whenever I wanted to, but that wasn't the case. I felt her slip away more and more and by the time I made the decision to leave, I couldn't figure out how to get out of this body, and I wound up killing—"

"I know," I cut her off, and pull her in closer. "And I killed my mother. We're both murderers."

"I needed to tell you, though. I need you to understand that I'm not a good person. I'm not a person at all, and I'm never going to be."

"That doesn't matter," I say, smoothing back her hair. "I spent so much time alone with my mother, so much time staring at words in a dictionary or words written out on a wall that I thought that's all I would ever have. My whole life, I thought that I'd read things and never get to experience them. And it would have been true if it wasn't for you. You got rid of something that had been feeding off of me for almost a year. You saved my life."

She turns to me and her eyes are so blue. They're clear pools of water, and even though her sclera—the whites of her eyes—are bloodshot from crying, they're the most beautiful things I've ever seen.

"I like you a lot," she says.

I lean in and my lips brush against her cheek. I want to say that I feel the same. I want to say that I understand, and that nothing will ever change what we went through here. We'll always be linked.

But I can't find the words.

There are no words.

"That's all super touching and everything, but we have unfinished business."

We pull away from each other and turn to Mason, who

stands in the middle of the room. He shakes his head out again and cracks his knuckles, flecks of blood freckling across the floor from the wound in his arm. His face is set into an expressionless mask, but there's a manic light behind his eyes.

"I didn't mean to be rude and ignore you for so long," he says. "I was hoping that Ana would get her ass over here or *somebody*"—he cranes his neck toward the ceiling again before looking back at us—"would tell me what to do. But since it's all quiet in here, and since we're alone in this lovely room after I've gone through a lovely metamorphosis, I figure why not have some of my own fun for once?"

He extends his wrist toward Gracie, who backs up as far as she can, her spine pressing into the skeleton of the cold chamber. I walk back with her, pressing my own body against the metal frame, wishing that we could squeeze inside one of the empty gaps and claw our way out of here—right through the belly of the hospital.

"I wonder what would happen if you went through the ritual," Mason says, a smile ripping across his face, tearing at the corners of his mouth. "Would it make you stronger, or would it destroy you?"

"Get away from me," she spits, releasing her grip on the metal frame. She pushes me behind her and takes a step toward Mason. "Get away from *us*."

My heart flutters at the way she says it. Us. Like there's a future in the word, an entire lifetime made up of her and me, and no one else.

"What's the matter?" he asks. "If you were able to hold your own against Ana, you should be able to handle a few drops of blood.

"And," he continues. "Rae told me earlier that she wanted to drink. Yeah, all that shit she was spewing about accepting you or whatever, she doesn't give a shit about you. She wants to claim our power for herself. Not that I blame her—the hospital really is the only one who deserves our unwavering loyalty."

His head lolls over to the side. It droops as if the bones in his neck are made of jelly and I'm sickened to think that I was half considering becoming like him.

Even if it meant getting to Gracie.

She frowns at me but I do my best to communicate what I can in a glance—that I never would have agreed to it if I didn't think it would help us get out of here, that it's okay that she's a monster, that I like her and I want to know her.

"Rae," he taunts, advancing toward us. "You seemed so excited before, what's changed? Your girlfriend can keep running all she wants, but all roads lead back here in the end. There's really no other choice. Eat or be eaten."

He stops in his tracks and swings his head to the side, tilting his ear toward the ceiling.

"What's that?" he asks, laughter trickling from his lips. "Oh, yes, of course. I'm glad you agree."

The morgue walls shake and strips of paint peel from the plaster. They drift like ashes to the ground, and the doorway— the pale hall shifts into a stone wall. We're boxed inside the morgue with Mason, and as he saunters over, his nails elongate and his neck continues to droop.

The tile floor shifts beneath him, carrying him forward on a ripple of dusty ceramic. It's as if the hospital is convulsing.

Gracie grabs my wrist and yanks me out of Mason's path.

The cabinet doors open and shut, and the paint continues to peel from the walls. Countertops rip away and the metal from the cold chambers drips down into the tile, reduced to liquid.

"I think Seaside State is panicking," I tell Gracie.

"She knows exactly what she's doing!" Mason howls. He lunges at us, but we swerve and his head snaps back into place.

He cracks his neck back and forth a few times and pulls at his cheek.

"Gosh, skin can be so limiting, can't it?" He tugs a chunk away from his mouth and now both rows of teeth sit exposed, his gums peeking out from beneath pieces of ripped flesh. "I never realized back when I was a *normal* boy, but it really is such a burden lugging all this meat around."

The hospital continues to peel around him, and as the cabinets slam at a quicker pace, as the walls are stripped down to the plaster, Mason becomes more and more frenzied.

"Rae, I know you still want to drink. This will make you better," Mason says, dragging his nail along the incision in his arm, reopening the cut. "This will make you better!" he screams again, his eyes bulging.

Mother used to tell me the same thing. Back when I had to take pills and drink sticky syrups and bitter tea. I would hide under my covers and scream until my throat bled. I was already so broken; I didn't want to make it worse. At this point I had been out of school for almost a month. Mother hadn't taken me to a doctor and instead was trying natural remedies for what she called "a case of bad karma." The school system didn't know I was sick; she had "withdrawn me in favor of homeschooling."

"It'll be better that way," she told me. "You don't want them thinking I'm a bad mother, do you? You don't want them to take you away, do you?"

I'd shake my head so hard I was afraid my brain would disconnect and roll around inside my skull.

"No, Mother," I'd say.

"Then take your medicine," she'd tell me, shoving a pill down my throat. "It will make you better."

"Blood connects kin," Mason croons, making another grab for us. His wounds send specks of red flying through the air.

The golden light continues to squeeze in through the

windows and the fresh cracks in the walls, and I wonder if Seaside State will collapse in on itself, chew a hole through the morgue and allow us to escape.

Gracie shakes her head as if she can read my mind. "The hospital may be panicking, but it's not about to let itself die."

Mason digs his fingers into the hole in his cheek, running them over his teeth.

"I can hear her!" he screeches. "I can hear Seaside State and she's telling me such glorious things!"

He pulls a tooth from his mouth, his fingers bringing a sticky glob of red saliva along with it.

He continues to ramble, his voice distorted from all the missing pieces of his face and all the blood spurting from his gums.

"She has such a lovely voice," he says. "She loves it when I make you squirm, she loves it when I make you sick, she loves it when I make you afraid. And she's telling me the truth. She says that I don't need Ana—I don't need all this rancid, stinking meat."

He pulls on the chunk of flesh hanging down over his upper jaw. "I don't need a body; she's the only one I need."

I'm focused on the blood, and Gracie, and making sure that even if we don't escape, we stay together until the end.

"He's lost his mind," I say, not sure if I'm in awe of what's happening, or horrified.

"Clearly. Whatever Ana did to make him like that knocked a few screws loose." Gracie grabs my hand and pulls me across the room. We stumble over broken tiles and beakers as they fall from the shelves.

One of the cabinets flies open, and Gracie tears it from the frame. She digs through a drawer for a few moments then throws it to the side, a scalpel gripped tightly in her fist.

She moves it back and forth in front of her face. The tip of the blade glistens in the amber light. She pulls her lips up into a smile, but it looks like it takes a great deal of effort. It looks more like an expression of pain.

"I don't think a scalpel is going to help us against the hospital, especially if it continues to convulse like this," I tell her. I'm terrified that Seaside State will pitch the floors forward again and she'll wind up digging the scalpel into her thigh or the center of her forehead, or worse—she'll follow Mason into that dark place at the center of the hospital, where the entry fee is final breaths.

Mason turns to us and makes his way across the tile floor. "She's still talking to me. She's saying that that *thing* wearing Gracie's face should put down the sharp object. She's saying that if she doesn't, then she'll make her."

"Please put down the scalpel, Gracie. It isn't going to do us any good; you'll only end up hurting yourself."

"Fuck that," Gracie spits, her brow knotted in determination. "I'm not going to let a building intimidate me. I'm not going to let a little boy controlled by some wannabe cult leader tell me what to do. I'm getting us out of here, Rae."

27

GRACIE

Even as the hospital shakes and its walls peel around me—even as Mason tears his skin from his face and his blood pools across the floor—all I can think about is Rae.

She stands behind me, her aura electric bright, a bite of citrus that explodes around her. A color that's equal parts love and panic. The panic won't last long, though; once I take care of things, it will fade.

She's better now, she's finally rid of that thing on her back, and I vow to myself that I'll never let her aura darken again. I'll never let anything hurt her again.

We're going to be happy, damn it. Both of us.

I advance toward Mason, twisting the scalpel round and round in my mangled hands, running my fingers over the blade. I cringe every time they graze the sharp edge. They're torn to pieces after my fight with Ana, and even though the wounds are beginning to scab over, they sting afresh each time the knife passes over them.

There's a sweet edge to the pain, though. It reminds me of the real Gracie and her infectious empathy. It reminds me of how I was able to fend off Ana. It reminds me of how I was able to fight my way to Rae through changing hallways and a hospital that wanted me subdued, repressed, subservient to it. Instead, I'm strong. Instead, I'm moving in for the kill.

I meet Mason in the center of the morgue, and he lifts his hands so that they're level to his chest, palms facing outward.

"I don't want to hurt you," he says. "Either of you. Drinking will help, and I'm only trying to help. Rae said that she wanted to try it. She wanted to taste, and to change. And Seaside State is saying that you'll benefit from it too. It'll bind you to us, it'll bring us all together. I'm sure Ana will forgive you once you drink too. After all, what's a little fighting between family? You learn to smile through the pain."

Rae steps up next to me, fists clenched at her sides. "Mother used to say that to me all the time—that pain was the price of family. But she was wrong. Family doesn't hurt each other."

Mason scoffs. "As if you would understand a thing about family."

Rae clenches her knuckles harder until they burn white, and I continue to advance until I'm inches away from Mason and the hospital stops shaking all at once. The walls stop peeling. The floors stop moving, and a cloud of dust rises from the damage.

"See?" He stretches his arms out to embrace me. "She wants you to accept our invitation. Just a drop of blood, and you'll be tethered to Seaside State. You'll be family. We'll *all* be a family."

"Gracie!" Rae cries and I look over my shoulder. She leans up against the wall, standing on top of a pile of paint chips. The wall behind her has been stripped back to the smooth plaster and her black hair is harsh against the white.

She's breathing heavily, the smaller items around her hovering an inch or so off the ground, but she doesn't seem to have the energy to direct them anywhere.

"Get away from him," she says, a beaker flying across the room and smashing next to his face. "The hospital's stopped moving. Maybe it's tired out. We should get going before it builds up its strength again." She reaches for me, but I shake my head.

"It'll be fine," I tell her. "Stay back and trust me when I say that this will all be over soon."

"Are you sure?" The items sway slightly, like she can't decide whether or not to let them go.

"Positive." I lock eyes with her and try my best to look confident, even though I'm not sure if what I'm about to do will work. "Watch. Everything will be fine."

She nods and I turn away.

Not because I want to, but because if I look at her for too long, I'll lose my nerve. I'll be too afraid of everything I could lose to fight for what we could gain.

"Sorry, Mason," I tell the mangled creature in front of me, the mess of blood and gore and half a face. "You were saying?"

He tries to smile but only succeeds in pulling back half of his chin. "I'm saying that I'm trying to help you. I'm saying that this is where you belong. What do you have waiting for you out there, hm? Some fake life that you stole. You're already one of us; why not make yourself a home, with others who know what it's like. We'll hunt for her, and in exchange we'll get a place to live, with people who understand us. We'll feed and be fed in return. Doesn't that sound perfect?"

"What are you going to do, force blood down my throat?" I ask, the scalpel poised in front of my face. It shines yellow, the pale color of the walls reflecting off the blade. "I took down Ana, someone who's been at this for a lot longer than you have —someone who's a hell of a lot stronger than you. Do you really want to challenge me?"

When it's clear that I'm not going to run into his arms, he drops them back to his sides and stands still in front of me. He's so close that my nose is almost touching his chin, and the rust-colored stain on his gray shirt almost brushes against my shoulder.

"Gracie," Mason says and places a hand on my shoulder, the dark fluids that coat it seeping into my shirt. "Show Rae that everything will be okay. Show your little girlfriend that we can be a family."

I look at Rae again. Rae, who, even huddled up against a wall, even with her dark makeup smudged around her eyes, looks beautiful.

I think of the life we'll build together once we get out of here and how crazy it is to feel so close to her when we only met earlier today—or was it yesterday by now? The pace of our relationship, if it can even be called that, has been frantic. It's been the quick thumping of a rabbit's heart, and the pounding of footsteps down long abandoned hallways.

Day-to-day life will be so much different. There won't be any dead mothers to exorcise, or dead girls to save. I'll head home to my McMansion, and she'll head home to her father's house. There will be long periods of time when we won't see each other because of family obligations or plans with friends.

Maybe we'll get into arguments.

Maybe after all this we'll realize that we don't get along so well after all, and maybe it will feel too awkward sharing a sandwich with her after everything we've been through together, but that doesn't matter.

What matters is that we have an entire span of mundane, hopelessly boring days stretching out in front of us. Ours for the taking. And we can spend them however we want.

Mason twitches his lip again, the gaping hole that used to be the right side of his face shifting with the motion, chunks of blood and spittle flying onto our shoes.

He reaches for me again and I lean in, the whole time thinking of Rae.

No matter what happens after this, whether our final breaths are drawn together, inside these walls or apart, outside of them, we'll be together.

Mason pulls me in close to him, and I dig the scalpel into his chest.

28

RAE

Mason falls back, hitting his head against the tile floor, and Gracie pounces on him. She pulls the scalpel from his chest and plunges it in again. She does this gracefully, with a natural cadence that mirrors a ballet dancer or professional musician. She slices him apart like she's painting a picture, like the hospital floor is her canvas and he's nothing but a tube of oil paints.

Then she frisks through his pockets until she finds the skeleton key Ana had before we entered the asylum, the oxidized ribbons of burnt orange scabbing over it. "Our way out of here."

She tosses it to me and I dive to catch it, only approaching her once she steps away from the corpse, wiping her hands on the thighs of her skirt.

"Are you sure you got him?" I ask, gesturing to where he's been reduced to a pile of meat on the floor of the hospital.

"He got the ball rolling for me," she says, no doubt referring to the chunks of flesh he pulled from his cheek. "I just finished the job."

"And he won't come back?" I poke the edge of the blood

pool with the tip of my boot. "Didn't Ana heal ridiculously quick after you fought her up on the roof?"

She flashes me the scalpel, now completely red. "I think I tore him up enough that we don't have to worry. He was never built to last anyway."

She drapes an arm around me and drops the scalpel to the floor, where it clatters against the tiles. I snuggle up against her chest even though her shirt is coated in a fresh spray of blood. It looks like a grotesque version of tie-dye at this point, with layers and layers of red.

"I thought you couldn't stand the sight of blood," I say, eyes still fixed on patterns that spread across the shirt, key clutched tightly in my palm.

"After everything that's happened today, I've kinda gotten used to it." She lets out a nervous laugh. "Don't get me wrong, though, after today I don't want to see so much as a paper cut for a long time."

"You and me both. The good news is that without Mother, I finally won't need to deal with any more nosebleeds."

"Thank goodness," Gracie sighs. "I don't think I'd be able to stand kissing you if there's a possibility that at any moment your nose might erupt like a volcano."

My heart flutters at the mention of kissing and I nudge her playfully. "I'll have you know that my nosebleeds were extremely gentle. There was nothing violent about them and they definitely didn't burst out of my nose like a volcano. If anything, they were like a leak from a very sad, very slow faucet."

She nudges me back. "I like this. It feels right to be able to joke around with you. It makes me feel like we're normal."

We stand in silence for a few moments, watching the pool beneath Mason stretch across the floor and lap at the bottoms of our feet. It's so strange to have a moment of peace together. Even though the hospital is still conscious, lounging like a lioness waiting to pounce, and Ana hides somewhere within its halls, it's nice to have a second to breathe—to be together without constantly worrying that one of us might die.

"Should we soak that up with something?" I ask, backing away from the pool, and she moves with me. "Won't the hospital drink it and go all batshit on us again if we don't clean it up?"

She shakes her head. "I don't think it will. I think it realizes that it's running out of options. Now that Mason's gone, Ana's the only one left to worry about."

"And you already did a number on her, so she should be pretty easy to take down," I say, giving Gracie a final squeeze before stepping back from her, away from the mess that used to be Mason. "The only problem is going to be navigating through the hospital to find her."

"No need." The voice rasps through the room, and we turn to see Ana standing at the entrance to the morgue.

Although her dress is splattered with blood, although her face is streaked with red, she appears fine otherwise, even amused. "Hope I'm not too late to the party. I was just taking a moment to collect myself."

She looks down at Mason's mangled corpse and clucks her tongue. "I should have known he wouldn't last long."

"You're not upset?" I ask despite myself. "He's been reduced to a pulp."

She waves her hand dismissively.

"He was way too clingy. Now," she says, clapping her hands together. "If you girls will follow me out into the hallway, we have some unfinished business to take care of."

Gracie comes up next to me and laces her fingers through mine. "Come on. This won't really be over until we deal with her."

We follow Ana out of the morgue and into the long, pastel-colored hallway. The door shuts behind us, locking Mason's remains inside. I know that he was trying to kill us, I know that he sold his soul to the hospital, but a pang still rings out inside my chest. He's a victim as much as we are, and now he'll never get a chance to leave this place. He'll rot within these walls, feeding the darkness inside until there's nothing left of him.

We follow Ana down the hallway and stand in an awkward cluster in front of a large set of double doors. She snaps her fingers and the hallway darkens, boards covering the windows so that only small shafts of light puncture the darkened hall.

"Look familiar?" she asks.

"It's the first-floor hallway from when we first got here," Gracie says, squeezing my hand again.

It's okay, her touch tells me. *We can still make it out of here.*

Ana turns toward the window and rakes her fingernails along one of the wooden boards, causing splinters to break apart into her palms and tear the pads of her fingers.

I'm tempted to grab the back her head and force it into the board, or whisper to Gracie that we should have taken the scalpel from the morgue—that she should use this opportunity to overpower Ana and ensure that we can make it out of here. But Ana's behavior is so unexpected, so different from anything that I could have imagined happening when we made it into the hallway, that I can't help but watch in wide-eyed surprise, uncertain of where this is leading.

"It's strange," Ana says, "Before I found this place, I never really cared much for permanent living situations. I'm sure you're the same way, Gracie. Our kind hates being tied down, after all; we're nomadic by nature. But ever since coming here, no matter how many times I leave, I never get tired of coming home."

Ana rips at her shredded fingertips, peeling pieces of loose, hanging skin off and discarding them like candy wrappers. They drift across the hospital floor, carried by some unseen draft of wind.

I release Gracie's hand, reach down, and pick up one of the pieces. It's thin; the delicate flaking, the transparency of it is beautiful. The careful swirl of her fingerprint, the patterns that weave through the thin flesh.

Gracie frowns at me through the dim light. "What are you doing, Rae?"

"She's curious," Ana says smugly. "You can fight the hospital for as long as you want, but there's no fighting it forever. There are too many delicious secrets here, too many possibilities. You want a taste of what it's like to not be held back by physical pain. You want to know what kind of place could give me the strength to rip myself apart and still stand tall."

"That's not it at all," I tell her. "I don't care about this place. I'm trying to figure out how you managed to convince yourself that this is a home, that this is your family. I think this place is taking advantage of you because it knows that you'll do anything for the smallest scrap of attention.

"Not that I blame you," I continue. "I was alone for a long time too. I was trapped by things that were outside of my control, but that's no excuse for refusing to make your own way in the world. And I don't think the hospital is as strong as it claims to be."

Gracie reaches her hand out to me, and I take it again.

"Something just occurred to me," she says quietly. "And it might be enough to get us out of here."

She steps out in front of me and looks Ana over, head to toe.

"That body won't last much longer. You can only hold it together with flies for so long. It'll decay at some point."

"And when that happens, I'll join the hospital. I'll live on within the walls of this building."

"No, you won't," Gracie says shaking her head. "You must realize on some level, otherwise you wouldn't be so desperate to get others to join you here and do your dirty work for you. You work them to their breaking point to put less strain on your own vessel. Even if you managed to cohabitate this building with the malum who got here before you, how would you both eat? If you're the only one out there fishing for meals, then what happens when you can't leave the grounds anymore?"

My eyes widen. It never occurred to me that, much like myself back when Mother was still attached to my back, Ana's days are numbered.

Her shoulders shake and she scowls at Gracie, her bared teeth gleaming in one of the rays of light coming in through the boarded windows.

"Seaside State is starving as it is," Gracie continues. "Even with the meals you bring it. They aren't enough to feed something of this size. If its little outburst earlier in the morgue showed me anything, it's how quickly it manages to exhaust itself."

"No," Ana shakes her head. "She's powerful, but she picks and chooses when to exert her energy."

She raises her bloody hands to the ceiling. She reaches as far as she can, stands on her tiptoes and claws at the peeling paint. Blood drips from her hands, thin streaks of red down her thin arms. As she reaches, her limbs elongate, and her jaw snaps so that her mouth falls open.

I press up against Gracie's back. "What's happening?"

Gracie takes me by the shoulders and spins me around in front of her. A streak of blood flakes from her left cheek, causing her eyes to look dangerously blue, even in the dim light.

"I need you to make a run for the door, Rae."

"What? No!"

Finished with her transformation, Ana screeches and hurls her body at us, a mess of limbs and claw-like nails.

Gracie pushes me out of the way and the bones in her left hand crack all at once, the joints splitting open, and her fingers grow longer, flies fanning out around them.

Ana claws at her cheek but she pivots and wraps her newly stretched hand around Gracie's neck.

I watch, horrified. Torn between their violent dance and the double doors in front of us. I'm aware of how the rusted, iron key sits in my back pocket like a stone, and I reach into my jeans and pull it out.

I hold the key out to Gracie as she continues to struggle with Ana.

"When we leave, we can lock the door behind us!" I tell her, my voice strained. "We can make sure that no one ever makes the mistake of coming inside here again."

"Then go!" she screams, her fingers still wrapped around Ana's neck. "Leave now while this damn place is still lying dormant."

"Not without you." I blink back tears and reach for her, my fingers pulling at the air.

"Rae," she says through gritted teeth. "I need you to go. Leave the door open for me but promise that if I'm not out in ten minutes, you'll lock this place up for good."

Ana kicks her hard in the stomach and Gracie falls back, releasing her grip on her throat.

Ana drops to the ground and rises, locking eyes with me. But before she can lunge, Gracie kicks her, sending her flying against the wall. Ana's spine bends backward as she hits the plaster, and paint chips fall to the floor next to where she lies twisted in a heap.

I take a moment to make sure that she isn't getting right back up before running over to Gracie.

She crouches close to the ground, her fingers elongated at the knuckle, her nails grown to sharp points. She turns her face so that her blonde hair obscures her features.

Her bones continue to pop and scream as her transformation continues.

"I don't want you to see me like this," she moans. "I don't want you to see what a monster I really am."

I crouch down next to her and place my hand over hers. Slowly, she lifts her head and I see the red tear marks where her skin has ripped apart around the mouth. I see the way her eyes shine like a jungle cat's and her cheekbones threaten to tear through her skin as if it's wrapping paper.

Her hair hangs in unsightly clumps around her head, dull at the roots, as if the transformation has knocked all the life out of her skull.

But the body is only a body; it's only a shell.

She's still Gracie.

"You're beautiful." I push a strand of hair back from her eyes. "You're always beautiful."

She pulls her hand from beneath mine and uses a claw to trace the outline of my jaw. "So are you."

She grimaces as her back gives a final crack. "I don't want to hurt this body like this."

"It'll be okay—it'll heal. And after today, you won't have to ever again. We'll do so many normal, boring things that you'll wish you could get the opportunity to transform. We'll cook dinner and do the dishes together. We'll ride bikes down to the waterfront and spend the day throwing shells into the ocean. But Gracie," I say, holding the key up to her. "We need to finish this. Together."

I wrap my fist around the key and concentrate, calling on all the damage, all the discomfort I've ever felt, and below me, the ground begins to shake.

29

GRACIE

Even as the foundation of the hospital rumbles, Ana advances on us, dragging her severed ankle behind her.

"What do you think you're going to do, little girl?" She sneers at Rae even as her arm hangs immobile at her side, barely clinging to its tendons. "You have no power here. And you." Her gaze rakes over me. "You're nothing but a shadow in a skin."

"And you're nothing but a swarm of flies puppeting a corpse," I spit.

"Soon you'll be a corpse yourself. You'll wish that you had a swarm of flies to keep your body warm; you'll regret not agreeing to join the hospital when you had a chance." Her flies circle her head, forming a halo around her pale blonde hair. Their buzzing fills the hallway and she grins, the flesh around her lips tearing. "Seaside State is waking up again and she's not going to like all the trouble you caused. She's going to punish you for what you've done."

It sounds pathetic coming from her, and even though the flies buzz around her, doing their best to clot her wounds and reset her bones, they only manage to make her look more grotesque as she falls apart.

I glance at Rae, standing with her spine straight, fist clenched tightly around the skeleton key. She looks so powerful as she pours her entire being into the hospital, splitting tiles and shaking the windows.

When our lips met, it was like nothing else mattered. Our kiss sharpened everything around me. The colors, the smells, the harsh panic that both of us were trying so desperately to keep under control. Our kiss made me realize that even after everything I've done, there's still hope for me. I can still live. I can still become something better than what I was before.

"You can't intimidate us," I tell Ana. "I don't know what you're trying to prove at this point, but it's over—you have nothing left."

The skin around her lips rips further and she lets out a guttural laugh. "I have everything. Even when this body is gone, I'll live on inside Seaside State. She'll take care of me. I shall live as long as she stands."

"I know," I say calmly. I reach into my skirt pocket and withdraw my lighter. It's red with delicate yellow flames painted on the side, a gift from my ex-boyfriend. Pete. He only lasted three weeks, but it might as well have been an eternity.

Given my history and the fact that I was, until recently, so convinced that I would expel myself from this body, I only dated to keep up appearances and keep the real Gracie's mother off my back.

All I remember from the Pete phase is his gelled hair and affinity for menthols. I don't smoke now, but I did when I was with him. I didn't like it then, but the real Gracie did. And the real Gracie liked Pete. It was strange, going out to the movies with him and then coming home and gossiping with her inside the head we shared. This was back when our connection was strong, and we would stay up late into the night chatting, and arguing, and lamenting the fact that I couldn't find my way out again.

Even though I quit smoking around the same time I quit him, I kept the lighter. The real Gracie loved it. She thought it was a way better gift than flowers or chocolates.

"I don't want to be the kind of girl who can be won over by stuff like that," she told me. "I want people to realize that if they mess up, I can't be bought back."

"But he bought this for you," I argued.

"Yeah, but I like it."

At her request, I kept the lighter in my pocket, and even though I refused, much to her dismay, to smoke any more cigarettes, I agreed with her that having it on my person made me feel powerful somehow. I had fire in my pocket. And it was something we could share, an inside joke as we struggled through our cohabitation.

I thought that when I finally handed this body back to Gracie, she deserved some sort of proof that I had lived life the way she would have. That even after I couldn't hear her anymore, I still took what she said into consideration.

A pang rings out inside my chest.

"I'm sorry I was too late," I whisper. "And I'm sorry that I'm fucking up your body right now, but I promise after all of this, I'll create a life that would have made you happy. I'll make it up to you one day."

I hold the lighter out in front of me and flick it once, twice, three times until a flame springs to life.

Rae's grip on the skeleton key falters and she rushes to my side, knocking the lighter to the floor. "Gracie, no."

"It's burned before, it can burn again. Besides, you said we should do this together. I need to help you."

"No, you don't," she insists, her voice steady and determined. "I'm strong enough to bring this place down. Just... just stay with me as I do."

She reaches out and grabs my hand, our fingers lacing together as, in her other fist, she tightens her hold on the skeleton key. A rush of power, a turbulent, warm wind moves through her. I feel it pulse through where our hands connect. It's a war cry, it's a reckoning.

The hospital reacts immediately.

Boards rip from the windows, the tiles shatter one by one as if they're being blown apart, and vicious fractures snake through the ceiling.

Ana takes slow, calculated steps toward us, her lame ankle dragging behind her. She spits a glob of blood and saliva onto the dusty floor and cracks her jaw, the sound lost in the cacophony of shattering tiles. Her wild eyes dart around the hall. "You will never know a love like this. You will never know a connection, a *family* connection like this. And you won't get out of this alive."

The hallway walls flake in thick chunks as if they're being skinned alive, strips of paint wilting down from where the molding meets the ceiling. It's grotesquely beautiful, like flower petals dropping from a blooming tree.

"You're wrong," I tell her as the floor quakes, tremors that radiate out from where Rae stands next to me, a look of stoic concentration on her face as she rips the hospital down around us. "You're the only one who's dying today, and once we get out of here, we're gonna dedicate the rest of our lives to fighting things like you."

The moment I say it, I know it's true. I'm going to make sure that a place like this never comes into existence again. I'm going to make sure that my kind doesn't find new, inventive ways of taking up permanent residence in any person, place, or thing. I'm going to do what I can to reason with my kind, to find them alternate ways of sustaining themselves. And maybe one day, far in the future, we'll no longer be parasites for pain. And Rae will be there by my side. Rae will help me.

She squeezes my hand and the hallway lurches.

Rae, beautiful Rae, ripping the walls down around us—grinding the hospital to dust. She doesn't have to worry about being eaten alive by a shadow or haunted by her family's history.

The building crumples in on itself, floorboards snapping back like hangnails, the ceiling splitting down the middle and collapsing in huge chunks at our feet. But through it all, Rae stands tall, and as if we're protected by an invisible force, none of the falling debris hits us. There's a two-foot radius fanning out around us, a perfect circle where we're completely untouched.

Rae squeezes my hand once, twice. Letting me know it's okay, we'll be okay. I just need to trust her. And I do.

I wish there was a way to tell the real Gracie how grateful I am for this body and the second chance this skin has given me. I want to tell her that I'm sorry it took me so long to try to save her, and that she's the reason I was able to save Rae. She's the reason why I tried so hard to be better.

The floors pitch, and Ana rears up like some horrible, mangled animal and lunges forward one last time.

Rae flicks the hand that grips the skeleton key in her direction, and she's thrown back into a yawning crater that's being gouged out around us. She struggles at first, scrambling for purchase and leaving streaks of red in her wake. Red like Rae's nosebleed, red like Mason, like my bloody knuckles.

Rae's power eats its way through distant halls, the hospital peeling back and collapsing into the hole that scores the earth around us, the ceiling ripping apart to expose the crisp night air, the stars.

Seaside State drops its veil as it's eaten away, and I can see its aura again clearly, for the first time since I stood outside its walls. Its aura burns. It burns in acidic, nasty colors and I've never been so proud in my life. I look at Rae with such pride, such raw admiration as the last of the hospital rips apart and the scraps of its corpse sink down into the earth until we're the last ones standing, surrounded on all sides by a deep hole roughly the width of a fresh grave. Everything that Seaside State was disappeared into those fault lines in the earth, and Rae heaves a breath as she finally releases the key, allowing it to fall into the depths of the chasm after Ana. Ana, who was swallowed by the ground along with what remains of the hospital she worked so hard to feed.

I need to keep reminding myself that she deserved everything that came her way, but at the same time, I know what it's like to feel desperate. I can't help but feel a little bit sorry for her.

Rae twists to face me, her eyes bright, a sheen of sweat glistening across her brow. Poor, poisoned Rae. A girl growing into her power. She scoops my free hand up so both my hands are clenched tightly in her fists. There are dried bits of blood under both our nails, little crescent moons that remind me that what we went through was real.

The wind howls through the empty expanse that once was the hospital. The cold air kisses our skin, and she grins as she brings my hands up to her face, gently pressing her lips to the backs of my knuckles, where more blood has begun to coagulate.

We stand, hand in hand beneath the starless night, and I lean into her.

"You were incredible," I breathe into her shoulder. "You're so strong."

I pull back slightly to look at her as she pushes the hair back from my forehead, and the gentleness of her touch is enough to crack my chest open and bleed me dry.

"I'd understand if you don't want anything to do with me after seeing me for what I truly am... After all, I'm a monster," I say quietly. Even though my features have snapped back into place, I'm still painfully aware of everything she witnessed between me and Ana in the hallway.

"Yeah, you're a monster," she says, her voice shaking. "My monster."

Tears prick the corners of my eyes and I bury my face in her chest again. I've never been so happy to be held by someone before. I've never wanted to draw someone in until there's nothing left between us, until our lungs rise and fall together, until they pump the same air and our veins pump the same blood.

"If you're sure," I say, voice muffled by fabric.

"I'm sure," she promises, and the air smells like salt and blood, but above all it smells like her. Like berries, and brightness, and new beginnings.

Rae's grip on me tightens.

Her arms are safety.

Her arms are everything.

ABOUT THE AUTHOR

Danielle Renino writes horror and speculative fiction. When she's not writing she can be found exploring abandoned buildings, eating her way around Boston, or checking for monsters under her bed. Find her online @daniellerenino on Instagram and TikTok.

www.ingramcontent.com/pod-product-compliance
Lightning Source LLC
Chambersburg PA
CBHW022127310726
48972CB00007B/2228